VEIL

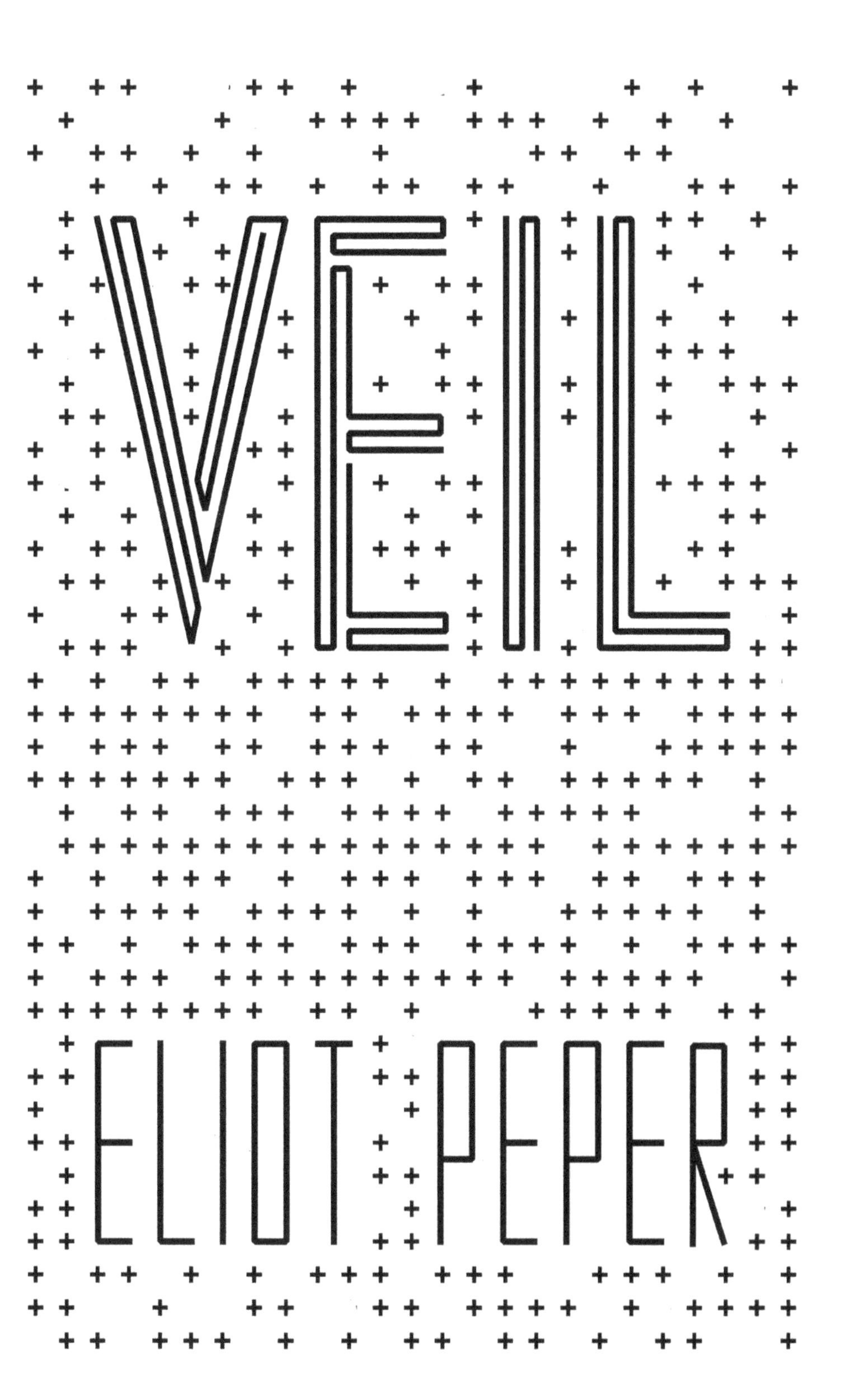
VEIL
ELIOT PEPER

Book design by Kevin Barrett Kane
Typeset in 10.5/15 Mercury Text G1

+

Also by Eliot Peper

Breach

Borderless

Bandwidth

True Blue

Neon Fever Dream

Cumulus

Exit Strategy

Power Play

Version 1.0

To all who have lost a loved one,
or are lost themselves.
You may be shattered,
but you are alive.
You can pick up the pieces.
You can make something beautiful.

+

PROLOGUE

SWEAT STUNG MIRANDA LEÓN'S EYES. BREATH CAME in shallow gasps. Mud squelched under her boots. Just after dawn and it was already forty degrees Celsius with ninety-nine percent humidity. Insects swarmed. The hot spot on her left heel chafed. She wasn't as young as she once was. And yet, there was nowhere else she'd rather be.

Swiping a dirty hand across her forehead, she peered up at the receding back of her guide. The bright yellow soccer jersey hung loose across Gilberto's narrow shoulders. He was nimbler in his plastic flip flops than she could hope to be with the best gear modernity could offer.

"Not much farther, Doña León," he called back over his shoulder. "It's just over the next ridge."

Doña. She really was getting old.

Snagging the water from her pack, she stopped to take a

sip. Jungle encroached on all sides, ten thousand shades of green bending, branching, reaching ever farther in an endless quest for light and water and nutrients—the basic ingredients from which life manufactured itself. How many undiscovered species called a single square kilometer of this tropical rainforest home? How many miraculous medicines might be derived from the biochemical exhalations of one of its undocumented leaves? How long did this rotting, teeming, fecund forest have before succumbing to the slash and burn of progress?

Stashing the water bottle, Miranda pressed on up the steep track. Her clothes were soaked with sweat. Her calves ached. Her spirit gorged on the lush fractals of gigantic ferns that had been gobbling dappled sunlight and releasing spores since dinosaurs roamed the Earth. Sixty-six million years after an asteroid drove them to fiery extinction SaudExxon was consolidating global concessions and squeezing every last drop of liquified dinosaur from their graves to power the churning, commodified madness people called civilization. Humans were their own meteorite.

Damn. That was definitely a blister. There was moleskin in her pack but if she sat down to take off her boot right now, she might not get up again. She'd deal with it when they got back to the village.

She stumbled around a sharp bend and there was Gilberto, grinning at her like the teenager he'd recently been.

"*Hijueputa*," she managed between panting breaths. "Is it always this hot?"

"Look," he said.

She did.

They had reached the crest of a hill and through a gap in the foliage the Sierra Nevada de Santa Marta mountains stretched away to the horizon. Birds darted through the canopy. Mist daubed valleys like sculpted meringue. Unidentifiable animal calls formed a soundscape as rich and tangled as the ecosystem of this unique Colombian coastal range rearing up almost six thousand meters from recently submerged Caribbean beaches, little sister of the Andes and mother of thirty-six rivers.

"Hijueputa," she said again, reverently this time.

Gilberto nodded, still smiling.

The epic view called to mind the epigraph of her work in progress—the description of a fictional astronaut's view of the Earth from space, gleaned from a 1983 short story by Don DeLillo. Reading that story had reignited Miranda's childlike curiosity, taking her back to the first time she'd gazed up at the stars through a telescope as a young girl, noticing their uniquely nuanced hues amidst the buttery glow of their respective galaxies, imagining the planets that danced around them and whatever beings might be gazing up into their own firmaments at the distant star around which Earth spun in all its verdant, multifaceted glory. At the end of the day, literature was nothing but a reminder that life was too big for language to contain.

Gilberto led onward. She had thought it would be easier going downhill but the rising temperature counterbalanced whatever respite descent had promised, and Miranda had to fight back dizziness as she focused on not tripping over rocks or slipping on roots.

Her previous books had cataloged humanity's self-inflicted wounds. The failing crops and rising seas. The water wars and megastorms. The stateless refugees and smoldering wildfires. An endless stream of canny politicians, frustrated scientists, slick lobbyists, outraged activists, cynical industrialists, and everyone else just trying to do their best in a world that always seemed to lie just beyond the edge of comprehension.

If she didn't have Santiago, Miranda knew she would be insufferable. *The future belongs to the optimists*, he would say. *What future?* she would reply. He kept her hopeful despite everything. She kept him grounded despite himself. They drove each other crazy and from their craziness had sprung one daughter, four-going-on-five books, and a trillion-dollar company.

This book, though... This book would be different.

"Da da da *da*," sang Gilberto, spreading his skinny arms wide.

Huffing, Miranda stumbled up beside him. The sight took away whatever breath she still had. These weren't trees. They were giants, monarchs, the ancient gods of this single, vast, variegated organism that humans called a forest. This stand of old growth monsters dwarfed the surrounding trees, forming a local mesa in the topology of the canopy that was so dense with other plants, animals, and symbionts that it made Singapore's famous arcologies appear to be little more than abandoned warehouses in comparison.

Yes, this. *This*.

Miranda reached out and touched the knobby, cream colored bark of the rubber tree. The trunk shot forty meters up before exploding into a luxurious crown that permitted only fractional glimpses of the blue sky above. She inhaled deeply and the hot, wet, pollen-laden air was the greatest gift she'd ever received.

This book was her way of paying that gift forward. She was tired of playing Cassandra, of being the sailor pointing out leak after leak to a crew that barely pretended to listen. So instead of highlighting the mass delusion that doomed future generations, maybe she could seduce humanity into sanity via that most slippery and profound of emotions—wonder. Could she capture natural splendor in narrative and, in doing so, provide everyone a taste of the overview effect experienced by DeLillo's astronaut? Could she craft a story that would burrow into readers' minds and inoculate them against the manic consumption that was the endpoint of so many commercial, social, and political vectors? Could she make them see this tree for what it was, instead of only the latex it produced?

This was the most ambitious project she had ever attempted. It was why she was here in a remote corner of a Colombian jungle with nothing more than a local guide and an open heart. It was way beyond what she was capable of. But she could hear Santiago: *The only way to find your limits is to assume you haven't got any*. She had poked him and told him he should hand over Interstice to a successor and start a self-help seminar. But she had started reading up on that initial intimation of an idea all the same, and the reading turned into notes, which turned into research, which turned into an outline, which turned into a proposal, which turned into her, here, now. If Miranda could accomplish even a vanishingly small percentage of her goal with this book, maybe Zia could leverage her soon-to-be-announced appointment as the youngest Costa Rican ambassador in history, recruit her friends from that elite Swiss boarding school, and force some common sense into the next round of UN climate negotiations.

See? Hope. Santiago would be proud.

"Ready?" asked Gilberto. "It'll take us three hours to get back to the village and we need to get moving before it really gets hot."

"It isn't already?" Miranda shook her head. "Okay, just give me a few minutes."

She explored the grove, savoring the mesmerizing intricacy of tessellated life. This moment. No, this one. This one. Each was a seed she would plant in prose, in the all-too-likely-vain hope that they might sprout and produce fruit of their own, pollinated by readers. She would walk a razor's edge. People were born. People had a succession of sensory experiences. People died. All the highs and lows and angst of life was nothing but an extended effort of wrangling meaning from step two. That's why art was dangerous. It was beautiful, it *felt* true. But the universe didn't conform to what humans found convenient to feel to be true. The universe was the universe. In trying to divine its secrets, humans projected themselves onto systems that transcended them. When DeLillo's astronaut gazed back at Earth, he saw himself reflected in it. How to inspire people to look beyond themselves and their petty squabbles, to see the beauty in the vascular patterns of this leaf, hear the music in the pitter patter of rain, imagine the dazzling scale of the cosmos and the quantum extending infinitely in more directions than there were words for?

"Doña León?" Gilberto's tentative voice intruded on her reverie, and she followed it back to the present as Theseus did his string out of the Minotaur's lair.

"Yes, of course. Let's go."

Climbing back up the ridge was a slog. By the time they reached the lookout, even Gilberto was sweating. Miranda was so taxed she felt like she might not be able to go on. Fantasies of being trapped in this sweltering forest invaded her thoughts. Insects crawling up her sleeves. Jaguars stalking in the shadows. A frog the size of a dime with enough neurotoxin to blow even Timothy Leary's mind. It was fucking hot—a sauna draped in vines.

"When we get back? AC baby!"

Gilberto was trying to cheer her up, and she was tanked enough to need it. He mimed drinking and Miranda took another deep pull from her water bottle. She was losing water, that was for sure. The heat and humidity and exercise were wringing her dry.

Then, onward.

Onward over hills, across streams, down gullies, and through thickets that Gilberto had to hack apart with his machete. Her joints ached. Her muscles bathed in acid. The blister grew and burst. Her vision narrowed and swam. Pain. The pain of creation. Zia would not exist but for the insufferable pain of Miranda's thirty-seven hours of labor. Miranda still remembered her astonishment when the doctor handed her the screaming, bloody infant. Another human. Another life. Santiago's hand on her shoulder promised that he felt it too, that their dreams, their desires, their fears, had suddenly found a center of gravity outside themselves, had transferred into this strange and wondrous being that was the farthest thing from cute.

Miranda belatedly realized that she was lying facedown in the mud. She pushed herself up and replayed the last few seconds. Her boot had snagged an exposed root. The world spun when she stood up and she pressed her eyes shut until it subsided. Gilberto was coming back up the trail, fear painted across his genial face. She waved him off, looking down at herself.

Bloody palms. Wobbly knees. Mud everywhere. Nothing serious.

"I'm fine," she assured him. "I'm fine."

Onward.

Up, down. Up, down. Up, down.

How much farther to the village? Miranda had lost all sense of direction. Trees leered at her. Spider webs laced her face in sticky strands. A waterfall roared and she looked around for it wildly before realizing that the sound was the rush of blood in her ears. The heat was a physical thing, a blanket that wrapped itself around her and squeezed, stronger than the four-meter boa constrictors that slithered through these woods. The air was thick and viscous. The leaves whispered to each other and Miranda could almost understand them, as if they were speaking a language with the same root as her mother tongue. She caught herself giggling and pressed her hand over her mouth before Gilberto could hear.

And then they stumbled out into brutal sunlight and there was the village with its huts and its bundles of electrical wires and its stray dogs and its abject poverty and Miranda looked up at the infinite, murderous blue and wondered if any of her husband's satellites were overhead right now and then she was the satellite looking down at herself from above and only then did she realize that Gilberto was the only thing holding her up, that he'd been half-carrying her for kilometers, that she was wasted and angry and dying and missed her family more than anything and that she wasn't the only one, there were people huddled in whatever shade they could find, there were men screaming at each other but no one was on the streets under the enormous cascading fusion explosion that dominated the sky, that nearest and dearest of stars whose thermal embrace was sucking the life out of her and—

"I'm freezing."

She was lying in the corner of an earthen floored room, mercifully dark, shivering violently.

"I'm freezing," she repeated. "Turn down the AC."

"No AC," said Gilberto.

He mopped her brow with a wet rag. There was terror in his wide brown eyes.

"No electricity, no AC."

Miranda tried to prop herself up, irate. "But I'm telling you I'm *freezing*."

Waves tumbling up the beach at her childhood home in Guanacaste, the one the bulldozers had demolished to build yet another cookie cutter resort. Santiago ending every argument with a ridiculously detailed plan for identifying and fixing the precise problem that had sparked the fight. Zia at sixteen, home on break from school in Switzerland, admitting to her horrified-but-trying-so-hard-to-hide-it mother, complete with air quotes, that yes, she was "sexually active." The curiously empty feeling inside Miranda whenever she completed the rough draft of a new book, a hollowness that was at once satisfying and tragic. The taste of trigonometry. The smell of pink. The color of jazz. The coruscating sheen of the amorphous shapes that were right here all the time but separated from us by the thinnest of membranes, that liminal, invisible *something* that was everything and nothing, impermanent and eternal.

By the time the medevac team arrived, it was already too late.

+

1

THE BORDER SECURITY FORCE OFFICER EXHALED A lungful of smoke at the perfect angle for the wall-mounted air-conditioner to blow it straight into Zia León's face. This was the man she was missing the reunion for. She wanted to cough. She wanted to snatch away the cigar and extinguish it on his forehead. Instead, she smiled.

"TCI informs me that you're refusing to release our containers," said Zia, careful to keep her tone neutral. "Is there some kind of problem?"

"Mrs. Lion," he deliberately used the wrong title and mispronounced her name, "there's no need to be concerned. We aren't refusing to release anything. This is standard procedure, nothing more."

"Standard procedure? Bilaspur Junction doesn't have any borders nearby. This is heartland."

“When it comes to protecting India, there is no such thing as too thorough,” he said with an expansive smile.

Himmat shifted in the seat beside Zia. “The shipment has a verified chain of custody and already passed BSF inspection at the Port of Kolkata,” he said. “You have all the paperwork and authorizations. Give us what we came for.”

The officer drummed pudgy fingers on the pitted Formica desk. “Random inspections can happen at any time. That’s why they’re called ‘random inspections.’” He took a puff. “I mean, she’s a foreigner”—shrugging derisively at Zia—“but I would expect *you* to know how these things work.”

Himmat leaned forward angrily but Zia put a hand out to restrain him. He was a good kid. He could even grow to become a good leader. No point in him making enemies until he absolutely had to, especially when he’d have to deal with the repercussions for years to come.

“This is the fourth consecutive year without a monsoon,” she said. “People are starving. Farmers are bankrupt. Topsoil is blowing away in the wind.” She touched her collarbone. “You may not like me, but India needs those seeds.”

“India doesn’t need you telling us what we do and do not need,” said the officer.

There it was—the thing that drove her mad: that wrapped in a desiccated husk of ignorance and petty viciousness was a kernel of truth.

“This strain was bred by Dr. Chou’s team at UC Davis,” said Himmat. “Drought resistant. High yield. No fertilizer needed. We *do* need this. Badly. If they aren’t planted in time, we’ll miss another harvest.”

“Farmers can plant what they’ve always planted.” Puff. “The monsoon will come when it comes.”

“If they do, and it doesn’t, next year will be even worse,” said Zia.

The officer tapped ash off the end of his cigar into a ceramic tray scarred by a network of thin cracks. "Funny," he said. "Nobody else seems to be able to predict the climate anymore, yet you seem so very sure of yourself. Coming all the way out here to appease your guilt and tell your rich friends back home that you're saving the world. Well, it's time to go back to America. Go home. Go."

"She's from *Costa Rica*, you imbecile," snapped Himmat.

"And *you,*"—the officer smacked his palm on the desk and the ashtray jumped— "cozying up to her like some kind of toy poodle, sucking the foreign aid teat. You are a disgrace. You should go with her, but the way things stand she probably won't even be able to get you a visa. If I had my way, I'd rescind hers preemptively."

Zia touched Himmat's arm to make sure he didn't say something he'd regret. A bead of residual sweat trickled down her spine, raising goosebumps in the air-conditioned chill. Her mother would have been able to make this scene read as profound. She would have teased out the irony and shown it to be a microcosm of the human condition, a reflection of the beautiful, fucked-up universe. Zia's father on the other hand—he would have noticed opportunities to exploit, sought clues that might suggest higher levels of abstraction, bigger pictures that only he could see.

The officer was leaning back in his chair, looking back and forth between them—savoring the flex of what little power he had. The chair itself looked like it might collapse if he wasn't careful. The walls of the room were bare, dirty white paint peeling back to reveal asymmetric islands of lime-green undercoat. The AC unit purred unevenly. The ashtray was the only thing on the desk, and there wasn't any other furniture besides the plastic chairs they occupied. It wasn't so much an office as a room hastily emptied to act as one.

She met the man's eye. This wasn't merely an exercise in fishing for a bribe. He was having far too much fun for something so quotidian. And she couldn't see why a BSF grunt would take the initiative to arrange an impromptu holdup in a borrowed room at a freight yard hours away from wherever he called home. If this little stunt wasn't on his initiative, then it was on someone else's.

"Governor Rao would like that, if you pulled my visa," said Zia quietly.

The officer grinned. "Just when you think all politicians are lying cheats, one comes along who knows what he's doing, who isn't afraid to stir things up."

Zia nodded. "And it seems to be working. All those rallies. I wouldn't be surprised if his party won a dozen more seats in the Lok Sabha in the next election."

"At last, an India for Indians."

Himmat stiffened at the slogan and Zia willed him to keep his peace.

"You're an enterprising man, officer," said Zia. This was just like when she'd been gearing up to represent Costa Rica in Colombo by special ambassadorial appointment of President Kim. "BSF is certainly thorough, but only through the efforts of high performers like yourself. And I'd imagine that Governor Rao might be able to put in a good word for a man like that, encourage the system to promote the deserving."

The man's face closed. "I wouldn't know about that," he said. "What I do know is that your shipment isn't going anywhere."

"Ahh," said Zia. "The shipment, of course. Given how well-informed someone in your position must be, you know that the Minister of Agriculture personally approved this project." The man's ruddy cheeks paled. "And the Minister of

Agriculture plays polo with the President, at whose pleasure Governor Rao serves."

"Rao is invulnerable," the officer snarled. "There'd be riots."

"As you say," said Zia. "But ask yourself—are *you* invulnerable? How far will the good governor go to protect your career, if this mission later proves politically inconvenient? He was appointed to appease a loud minority. Why do you think he's stationed here in Chhattisgarh? Because the governorship is a figurehead position and the woman with the real power here, the chief minister, hates everything he stands for."

The cigar smoldered, forgotten, ash flaking onto pressed khaki pant leg.

"Now,"—Zia offered him a small, close-lipped smile—"as I said, you're an enterprising man, a man with *intuition.* If I was in your shoes and possessed a similar gift, I might take this opportunity to suggest that perhaps the best way to serve Governor Rao would be to release the shipment to us so as to spare him the unpleasantness of a browbeating from Delhi. You can still tell him you held it up and that I had to come down here personally to get it released, disrupting our field operations. Tell him whatever you damn well please. But give us our containers, and sleep soundly tonight knowing that you saved your career and did your part to prevent a famine."

All trace of good humor had evaporated from behind his eyes. You could almost hear his thoughts racing around the cul-de-sac, probing for a hidden exit. Zia didn't want to have to make good on her threat. That would mean asking Vachan for a favor. A big one. She was here to offer help, not ask for it. But if she couldn't make this suit-stuffer see reason, she'd have no choice.

The officer broke eye contact and ground out his cigar in the ashtray with unnecessary force. Although his shoulders remained pointedly un-slumped, his presence deflated like a punctured party balloon. Without looking up, he raised a hand and waved them from the room.

+

2

"DID YOU SEE HIS FACE?" HIMMAT'S OWN EXPRESSION was rapturous as he offered Zia a fresh coconut. "It was *priceless.*" He shook his head. "I don't know how you do it, but when there's so much bullshit to crawl through, it feels good to see the jerks heaping it on fall into the muck themselves once in a while."

Zia accepted the coconut. Drank. Tried and failed to appreciate the cool, sweet water in the sweltering afternoon heat. Outside the station the air was thick with dust and humidity—it felt oily on the skin, more liquid than gas. Buses, trucks, taxis, bicycles, scooters, and rickshaws roared by in a haphazard mass migration. The smell of rubber, melting asphalt, and VOCs went to her head like so much champagne. Was this what her mom had felt like just before the Heat Wave had claimed her and twenty million other souls?

"What's wrong?" said Himmat, his gaze sharpening.

There was something inside Zia peeling away like the paint on the wall of that sad little room, but it was too early to see what color lay beneath. And just because Himmat was onto something didn't mean she wanted to admit it, even to herself.

Zia forced a smile. "Oh, it's nothing."

He raised his eyebrows. "Come on," he said. "We've been working together for what, two years now? You just showed that asshole what's what and snatched the seeds from his clutches. Once this cohort finishes training, our volunteers will be able to distribute them just in time for planting. You should be celebrating, but you look like a doctor just gave you a terminal diagnosis."

Despite herself, Zia chuckled. She gave Himmat a once over. Thick wavy hair, large eyes and sharp features that brought an owl to mind, loose linen shirt over jeans and battered work boots. Smart. Earnest. Hardworking. Penchant for Aperol Spritzes, which he singlehandedly prepared for every graduating class of their dryland farming training program. He'd proven himself as her lieutenant here. Which meant he deserved to continue growing, even if it made her uncomfortable.

"Take it further." She took another swig of coconut water and drew circles with an index finger.

When he opened his eyes wide, it accentuated the owl.

"You might be happy to have overcome this hurdle, but you know it's just one of many," he said slowly. "You love your work, but you've been chasing disasters for so many years that they're starting to blend together. The satisfaction you take in helping people wilts in light of the fact that you can only offer stopgap solutions to systemic problems. You're treating symptoms instead of addressing root causes, and you have to beg donors for the privilege of doing so. Your energy is flagging. Your compass is spinning. Am I getting somewhere?"

The corner of Zia's mouth quirked to accommodate her burgeoning pride and melancholy. "Yeah, you're getting somewhere," she said. "My first field op was typhoon response in Taiwan. Flash floods took out all the bridges in Hualien and debris flows wiped out entire neighborhoods in seconds. Afterward there was this huge international response as footage went viral. We had more donations than we knew what to do with. We started with direct relief—just getting people fed and sheltered. But once we had things more or less sorted and were trying to get started on long-term recovery, the mayor's office kept dawdling. We'd get a permit for our reconstruction plan but without a start date, approval for one site but not another, requests for additional impact reporting when the proposal was already thoroughly vetted. I spent months in extended dinner meetings trying to figure out what the problem was, why they wouldn't let us get to work. But I couldn't get a straight explanation, only promises that weren't really lies but never quite came true either. Drove me batshit. Finally, a politically connected friend from Taipei came for a visit and tagged along to one of the banquets. Afterward he took me aside and patiently explained that there was a consortium planning to build a new casino in town, an initiative the mayor's office secretly backed because of the jobs and tax revenues it would bring, and that the project was contingent on buying up the destroyed homes for redevelopment before people could rebuild them." She could still remember Li Jie's pained expression as he dangled his feet over the seawall, face illuminated by the glowing ember of his cigarette and tongue loosened by their host's liberally dispensed *baijiu*.

"They wouldn't let us rebuild because they didn't *want* to rebuild. They wanted to put a casino there instead."

Zia drained the last of the water and handed the coconut back to the vendor.

"He gleaned all that from one dinner?" asked Himmat.

The vendor raised his machete and split the coconut with a *thwack*. Then with a practiced twist, he carved out the thick white meat and presented it to her piled up in one of the hemispherical halves. She chewed on a fatty piece. Swallowed.

"I was a hamster that didn't realize it was on a wheel," she said. She turned to the side and spat into the dust, which flashed ever so briefly scarlet before the parched earth sucked up her saliva in front of their eyes—molten lava hardening into basalt. "All that wasted effort. All those missed opportunities to actually do something that mattered, to serve the people I sought to serve."

Zia squeezed Himmat's shoulder. "Listen to what people mean instead of what they say. Pursue subtext. Don't just speculate on motive, ask what context shapes the motives on offer. Reframe that context. You've got a knack for it. Now you need to develop it into a superpower. In this job, it's everything."

Even in the chaos of the street, the moment held like an expanding soap bubble—until a chirp from her phone popped it.

A text. Not the group chat, but a direct message from Selai. The profile picture next to the notification set off a cascade of memories. Bleached reefs. Quantum theory. Singing along to Disney songs. Impossibly elegant proofs submitted in response to rudimentary math assignments. A dizzying ascent to internet stardom. *Don't you dare bail,* Zia read. *No excuses of any kind, especially of the long-suffering savior variety.*

There's a new project I want to tell you about.

The reunion. Zia checked the time. This debacle had resolved itself faster than expected. She could still make the flight to Zürich if she went straight to the airport.

She shouldn't. She should. Fuck it, what did "should" mean anyway?

Zia looked up at Himmat, who was peering at her quizzically.

"You're in charge," she said. "Effective immediately. I'll be back in a few days."

His eyes widened.

"And you're right," she continued, raising a hand to hail a cab. "I don't know what I need right now, but maybe a change of pace will help."

3

+

ZIA TUCKED AWAY HER DOG-EARED COPY OF *The Princess Bride*, muscled her carry-on out of the overhead bin, and triaged her inbox as she walked up the gangway into Zürich International Airport. There was a message from Jason right at the top. The subject read, "You're gonna hate this, but" with a shrug emoji appended to soften the blow.

Zia opened the email.

Z, sorry to bug you during PTO (which you should take more of), but we've got a new major donor prospect who wants to press flesh. Apparently he's also flying into ZRH this afternoon. Assuming your flight arrives on time, can you swing by to meet him at the Blue Bottle in the international terminal before you head off to the mountains?

Says you'll recognize him. Asked me not to mention his name, wanted it to be a surprise. Weird, I know, but whales are always odd ducks if you can forgive a mixed metaphor.

Thank you, thank you, thank you, thank you, thank you. You know I wouldn't ask if we didn't really need it. Wish I had stayed in the field like you. Fundraising = gargling sweaty balls with strep throat.

Please don't murder me in my sleep, J

P.S. Yes, I will make you my special tacos al pastor next time you visit. Promise.

Damn.

Zia belatedly realized that she had stopped right in the middle of the bustling terminal—a boulder in the stream of other travelers. A beleaguered mother pushed a stroller with twin toddlers. A lithe woman with amber eyes looked away as soon as Zia met her gaze. A squadron of Japanese bankers argued as they hurried to their gate, the lack of overt labeling on their secret brand suits signaling just how extravagantly expensive they must be. All of them buoyed along by a ghostly Brian Eno ambient album that was glass and steel and time melted down and transmuted into music.

Zia wanted to see her friends, wanted to hear whatever it was Selai wanted to tell her. Zia did *not* want to schmooze with yet another billionaire looking to assuage a guilty conscience or launder a dirty reputation. How had Himmat put it? *You're treating symptoms instead of addressing root causes, and you have to beg donors for the privilege of doing so.* He really was learning fast. Maybe too fast.

She sighed, scanning the terminal for a map. No need. There was the Blue Bottle sign, just around the bend toward baggage claim and across from a full-wall ultra-high-definition photographic print that must be one of Selai's—a red gummy bear perched on a craggy peak overlooking an Arctic fjord with water so absurdly turquoise it might leak out of the frame.

Zia set out toward the coffeeshop, then faltered again as an even more disturbing thought struck. *Says you'll recognize him. Asked me not to mention his name, wanted it to be a surprise.* Could her dad be nursing a macchiato, waiting for her to waltz in? Her stomach twisted. It would be just like Santiago, wouldn't it? Manufacturing an excuse to show up one day after years of silence. Buying his way back into her life despite his tacit disapproval of her choices. How appropriate that he would appear right here right now, just as she was en route to a reunion at the boarding school he'd shipped her off to a lifetime ago.

No. This wasn't a conversation she wanted to have right now.

Or ever.

The worst part was that she knew she was being unfair. That the silence had been mutual. That both of them had helped erect the wall that had grown between them. But what gave him the right to tear that wall down just because he felt like it?

The café drew Zia like a magnet, her body falling toward it through the crowd, against her will. One foot in front of the other across the agglomerated marble floor, carry-on humming along behind. The sleek espresso machine shrieked as she crossed the threshold into an airy space that was all blonde wood and polished concrete—every detail designed with self-conscious obsession.

There he was. Corner table. Complete with the prophesied macchiato and apologetic lopsided grin.

Not her father.

Maybe worse.

Tommy.

+

4

"FIRST OFF, I WANT TO SAY I'M SORRY," SAID TOMMY, his blue eyes clear as cut glass. "I didn't want to ambush you like this, but I was worried that you might not come if you knew it was me."

Instead of responding, Zia sipped her pour-over—black—and remembered their first date. With butterflies in her stomach, she'd squeezed out of the window and climbed down the rough stone wall into the orchard, where Tommy had been waiting with a fresh Guaria Morada orchid. He'd led Zia by the hand through the shadows, along the lake, and into the forest.

She'd seen the glow long before she could figure out the source. They'd pushed through a patch of brambles and emerged into a clearing with a French bistro table and two chairs standing in the middle. Lights were strung through the branches of the surrounding trees, as if stars had fallen from the sky just to illuminate their meal. White truffle salad. Beef carpaccio. Fresh sourdough smothered in cultured butter. An assortment of raw milk cheeses and homemade jams. Beluga caviar. A twenty-sixteen Loire Valley pét-nat. Ridiculously over the top for a pair of fifteen-year-olds, but ridiculously over the top was precisely the impression Tommy had hoped to make. Corporoyals were like that, and Zia had appreciated the gesture more than she'd like to admit. Everyone wanted to feel special sometimes. What got you in trouble was believing you were better than everyone else.

Tommy cleared his throat. "Jason sent over the draft annual report. You're doing incredible work in Chhattisgarh. Nine thousand farmers trained. Twenty-five hundred rescued from the brink of bankruptcy. Open source gene license on Dr. Chou's new miracle seed. Looks like what the Green Revolution was *supposed* to be. And before that: Ghana, Sri Lanka, Fiji, Bolivia, Taiwan, Guatemala, and the Maldives." Memories flashed through Zia's mind—vestiges of doing what little she could to help hollow-eyed survivors in her friends' respective homelands. "More rigorous program data and better impact metrics than any comparable NGO. You've been all over the map tackling every kind of disaster." He golf clapped. "Kudos, seriously. We need more people like you."

Zia tilted her head back and gazed straight up into the tastefully recessed light. That's what everyone was doing all the time: shining forth from a certain remove—dimmable, perhaps, capable of coloration, refraction even, but never dark, never off, until the reaper threw the final switch. She looked back at Tommy. Blinked. Watched his face fade in through the negative after-image the light had impressed on her retinas.

"So, SaudExxon is looking to buff up its rep, or is it you personally?" she asked.

"Changes are brewing," he said. "And it's past time we got out ahead of something. Being a laggard gets old."

"Being a laggard makes sense when you have everything to lose."

He raised his diminutive cup. "My glass is half-full," he said. "How about yours?"

Zia stared at her coffee, wishing she could read the shimmer of light on its dark surface like a psychic could tea leaves. Galang was going to flip out when she told him about this.

"For your sake, I hope your reservoirs are too," she said.

"Ahh," said Tommy, pushing back a floppy lock of blond hair. "Now we get to it. Oil money too dirty for you? You do the Lord's work, no ill-gotten alms accepted? That's how this goes, right?"

"Tommy," Zia kept her voice as gentle as she could. "Why are you here, really?" She leaned forward. "And don't try to sell me the same bollocks you did Jason."

He opened his mouth. Closed it. Shut his eyes for a moment during which Zia suddenly noticed the crow's feet that had formed at their corners, the streaks of silver in the blond. The old Tommy hadn't known how to rein himself in, hadn't *wanted* to know.

When he spoke his voice was rough. "Look, I just—" He stopped, started again. "This reunion. I know it's silly, but I've been thinking about it a lot. I've been thinking about *us* a lot. And that's even sillier—laughable, even. But I— As the date got closer, I just couldn't get it out of my head. I was such a total ass back then. To you. To everyone. And I just couldn't bear the thought of sipping cocktails and pretending to be interested in all the bullshit catch-up. And I know we would never have a chance to really talk, that you wouldn't want to anyway. So I just figured—"

"That you'd lie to my boss to trick me into meeting you here?"

"It wasn't a lie," he said. "Honestly, I'd love to support your work. And I have the resources to do so in a big way. I wasn't kidding about being impressed. But I would never do it without your blessing. This conversation isn't for me to vet you. It's the reverse."

Zia thought of Himmat, what it would mean to him if they could increase their headcount. They could expand the test program in West Bengal, lower the threshold for loan forgiveness. Jason would be able to make his fundraising quota, at least until the whole dance started again next year. Zia would... Zia would be able to keep doing what she'd been doing—pretending to scratch an itch when she was really picking a scab.

"You want to know the real reason I'm here," said Tommy. "Well, I don't know if I realized it until right now, but the reason I'm here is to apologize." He stood, knocked on the tabletop. "My offer stands. Good to see you, León. Really. Have fun tonight."

"You too," said Zia. "And... I'll consider it."

There was that grin again.

"All a man can ask," he said, and was gone.

Zia watched his retreating back, noticed how the crowd parted unconsciously to accommodate the supreme confidence of his gait, the precision with which he hewed to his own line.

High school was a long time ago. Sometimes, people changed. She had.

Hadn't she?

+

5

"IT'S A PHYSICAL MANIFESTATION OF THE GROUP chat," said Li Jie.

"I prefer to think of the group chat as a digital instantiation of us," said Selai.

"What's the difference, really?" asked Daniela. "We contain multitudes."

It *was* hard to believe. Zia, Aafreen, Galang, Kodjo, Selai, Daniela, Vachan, and Li Jie all in the same place at the same time. The band was getting back together, and Zia silently thanked the gods of red tape that the obstinate BSF officer hadn't made her miss this. Then she silently thanked Himmat for pushing her to actually go when she finally had the chance.

"So this is what high school reunions are like," said Kodjo, looking around at the campus from which they'd graduated a decade and a half ago. "Nicer venue than in the movies, but they nail the ambient level of social anxiety."

The reception was staged in the tiered garden in front of the school. A repurposed thirteenth century château, the fortress now struggled to keep its elite students in rather than invaders out. Torches burned in brackets along the exterior walls and braziers smoldered throughout the garden, illuminating guests and setting in flickering firelight. Servers prowled with trays of hors d'oeuvres. A live chamber orchestra soared through Vivaldi's *The Four Seasons*. The drinks were appropriately strong, and Zia was sipping a rather excellent Old Fashioned.

"Hard to believe we spent four years here," she said.

"Felt like a lifetime," said Vachan.

"Feels like a lifetime ago," said Aafreen.

"Sometimes, I wish I could go back in a time machine," said Kodjo. "Then I remember how awful teenagers are to each other." He grimaced. "And if Lucy is any indicator, it isn't limited to teenagers."

"Want to talk about it?" asked Zia tentatively.

Kodjo swallowed the rest of his gin and tonic. "She's got a bulldog of a lawyer. They're shooting for full custody, the house, everything."

"For fuck's sake," said Vachan.

"But the boys," said Kodjo, shaking his head. "I'm amazed at how calmly they're dealing with it all, even if their classmates are at least as bad as ours were."

"Kids are more resilient than we give them credit for," said Li Jie.

"I mean, we survived, right?" said Aafreen, with a crooked grin that accentuated her almost painfully intense beauty.

"There's that." Kodjo chuckled. "But let's not get caught

up in my divorce proceedings. I spend enough time thinking about that as it is. Daniela, I hear rumors the new label you're shepherding is really taking off."

"Oh, nothing serious yet," said Daniela.

"If three Grammys in one year isn't serious for an indie, what is?" said Li Jie.

"Breakeven," said Daniela. "You're not truly independent until you're profitable."

"Spoken like a real artist," said Vachan.

"Real artists hit the black," said Daniela, the promptness of her response reminding Zia of the ever so brief period when Vachan and Daniela had dated.

"Amen," said Selai.

"And they definitely wear leather jackets," said Galang, tugging on Daniela's sleeve with a wink. "Always patinated. Never distressed."

"That's right," said Daniela, with an infectious laugh. "The secret to making great art is to look good doing it."

These were Zia's people. She felt an ease in their presence she hadn't felt in years, but also something more, as if, while taking a breather from constructing her house of self, she'd noticed that said house had accrued enough moats and fortifications to rival this chateau.

The conversation ebbed and flowed between reminiscence and personal updates, jokes and pathos. Li Jie was writing a new programming language that he hoped would be as groundbreaking as Lisp. Aafreen was in the midst of renegotiating half a dozen Maldivian emigration treaties. Vachan was slowly but surely taking over the family business, which involved bitter fights with his grandmother over his decision to increase wages for migrant laborers at the tea estates. At one point, Tommy strolled by talking animatedly to two of his old lacrosse teammates and nodded to Zia surreptitiously.

This conversation isn't for me to vet you. It's the reverse. Zia was still trying to parse the surreal airport rendezvous. Per Kodjo's point, teenagers were awful to each other. Was the fact that she wanted so badly to hate Tommy blinding her to the fact that he no longer deserved it? Zia knew how painful snap judgements could be to the person on the receiving end. If she declined his offer, was she avoiding an elephant trap or slapping away an olive branch? Was it even ethical for her to refuse, no matter the source of funds, given how many people they could use the money to help? But wasn't that an argument for taking blood money? Where did you draw the line? These were precisely the sorts of questions she was getting tired of asking herself.

Aafreen was talking, but Galang was gazing at Zia curiously. He'd noticed the nod. She returned his look to implicitly promise a tête-à-tête. It was surprisingly easy to fall back into the telepathy routine they'd developed while jointly editing her mother's book. Hard to believe they'd get to see each other in person again in less than two weeks when he'd promised to drop by Chhattisgarh en route to a new assignment. They'd have time to really talk then.

Li Jie rattled the ice in his empty tumbler. "Seriously though," he said. "If it weren't for you all, I honestly don't know if I would have made it through this joint."

They looked up at the ramparts, which the torchlight just barely kissed.

"I feel you, brother," said Vachan.

"I wouldn't have admitted it then, but I had never been more scared than the day we arrived," said Zia, remembering the disorientation of leaving everything and everyone she knew behind. She'd held back tears until her parents were out of view, then found a bathroom stall to sob in. She'd imagined that she was the only one, that the confidence her new classmates projected was sincere. The truth was many of them were in far worse shape than she was. Nobody had their shit together, least of all those who seemed to. Life was one big exercise in making things up as you went along.

"Second that," said Kodjo.

"Toast." Selai raised her glass, catching Zia's eye as she did so and managing a similar feat of telepathy, with a similar message: time to sneak off for a sidebar. Whatever it was she had up her sleeve, Zia was about to find out. "May the wind fill our sails, the stars guide our voyage, and the bottles of rum never run dry."

"I still can't quite believe we're all here," said Aafreen.

"And it's not even a wedding," said Daniela.

"Or a funeral," said Galang.

"To friendship," said Zia. "Until death do us part."

Memories swirled and glasses clinked.

6

+

ZIA PULLED HER DRESS UP AND OVER HER HEAD IN one smooth motion. Next to her, Selai did the same. Then off came the bras and underwear. No jewelry. Neither of them ever wore jewelry. They piled the clothes on top of their discarded flats and stared out into darkness.

"I can't believe we're doing this," said Zia with a giddy laugh.

"I can't believe we waited so long," said Selai.

"Okay," said Zia. If they waited any longer, she might chicken out. "Ready? One, two, *three*!"

A split second of free fall, then Zia hit the water.

It was so cold that it didn't feel so at first. There was just the visceral shock of sudden submersion.

They both came up spluttering.

"My nipples could cut steel right now," said Selai.

"You're not in Fiji anymore," said Zia.

"That's for fucking sure."

"I've had exactly the wrong amount of liquor—enough to make me do this but not enough to keep me warm."

"Fucking glacier melt," said Selai.

"Hey, at least there are still glaciers to melt," said Zia. "Now, let's get this over with before we succumb."

Selai didn't need to be told twice. She swam with the grace and power of an Olympic athlete. Kicking hard and gasping for breath, Zia followed in her wake.

Breath.

Stroke. Stroke. Stroke.

Breath.

Stroke. Stroke. Stroke.

Breath.

Stroke. Stroke—and then there was mud between her toes and algae-slick rock under her hands and they pulled themselves up onto the little island hidden among the reeds.

"Remember when we'd swim out here to smoke joints?" asked Selai as they sat back on the grass.

"You'd seal them in a plastic bag with a lighter and carry it between your teeth."

"And you'd unleash those truly epic philosophical rants."

"I had to do something," said Zia. "Otherwise you'd melt my brain by taking us down another theoretical physics rabbit hole."

"Nothing is sweeter than the memory of a misspent youth."

"If you're going to take up poetry, we really do need a joint."

Selai snorted and threw an arm around Zia's shoulders, scooting over so their bare sides and legs pressed together to share warmth. Where skin touched, they could feel each other's goosebumps recede.

"How are you holding up, really?" asked Selai. "Not the cocktail party version. The DL."

The standard anecdotes came to mind, the ready answers that would move the conversation along at a steady clip. And they were all accurate, or at least they used to be. But somehow, here, Zia couldn't bring herself to voice them. It was as if all their narrative substance, everything that made them not only factual but also true, had been shed along with her clothes.

In a flash of terrifying clarity, Zia understood what it must be like for Natalia Lafourcade to play "Hasta la Raíz" at every stop on every tour, repeating a hit written so many years before because the audience wanted it so badly, wanted the way her singing it made them feel. Just because you outgrew your own work didn't mean anyone else did. The better the work, the bigger the problem.

Across the water and up the hill, the chateau was bathed in torchlight. A few strands of Vivaldi twined through the chorus of frog song. Time thickened—as if the right word spoken in the right way might transport them across millennia.

"The DL"—Zia sighed—"is struggle city."

"Yikes," said Selai, shaking her hand as if she'd burned it. "That bad, huh? I've taken a few excursions there myself. Nasty neighborhood."

"I almost didn't come," said Zia. "To the reunion, I mean. I was planning to, but then this asshole border guard swoops in and seizes our latest seed shipment. I had to go get it released."

"Did you eat his soul, or merely rip his throat out?"

"Just made threats I didn't want to have to make good on," said Zia. "And luckily for him and me, he didn't force the issue. But afterward, I felt... nothing."

"Nothing?"

"Nothing," said Zia. "Just tired. Tired of corrupt officials and prissy donors. Tired of systems just broken enough to keep chugging, regardless of who they hurt, as long as the people who benefit from the status quo oil the gears once in a while. Tired of breathing topsoil. And my deputy—Himmat—he saw it in me."

"Smart kid," said Selai. "Promote him."

"You know what? I should," said Zia.

Selai hugged Zia's shoulder and rocked from side to side. "So, where do you go from here?"

Zia tore her eyes away from the glimmering fortress. She looked up to the constellations, brilliant without city glow to dull them, shining down through the thin alpine atmosphere, their light having traveled for aeons across the depths of space to gleam off the ring of snowcapped peaks that surrounded this remote valley. Interstice's satellites were somewhere up there, falling, forever falling, around the planet whose denizens they stitched together into a single vast tribe.

"Fuck if I know," said Zia. "But enough about me. You've kept me in suspense long enough. What's this new project you're so keen on?"

"It's..." Selai paused, uncharacteristically shy. "It's a bit of a weird one."

Zia rolled her eyes theatrically. "After surviving this place, you earned a doctorate in physics from MIT. You identified the perpetrators of the Great Parmigiano-Reggiano Heist fourteen years after the crime took place. You built up so many millions of followers for your Gummy Bear World Tour stream that Haribo had no choice but to sponsor you. You swim like a goddamned otter. What does weird even mean to you, sweetheart?"

Selai laughed. "It's like you're my agent, but I'm the only person you're selling me to."

"If I'm your agent, do I get to order you to stop beating around the bush before mine freezes off?"

"Okay, okay," said Selai. She took a deep breath. "It starts, as all truly great stories do, on a dark and stormy night—better yet, it's about why we can't seem to make sense of how nights get all dark and stormy in the first place."

+

7

"ARE YOU FUCKING KIDDING ME?" ZIA LEÓN couldn't repress a laugh as she opened the cardboard box to reveal a frozen deep-dish pizza wrapped in tin foil. It couldn't be more out of place in the only cafe in the rural Chhattisgarhi village she called home—which itself couldn't have been more different than the Swiss mountain hamlet in which she and Galang had last seen each other at the reunion ten days ago. "How did you get this on the plane? It must weigh twelve pounds."

"Cut it in half, packed each half with icepacks in a thermal lining, and stuffed it all into my checked luggage," said Galang with an extravagant eye-roll. "Duh."

A lump rose in Zia's throat. After months of *muthia* with a brief intermission of reunion finger food, pizza was a mythical creature from a parallel dimension, half-nostalgia and half-carbohydrates. Galang had even brought the box so it could be presented in its authentic packaging. "I would never—"

"I know you wouldn't, you silly bitch," said Galang as he took a prim sip from his cup of steaming chai. "Which is precisely why I brought it. I stopped in Oakland for a meeting on the way down here and I remembered the unadulterated joy on your face when I came out to visit you in college and you introduced me to this place. *Manna from the gods,* you said. Yes, exactly that look, but with less of the *I'm about to break down and cry.* For heaven's sake, Zia, pull yourself together."

Zia's snort squeezed out a tear and Galang reached over to wipe it away with the pad of his thumb. People relied on her, which made it hard to let go. Rocks don't cry, except, apparently, when a dear friend shows up bearing gifts from a past life.

"I hope your clothes don't smell like pizza," said Zia. "If you meet any cute boys on this trip, what will you tell them?"

"There is no sacrifice too large for Zachary's," said Galang like a captain going down with his ship. "And any boys that don't appreciate the incomparable pheromones of tomato and basil don't deserve my attention anyway."

Zia looked up into Galang's wide eyes. His chestnut irises were twin time machines that took her back two decades. Instead of Galang the Pulitzer Prize-winning investigative journalist, she saw Galang the gangly fourteen-year-old showing up with the rest of their privileged, abandoned cohort to run the petty, savage, searing gauntlet of boarding school.

"You," Zia punched Galang's shoulder, "are a *very nice* person."

Galang batted her hand away.

"Oh, come on," he said, but his cycs sparkled.

"So, what is it this time?"

Galang stretched luxuriously. "Gonna chill by the pool and get my tan on."

Zia just raised her eyebrows.

"Okay, okay," said Galang. "You know how the Maldives anchored their floating city to the submerged islands? Well, a few years back they decided that New Malé would never be anything more than a stopgap, so they started a resettlement program. The government signed treaties with other governments trading certain rights for special displacement visas. Buuuuuuuut, as you might have guessed, those visas haven't been distributed as originally intended. A ring of officials has been accepting bribes for the prime spots and simultaneously siphoning off funds intended to make good on the treaties." Galang waggled a finger. "Naughty, naughty. A steaming pile of blatantly selfish bullshit. Anyway, I've been tracking it for nine months now and Aafreen just hooked me up with some local sources, turns out one of the dickwad crooked officials is her second cousin, so I'm heading down to flooded paradise to rake some motherfucking muck."

Zia shook her head. "I worked on the island evac."

"I know," said Galang quietly.

The sour tang of brine and flooded sewer. An old fisherman, skin a contour map of wrinkles, his arthritic claws latched onto the railing in front of his hut as storm surge lapped at his bony hips, fighting off Zia as she attempted to pull him aboard the Zodiac. Kneeling in front of a child in an oversized life jacket and telling the little girl with the scared eyes and the heart-shaped face to think of this as an *adventure*. Boat after boat disgorging blinking, confused refugees into the floating capital to face the arbitrary bureaucratic fate that lacked the clarity but retained the powerless terror of the natural disaster they had narrowly escaped. Zia's frustration at the need to appeal for public support, the money flowing in from all over the world when she managed to pluck a few heartstrings. The late night sessions working with Aafreen to try to create a better process for getting people back on their feet, a process that didn't suffer from the same mistakes that sabotaged so many well-intentioned programs, the over-caffeinated tumble of ideas reminding them both of rehearsing declensions for Latin exams.

"Give her a hug from me," said Zia. "It was so good to see her in Switzerland."

"I know, right?" said Galang. "We can't depend on the odd high-school reunion. We need to get the old gang back together more often."

"It's hard. We're all scattered around the world and everyone's got their own jobs, worries, and even kids. Life, right?"

"Despite my fervent intention to avoid such a catastrophe at any cost, we are getting old."

"I feel terrible for Kodjo," said Zia. "The whole situation sounds like a shit show."

"Phew! It's about time," said Galang. "Lucy was a devil in disguise. Did you know that she cheated on him with the agriculture minister and they colluded to have Kodjo thrown out of office?"

"Seriously? I mean, I knew she was a snake, but I didn't know *that*."

"And Vachan finally standing up to his cci." Galang let out a long, low whistle. "I never thought I'd see the day. Have you met her?"

Zia nodded. "They had me over for string hoppers when I was stationed in Trincomalee. She is a force of nature."

"I just hope he doesn't pull any punches. The way their family works, if he shows the slightest sign of weakness, she'll build a coalition among the cousins to replace him. If fortune had played a different hand, that woman could have dominated the Kremlin. She's a born autocrat."

"Daniela is killing it though."

"She played me a few tunes from their next batch of albums," said Galang. "There were a few super trippy tracks, but for the most part, I didn't quite grok it. Of course, that means less than nothing because I've never had an ear for cool. What I do know is that Daniela has such a finely tuned ear for cool that I can't tell whether she's identifying trends before they break out or whether it's her blessing that makes them pop."

"Both," said Zia.

Galang laughed. "Good point. The zeitgeist is the zeitgeist is the zeitgeist."

"You somehow always manage to know everything about everyone."

"That's why you need me around, sister. Ears to the tracks."

Zia laughed. "Some things never change. You're still trading gossip like a prying teenager."

"Gossip gets a bad rap," said Galang. "Love, war, art, all the important things in life are gossip. We're like electrons, we only exist in relation to each other."

"Yet another thing that never changes: you always have a response to everything."

"A professional hazard, I'm afraid."

"Well, I guess it's journalism that's kept you in touch with folks. Chasing stories around the world. Shining a light on abuse of power. You better watch out, somebody's going to turn your life into a blockbuster biopic one day."

"Yeesh, I hope not. But... If they do, promise me that you will personally ensure they get Hasan Herianto to play me.

He's so dreamy."

"Hah, like I have Hollywood hookups."

"It's far more likely that they make the movie about you." Galang wiggled his fingers and dropped his voice an octave. "Zia León travels the world rescuing people from disaster. Daughter of a tech billionaire and an environmental luminary, she fights to relieve the suffering of strangers amidst the wreckage of a dying planet."

"Oh, the melodrama," said Zia. She didn't show it, but the joke stung because it hit a little too close to home. Decade-old headlines scrolled across her vision whenever she curled up on her hard cot and closed her eyes. *Electrical Grids Fail Across the Tropics as Temperature Spikes. Nineteen Countries Declare State of Emergency. Heat Wave Death Toll Hits 20 Million.* The maddening pity of the Costa Rican president elect as she accepted Zia's withdrawal from ambassadorial appointment. The impossible chasm that had opened between Zia and her father, grief wrenching them apart along an invisible fault line. She took a sip of chai, letting the spicy, creamy, sweetness wash away her angst. "Production would stop as soon as the film crew discovered how mundane humanitarian aid really is. Logistics isn't particularly cinematic."

"Meh," Galang waved away her objection. "Montage, montage, montage. They'd need to inject some drama though, maybe a spurned lover? Or is there something along those lines already developing?"

Zia guffawed as Galang leaned in conspiratorially.

"Alas, no," she said. "I'm super boring. All work, no play. Hardly worth your layover."

Galang gave her a look that communicated his deep concern that Zia was turning into an ascetic monk suffering from that strangest form of sexual perversion: celibacy. She responded with a lascivious wink that she hoped implied a whimsical preference for the freedom of un-attachment. She wasn't a monk, she was a knight errant. Or at least that's what she tried to tell herself on the rare occasion that she actually had time to entertain such banalities.

Galang leaned across the table. "Speaking of drama, have you decided what to do about Tommy?"

Zia rubbed her forehead. "Shit. Jason's been harassing me about it almost daily, which is maddening but understandable. We could really use the money. We can *always* use the money. But taking oil money to respond to climate change catastrophes?"

"It has a certain twisted logic."

"And then there's the fact that it's Tommy."

"You know what I think of him," said Galang. "But you probably shouldn't be taking financial advice from a journalist, we're barely managing to keep our industry afloat as it is."

"*You* know what *I* think of him," said Zia. She shook her head. "Twisted logic seems to be precisely what my job requires these days."

"I hear you," said Galang with feeling.

"Maybe that's why I've been distracted lately."

"With what?"

The chill of alpine breeze on naked skin, stars wheeling above. *It starts, as all truly great stories do, on a dark and stormy night—better yet, it's about why we can't seem to make sense of how nights get all dark and stormy in the first place.*

"So you know how global temperatures have leveled out over the past few years?" asked Zia.

Galang nodded. "No scientist I've interviewed has been able to fully explain it. Lots of handwaving."

"Right," said Zia. "Selai has made it her mission to figure out why, or at least why scientists can't explain it."

"Really? Now that's interesting. When she sets her mind to something..."

"...something usually gives before she gives up," said Zia.

"Exactly."

"What about Haribo?" asked Galang. "Isn't she being paid gobs of money to gallivant around the world taking exceptionally gorgeous photos of gummy bears?"

"Well, that's the other thing about Selai," said Zia. "As soon as she masters something, she moves on. This is me reading between the lines, but I think she wanted to treat social media virality as a problem she could solve. Once she broke the internet, Haribo got excited and Selai got bored. So when she started hearing from her uncles in the Fijian cabinet how unreliable climate models threw off all their infrastructure plans, she started digging. You know how serious Fiji is about climate science."

"It's never fun to be a canary in a coal mine."

"Right. She's read every paper, ripped out the innards of every model like a mechanic gutting a clunker, and done her own tests running open-source Mozaik architecture on top of the Interstice research data pool. She told me about it at the reunion and I've been reviewing her materials."

"And?"

"The upshot is that the numbers just don't add up," said Zia. It had felt good to dig so deeply into something that her mind began to run scenarios on autopilot. "Until a few years ago, climate models made somewhat different projections from each other but generally agreed on what direction we were headed and what inputs were causal. But none of them projected global temperatures leveling out, and nobody has been able to identify why they were wrong. There are a lot of folks tossing around theories, but when you do the math, none have enough explanatory power to make sense of it."

"Hence the handwaving."

"Correct," said Zia. "Selai's still doing mathematical forensics. The models are insanely complex, so there's a lot there. But I started thinking about you and me, all the scientists we talked to while editing my mom's book."

"Uh huh."

"And I'm wondering whether the problem isn't in the models themselves, but in the inputs. What if the math is right, but the models are reflecting reality imperfectly? What if a flaw in the models' descriptions of nature is the source of the disconnect? I've been making a list of the researchers we can introduce Selai to."

"The earth system is a big haystack in which to find a needle," said Galang.

"Which is why she'll need all the help she can get," said Zia.

"I have a serious question," said Galang.

"Yes?"

"When do you sleep, woman?!"

Zia laughed. "Who needs sleep when things need doing?"

"You crazy," said Galang, shaking his head. "I require all the beauty sleep a man can get."

"I just can't stand the feeling of surplus bandwidth," said Zia, a brittle truth. "If my job isn't all-consuming, why am I doing it?"

"As the coach I never had would have said: leave it all on the field, or don't play," said Galang. "I guess your work does have its upsides, though. I get to see you, Aafreen, Kodjo, Daniela, Vachan, Selai, Li Jie, and the rest whenever a story takes me to the right place. It's always like this, a brief opportunity for catch-up. Honestly, if it wasn't for the group chat you set up, we would all have fallen out of touch with each other. But you've spent months at a time with each of them at various points over the years."

"Directing disaster response in their respective countries isn't exactly the kind of bonding opportunity any of us are looking for," she said. Typhoons. Fires. Floods. Droughts. Ecosystem collapse. This was the montage Galang wanted screenwriters to dramatize.

Galang shrugged. "Well, I'm only here because of corrupt assholes, so take what you can get, I guess."

"Fair enough."

"How's this particular catastrophe treating you? I was hacking up a lung from all the dust on the way out here from the airport. And the lines out of your supply station are insane."

Zia winced. "That dust is topsoil lost to wind erosion. This region is an agricultural breadbasket, but it's been three years since the last real monsoon. Crop failure. Bankruptcy. Malnutrition. We're focused on distributing supplies to the needy and teaching dryland techniques to farmers so that India doesn't turn into a Dust Bowl."

"Fuck."

"That's about the size of it."

Zia hesitated.

Galang narrowed his eyes. "What is it?"

"It's just..."

"Yes?"

She thought of Himmat. Of Selai. Of paint, peeling. She hadn't meant to bring this up, hadn't even really admitted it to herself. But Galang had this way of drawing her out. For all his little jokes, he was a good listener. That, more than anything, was what made him such a great reporter.

"I started doing this work after my mom died," said Zia, stumbling over the words as she tried to navigate a slew of muddled feelings. "After the funeral... I just couldn't imagine dedicating my life to diplomatic cocktail parties, you know? Better to wade directly into the fray, serve the powerless and save the day. Basically, how all twenty-three-year-olds get into humanitarian aid." Her laugh rang hollow. "If I couldn't bring back my mom, maybe I could rescue others from similar fates. The disasters I've responded to are bad, but thank God we haven't had anything anywhere near the scale of the Heat Wave."

Galang reached across the table and put his hand on hers, which further constricted her already tight throat. She took a steadying breath, then continued. "After responding to natural disaster after natural disaster you eventually start to realize that there's no such thing as a natural disaster. There are only human disasters revealed by nature."

"What does that mean?"

"When New Orleans is destroyed and rebuilt again and again, is that a failure of the Army Corps of Engineers, or is it the inevitable result of trying to build a coastal city below sea level? When that earthquake hit Ecuador, every death could have been prevented with better building codes. Those wildfires in British Columbia wouldn't have been so destructive without decades of counterproductive fire suppression. I mean, look at the story you're working on. How much less screwed would most Maldivians be if their own government wasn't trying to profit from tragedy? The real disasters are poverty and shortsightedness. Systemic injustice turns the disadvantaged into human shields against the brute force of nature pursuing its normal course. We create victims, and then we congratulate ourselves when we show them small mercies."

"You got out of politics only to realize that the real challenge of humanitarian aid is... politics."

"Exactly!" It was as if the scab Zia had been covertly scratching had finally fallen away. She tapped a finger on the table. "Right here, the people suffering the most are the poor farmers who had no savings or other skillsets to rely on. I come in with my team and treat the symptoms without ever getting close to affecting the real cause. And what makes it even worse is that people resent us. Nobody wants to be a victim. And the people with real power, the power to make a difference, they hate the fact that they need foreign help. My personal political toxicity prevents me from making progress toward any longer-term solutions. Most of the officials I deal with are looking for an excuse to fire me, so I wind up running air cover to give my own people the space they need to get anything done at all."

"Have you asked Vachan whether he knows anyone in Delhi who could help?"

Zia pressed her lips together into a tight line.

"Oh right, of course not, because you're Zia."

"Isn't it bad form for journalists to pass judgement?"

"Is that what I am to you? Just a journalist?" Galang shook his head and donned a mask of ridiculously overdramatic pain. "Would *just a journalist* have brought you Zachary's?"

Zia laughed. "So you do bribe people for scoops!"

"If it's any consolation as you cross your existential Rubicon, I've been trying to ford a similar stream," said Galang. "I work my butt off exposing the wrongdoings of some politician or CEO and then when the scandal fades, some other jerk takes their place and the whole cycle starts all over again. It's like I'm on a treadmill powered by the dark side of human nature. Bonnie, my editor, says I need to chill out and come to terms with the fact that journalism is and always has been a Sisyphean task suited only for workaholic attention seekers with guilt issues." Galang heaved a sigh. "Sometimes I wonder whether my heart's still in it. Will I ever write a story that makes a real difference?"

"Well, you've won a couple of Pulitzers."

"Which makes it all the more maddening. Every aspiring reporter puts you up on a pedestal and thinks you've got some secret sauce that they just want a taste of and I'm all like, *My secret sauce tastes a hell of a lot like self-loathing.*"

Zia raised her chai. "To commiseration."

"I'll drink to that."

They drained their cups and enjoyed a moment of companionable silence.

"Hey," said Zia. "This is fun. Seriously. I miss this."

Galang's smile was melancholic. "Me too, love. I wish I didn't have to go to the airport."

"Go on, then," Zia shooed him with her hands. "Don't let me make you fall off your treadmill. There's a scandal for you to expose. It's getting late, and I need to get back and figure out who's going to step in for my supply chain manager who just went on maternity leave."

They stood and hugged.

"You're an angel," whispered Galang.

"And you're the best kind of devil," she whispered back.

They gave each other one last squeeze and then released. Galang retrieved his bag and headed for the door.

"Don't forget to tell Aafreen I say hi," said Zia. "And thanks again for the pizza."

Galang looked back over his shoulder. "Don't forget to cut yourself some slack."

Zia settled the bill and decided to walk home. Their "hotel" was more like a barracks and she wanted some time to think before running into Himmat and the rest of her overworked team. The night was hot and humid. The pizza was heavy and awkward to carry. She could taste the mineral funk of soil on the breeze. The gibbous moon shone through a thin sheen of clouds—reminding her, as the moon always did, of sitting beside her father at his beloved shortwave radio set, learning how enthusiasts bounced signals off the lunar surface to communicate across oceans and continents. Beneath the pulsing cricket song, memory's chorus swelled, serenading her meander down forking paths through the garden of the mind. That was why, despite her security training, it took Zia so long to notice that she was being followed.

8

+

THE MAN WAS TWO BLOCKS BEHIND HER. ZIA WOULDN'T have noticed except that she glanced up at a chaotic bundle of electrical lines pirating electricity from the grid and saw movement in her peripheral vision. Maybe he was just another pedestrian walking home after a long day's work. But the café she and Galang had just left was the last thing open in the village and there was no night life here to speak of.

Paranoia is your first line of defense, she remembered the friendly smile and hard eyes of the Interstice security coach. *Once you second guess yourself, it's already too late. Acting on a bad vibe might waste a little time. Failing to act might just cost you your life.* Tennis. Math. Boarding school. Company events. Security training had been just another hoop her dad was forcing her to jump through.

Zia turned right at the next corner. It was probably nothing. But better to be sure before reaching the border of town and setting off up the country road to the hotel. She forced herself to slow her breathing. Everything was going to be fine. She was just amped up. Seeing Galang had momentarily revived the emotional rollercoaster of her teenage years.

She turned right again at the next corner and then doubled back to peer through the drooping foliage of a pepper tree. Nothing. Just an empty street in a sleepy town. Inhale. Exhale. Relax. Far off, she heard the whine of a motorbike over the cricket choir. She'd loop back around the block and continue on to the hotel, maybe join Himmat for a glass of arak and laugh about her little freak-out. The hairs on the back of her neck rose. Through the veil of hanging stems studded with pink peppercorns, she saw a figure jog around the corner after her. Then a second figure appeared from the direction toward which she'd been walking.

Shit.

She turned and hurried up the street, heart hammering like it was trying to escape her ribcage. If she had forgotten something at the café and a member of the staff was trying to return it, then who was the second pursuer? Could Galang have been followed, was he trying to set her up? But why? And for what? No. Paranoia was a useful tool, but left unchecked, it would paralyze her. Perhaps the Indian Intelligence Bureau had put her under surveillance, egged on by Governor Rao? Could be. Maybe an organized crime outfit was hoping to hold her for ransom and loosen daddy's purse strings? Always a possibility. But Occam's razor would suggest that her stalkers might just be angry young men, embittered by lack of prospects, looking to teach the foreign woman a lesson with a good beating and a side of rape.

Zia accelerated into a jog and catalogued her assets. There wasn't much. Phone, but no time to call for help. Pizza, but whoever was chasing her probably wouldn't be won over even by Zachary's. She threw a glance back over her shoulder and saw the two men emerge from beneath the pepper tree. A few blocks behind them, a headlight tracked across the cinder block buildings as a motorbike turned onto the street.

Fear curdled in Zia's gut, and she weaponized it, transmuted it into fury, used it to fuel her churning legs. She was a *León*. Whoever they were, she wasn't going to make this easy for them. One more block, and she turned right again, shaking the hair out of her eyes. One last right and she was back where she'd started, banging into the café, shouting a warning at the shocked proprietor, ducking behind the counter and barging back through the kitchen, out the back door, and up the dark alley, squeezing into an alcove in the scarred wall of a mud brick building.

Had they seen her? Laundry fluttered on lines strung up over the alley, textile ghosts haunting a tropical night. She strained to listen over the throbbing bassline of her heartbeat. Only now did she realize that the kitchen must have had knives. She cursed herself for failing to grab one.

Shouts out on the street. Maybe her ploy had worked. Maybe they'd give up, decide to try another night. The whine of the motorbike was joined by the roar of a larger engine. Zia laid the pizza box on the ground, opened it, and picked up one aluminum-wrapped half in each hand. The frozen pizza immediately numbed her fingers. She hefted them. Better than nothing. Why had she so adamantly rejected her father's repeated demands that she accept a personal bodyguard? Was her pride, her perceived autonomy, worth so much? The fierce joy of freedom won crumbled to dust at the prospect of actual violence.

Zia's entire body clenched as a shot rang out. Then another one. Guns? What the fuck was going on? Why were they shooting? Who were they shooting at? More shouting.

Footsteps pounded up the alley. The beam of a flashlight swung wildly, stabbing at billowing laundry and rotting garbage.

Zia had to do something. She couldn't just wait here and get captured. She estimated when the footsteps would reach her hiding place, then heaved one half of the pizza up and over the alley. It thunked into the opposite wall and fell into the dust. The man charging up the alley grunted in surprise, spun to aim his flashlight and pistol at the source of the sound, and yelled, "Stop, don't move!"

Zia leapt from her hiding place and brought the other half of the pizza around in a vicious forehand swing. *Follow through,* her dad yelled at her as they ran drills on the clay court. Seeing that he'd been fooled, the large man turned back toward her just as five pounds of frozen deep dish connected with his face, crushing his nose and snapping his head back. He toppled back into the dust with a heavy thump.

Her chest rose and fell. Icy adrenaline surged through her veins. In the light of his own flashlight, Zia could see the man was dressed in matte black clothes that definitely weren't local. For a brief moment she considered stooping down to scoop up his gun. But the man was already writhing on the ground, trying to find his bearings and wipe the blood from his eyes. She needed to move, to get out of here, to find a hole to disappear into until she could figure out what was going on.

An arm locked around her throat.

"Gotcha," a voice rasped in her ear.

Zia tore at the arm with her fingers, but it just tightened around her neck like a vice. She tried to punch behind her with her elbows but struck only glancing blows.

"That's enough," said the voice. "It'll go easier for you if you just relax. This should help."

Something stabbed Zia's deltoid and a warm feeling spread out to the tips of her fingers and over her scalp and down her legs until her knees turned to Jell-O and she was hanging limply from the crooked arm instead of struggling to escape it.

A vehicle rumbled up the alley and Zia's limp body was dragged into the back of a van. She tried to scream, to fight, to flee, but her muscles didn't respond. Stars sparkled in the narrowing tunnel of her vision. Her assailant helped the injured man up off the ground.

She should have been terrified, but Zia felt removed from the situation, as if she was looking down on herself from above. Her soul was a still pond, its surface glassy in the gray of impending dawn. This wasn't the death she had wanted or expected. Maybe her mother had felt like this as her body shut down organ by organ, slain by the very disaster she was hoping to document. Death didn't conform to human will. There was something oddly comforting in that hard truth.

The heads of the two men scrambling into the van seemed to explode, but it must have been an artifact of the brilliant light show that occluded Zia's vision as time spiraled back on itself and consciousness slipped away like a stray cat.

+

9

ZIA STOOD AT THE EDGE OF A MESA THAT TOWERED kilometers above the surrounding rocky plains. It was high noon and the sky was a clear baby blue but rainbows of every conceivable size and angle arched across the landscape in all directions, their multicolored curves doubling and crisscrossing—bolts of lightning writhing between heaven and earth at each point of intersection like ropes between teams playing at tug-of-war. It smelled of roses and ozone. The air was alive with current, burning and buzzing against her skin.

Looking down at herself, Zia saw that her body was not her own, and that she was surrounded by people, that the top of the mesa was packed with them—Aafreen, Jason, Kodjo, Galang, Li Jie, Daniela, Himmat, Vachan, Tommy, Selai, the BSF officer, the girl Zia had beaten to win her first tennis tournament, Vizzini from *The Princess Bride*, the volunteers from last week's training—none of them in their own bodies but somehow identifiable nevertheless, all of them naked, touching, probing, kissing, fighting, flailing, tickling, fucking—backs arched in ecstasy, cheeks streaked with tears, sweat and blood and cum commingling to stain the sunbaked stone.

One of the bolts of lightning frayed, sending sparking tendrils in search of a new point of connection. It found Zia. Energy flowed into her. The more there was, the more she wanted. Lust. Rage. Transcendence. More bolts wavered, then one by one they snapped home to send their charge coursing through her. She swallowed them all, demanded more, channeled the electricity into everyone around her, her consciousness merging into theirs as their passion became a single pulsing entity all its own.

Reality's fabric rippled, ineffable patterns suggesting the shape of the feral gods that hid behind it.

Seedlings sprouted from the teeming mass of humanity. Vines curled out of ears. Saplings rose from open mouths. Wildflowers bloomed in pubic hair. Rivers flowed from tear ducts. Teeth hardened into crystal. Raised arms ossified into spires of granite, breasts rolling hills, and shoulders mountain ranges. Moss spread across boulders that had once been knuckles. Ribs became sedimentary layers folded by tectonic forces.

The transition was at once violent and seamless. Nothing had changed and everything had changed. The jungle was a throng. The people were a jungle. Zia stared down at them from among banks of invisible clouds. Déjà vu like the flutter of a moth's wing. With mounting horror, Zia realized she knew this jungle. She hated this jungle. She feared this jungle more than anything. She thrashed, but could not tear herself away.

If she pretended it couldn't happen.

If she wished hard enough.

If she summoned an act of will that could rewrite history.

This time could be different.

This time *would* be different.

Maybe.

Yes.

Then there was a flash of movement at the edge of the jungle. Two figures stumbled out from the verdant collage, Gilberto half-carrying Miranda, trying not to lose his footing as they pushed through the solid, impossible heat toward the ragged edge of the village. They crossed the gap in less than thirty seconds, but Zia knew it was already too late. The moment they made it through the door of the first hut, they stumbled out of the jungle again. Jungle. Stumble. Building. Jungle. Stumble. Building. Over and over and over and over and over.

Stop, Zia screamed, though no voice would come. *Stop. Please.*

But it didn't stop.

It was always the same.

Always.

A single endless loop.

10

+

THE FIRST THING ZIA DID WAS KEEP HER EYES SHUT. The second thing she did was keep her body still. The third thing was throttle her brain into overdrive.

Without the dam of unconsciousness holding them back, memories flooded through her. The moon hanging cold and bright behind a thin patina of clouds. The earthy fragrance of chai. The poignant luxury of getting to see Galang. The glimpse of movement through the drooping foliage of the pepper tree. The ghostly flutter of laundry in the evening breeze. The crunch of cartilage. *Gotcha.* She had to fight to keep her heart rate and breathing even. If they had hooked her up to biofeedback equipment, she couldn't afford to give herself away.

Kidnapping was just so... cliché. It echoed teenage boasts whispered after curfew as snow swirled outside the chateau. *The FBI briefed my family before Thanksgiving because we are high value targets. Oh yeah? We have a full-time white hat team at our family office because Russia-sponsored hackers keep trying to crack our files. Well,* my *uncle was* assassinated *last year.* Sad, lonely, astoundingly privileged children trying to ward off corrosive insecurities by bragging about how they were so important that the world was out to get them. Being born into power bought you opportunity and illuminated your flaws in stark relief. Kidnapping was the ultimate vanity daydream for the entitled, to be torn from your life so that your loved ones would have to prove once and for all just how much they cared, moving heaven and earth to get back the child they'd ignored for so long. It was deeply embarrassing to Zia that she'd once indulged such fantasies, all the more so now that they were coming true.

Time to take stock.

She was lying in a bed, her head resting on a pillow. Not her bed. Not her pillow. It smelled wrong. This wasn't Chhattisgarh. Her secret wish that everything would prove to be nothing more than a bad dream faded. No sounds except for her own breathing and the gentle rasp of sheet against skin as her chest rose and fell. She varied the pace of her inhalations and exhalations ever so slightly just in case they were in sync with the breathing of someone standing guard, but if someone was in the room with her, they were being extremely quiet. The air was cool and dry from AC and tasted clean, so if she was in a torture chamber it was a top-shelf torture chamber. Ever so slowly, she twisted her wrists and ankles. No restraints. They knew they had her. When she relaxed again, she felt a gentle tug against her right forearm and realized she must be hooked up to an IV or some kind of sensor. That meant it was possible that her micro movements had already given her away, so she lay still and counted to ninety-nine.

Nothing.

Well, the room might be monitored remotely, but she couldn't just lie here forever. She cracked her eyelids, letting her eyes adjust to the light before opening them completely. Mahogany beams lined the high ceiling. Sunlight poured in through the shutter slats of wide windows. Historical photographs of rainbow-colored reefs overflowing with marine life hung on the walls. She couldn't identify any cameras or surveillance devices, but that only meant that they might be going for subtle. An IV did indeed run from her right arm up to a bag hanging from a stand next to the bed. The door to an en suite bathroom stood open. The door to what was probably a hallway was closed. It might be a boutique hotel, or maybe a villa. But a plush cell was still a cell.

In a flash, terror subsumed her. She had never wanted more badly to be back in her cramped room in India, woken up by the rooster's crow and the murmur of her colleagues' good-natured bickering filtering through the thin walls. These sumptuous surroundings were far more disturbing than a dank basement would be. This wasn't the kind of everyday crime that filled the headlines. These weren't local hoodlums trying to scare her off. Her abductors had resources and their gambit must have some larger game behind it. She was not just a victim but a pawn.

And there was nothing, absolutely nothing, that Zia hated more than being controlled.

Zia tore off the sheets and sat up. Her head swam and her temples thrummed like gongs under a monk's mallet. Breathe. Breathe. Okay. The longer she stayed here, the more likely it was that her captors would check in on her. Right now, she had an opening. How many victims had sealed their own fates by procrastinating escape or resistance in the vain hope that the situation might improve? She would get out of here and when she did, she would find out who had done this and make them pay.

Peeling the medical tape from her forearm, she gently removed the IV. Then she knotted the plastic line to stop the flow and yanked off the needle. It wasn't much of a weapon, but it was something. She looked down at herself. They had dressed her in a loose-fitting linen tunic and pants that split the difference between resort wear and hospital gown. At least the pants had pockets into which she could slip her needle. Careful to move more slowly this time, she swung her legs off the bed and donned the waiting slippers. Nothing on the bedside table except for an extravagant Guzmania in full bloom. The drawers were empty.

Zia stood, steadying herself with a hand on the bed. She could do this. She must do this. It might be her only chance. She just had to give her body enough time to pull itself together.

Somewhere in the building, she heard the faint sound of a toilet flushing and water running in a sink. Her palms began to sweat. She held her breath and froze, listening. A door closed and footsteps approached up the hallway.

Fuck.

Should she return to bed, pretend she was still unconscious? Wait behind the door, slip up behind whoever entered, and stab the needle through their eardrum and into their brain? Hope that they weren't coming here to check on her?

Zia's hands curled into fists. Who was she kidding? She was a humanitarian aid worker, not a secret ninja trained in an ancient mountain temple under the tutelage of stern grandmasters from an unbroken lineage going back millennia. If she could overwhelm her attacker with her expertise at navigating arbitrary bureaucratic labyrinths, she'd be all set, but if it came to actual physical violence, it might as well be over already. She'd gotten ridiculously lucky with the pizza ambush, and had been kidnapped anyway.

The footsteps were getting closer.

Fight or flight? The answer was obvious.

11

+

ZIA STEPPED TO THE WINDOW AND OPENED THE shutters. Sunlight drenched her. She was on the second floor. A path ran along the side of the building. Beyond, lush jungle rose up to mist-shrouded peaks. Off to the left, sparkling waves crashed against a crescent beach. Where in the world was she? But there was no time for speculation. She only had a few seconds.

Undoing the latch, she pushed the windows open, swung her legs over the sill, reached back and pulled the shutters closed from the outside, only to discover that there was no drainpipe to slide down or convenient handholds. If Galang had his way and screenwriters adapted Zia's life story, they'd really need to do a better job adding useful props.

Banana trees lined the side of the building, which really did appear to be a villa. The nearest one was a few feet away.

Last chance. Go. Now. Do it. Throwing caution to the wind, Zia pushed herself off the sill. She hit the tree at an awkward angle, limbs flailing. But the big leaves slapped at her, breaking her fall as they bent under her weight, and she was able to hook one elbow around the trunk. The combination slowed her down enough that she didn't break her ankles when she landed on the loamy, moss-covered ground.

For fuck's sake.

Zia pushed off the trunk and sprinted across the flagstone path, through a mat of hanging vines, and straight into the undergrowth. She plowed forward through a claustrophobic tunnel of dappled green, every root trying to trip her, every branch trying to snag her, every thorn trying to bloody her as she stumbled onward, ever onward, never once looking back over her shoulder, reserving every particle of willpower for the increasingly impossible endeavor of keeping her legs moving, her head clear, her lungs full.

And then, all at once, it was too much. Zia collapsed. Her limbs ached. Her throat burned. The world spun as if it were a die on a craps table.

Darkness.

Zia coughed and spat. She rolled over onto her back in the muck. The racket of birds, animals, and insects made her temples throb. She had had quite enough of returning from unplanned bouts of unconsciousness for one day. Light filtered through the canopy above her, sliced into thousands of glittering shards by soaring trunks and whispering leaves.

Zia's mom would have loved this place. She would have been able to name every species and trace it back through genus, family, order, class, phylum, kingdom, and domain to the roots of the tree of life itself. She would have taken Zia's hand and traced her daughter's finger along the fractal patterns of compound leaves, explained how the plant was a distant cousin that shared a quarter of its genes with humans, and joked about science fiction stories that imagined humanoid aliens arriving from distant galaxies when far more exotic lifeforms were going extinct every day here on Earth. Their laughter would have been shot through with awe at the extraordinary imagination that was humanity's greatest strength and flaw, and her mother would have captured everything in prose that transcended the experience itself and invited others to share it. It was a place like this that had claimed her mother's life.

Zia pushed herself up and leaned against a tree she couldn't name. She was caked in mud. Her clothes were torn and her skin was scratched and bloody. She must have stubbed her toe on something because the nail was split straight up the middle. It was incredible that the slippers hadn't disintegrated entirely and that the needle in her pocket hadn't stabbed her when she fell. Even more incredibly, there was no sign of pursuit. Or maybe that shouldn't have been so surprising. The forest around her was so loud that she couldn't hear herself breathe and so thick that she couldn't even identify which direction she had come from.

She had lost her jailers by losing herself.

If her mother were here, they could have lived off foraging indefinitely. As it was, Zia was more likely to poison than nourish herself by harvesting nature's bounty, and she was acutely aware of the short half-life of whatever calories and hydration remained in her system.

Shadows deepened and swirled around her. She was alone in a dangerous forest that could be anywhere on this miserable planet. All she knew was that there were people trying to abduct her and all she had was an IV needle and a pair of what might as well be pajamas. Fucked didn't even begin to cover it.

If only she had accepted her father's protection. If only she hadn't decided to walk home from her date with Galang. If only this nightmare would turn out to be nothing more than a bad trip brought on by an experimental psychedelic cooked up in a distant lab that the *chaiwala* had slipped into their teas on a dare. The air was thick in her bruised and swollen throat. Her stomach performed a Cirque du Soleil routine. The cornucopia of vegetation induced a bout of vertigo.

Focus on your breath. She could hear her dad's voice, feel his hand squeeze her shoulder before she stepped out onto the court for her very first tournament. *But there are so many* people, *Papi. And the other girl is* twelve. *I can't*— He knelt in front of her. *Look at me, sweetheart. Look at me. Who cares what they think? Fuck them.* She had never heard him swear before. It felt dangerous and raw and special. *You're a León. The only important games are the ones we play against ourselves. Nothing else matters.*

One thing at a time. One thing at a time was the only way anything got done in this world. If she could find some higher ground, she would be able to orient herself. Zia's hand clutched at the memory of a racket. *Not too tight. Not too loose. Just right. Imagine you're holding a delicate little bird.*

Nausea receded. Zia took one step, and then another.

12 +

ZIA HAULED HERSELF UP ONTO THE NEXT BRANCH, breathing hard. *Whatever you do, don't look down.* She looked down. The forest floor was twenty feet below. Her stomach jumped into her throat and a wave of dizziness washed over her. She forced her gaze up to look at the gnarled burl six inches from her face and then pressed her forehead against it until the world stopped spinning. This tree was her Cliffs of Insanity. Just a few more branches and she'd have the perspective she needed to orient herself. Reach. Grab. Heave. Her hands were raw and sticky with sap. She hadn't climbed a tree since she was a little girl.

With a grunt, she reached the fork in the trunk facing the gap that a falling branch had torn in the canopy. She wedged herself into the fork, wrapped her arms around the nearest boughs, and squeezed her eyes shut. Then she opened them and stared out through the leafy aperture.

Zia had gotten lucky, or chosen well. Maybe both.

This tree stood on a steep section of sloping ridgeline and she had a commanding view. The ocean stretched to the horizon, a patchwork of blue, green, and gray traversed by measured sets of waves that reared up before crashing down the line of the cove, whitewash churning up onto the picturesque sliver of beach. Natural beaches had all but disappeared as sea levels inched higher and higher. That meant that this one was probably artificial, and absurdly expensive to maintain. That it appeared to be natural underscored its opulence.

Up from the beach was a cluster of luxurious villas connected with pedestrian paths and gardens. In the afternoon sun, the red-tiled roofs and creamy stucco appeared to glow from within. After a moment, Zia picked out the house she had escaped from. She hadn't come nearly as far as she'd thought. Sun glittered off the surface of a shared pool and two players volleyed on a clay tennis court. Zia's skin crawled. Uniformed security guards were jogging up and down the paths and along the beach. Drones buzzed above them, clearly running a search pattern. Zia pressed her palms against the rough bark and forced her muscles to unclench. She was in enough trouble as it was. A panic attack would only make things worse.

The whole scene might have been a posh resort except for the high-tech industrial facility that lay beyond the villas. Massive hangars lined an airstrip. Antennae sprouted from rooftops like technological fungi. Solar arrays tracked the sinking sun. A small marine tanker was pumping off liquid into pipelines at a harbor built into the next inlet.

What the hell was this place? Who ran it? What could they possibly want with her? Impossible questions metastasized. She had been thinking that she might be the victim of a professional kidnapping by an organized crime ring, but this facility went beyond the scale of any cartel she was aware of. This looked military, or something close. Nation-state level stuff. She remembered Li Jie dropping hints about the various clandestine projects his parents' intelligence network was tracking in Beijing. But there were no flags anywhere, so a black program? What were they doing? Maybe an off-book signals intelligence facility? And why would a country want to abduct her? As a high-profile humanitarian aid worker, she'd annoyed politicians the world over demanding meaningful reform, but surely they had bigger fish to fry, not least each other.

Zia thought of her team in Chhattisgarh. How long had it been? What would they be thinking? Would Himmat sound the alarm? Would it matter if he did? She thought of her father. No chance that he'd notice her absence. They hadn't talked in years. She thought of Galang, off chasing leads in New Malé. Was this connected to him somehow? Did he have dirt on someone dangerous whose strike team accidentally targeted her instead? Guilt twisted her stomach. What if they had Galang too? What if he was even worse off than her? Zia had been so worried about herself that she hadn't even considered what might have happened to her friend. There were too many threads, and no way to weave them into a pattern.

A glint of silver caught her eye. A plane accelerated down the runway. It wasn't a commercial or military model she recognized. Its wingspan dwarfed any aircraft she'd ever seen. Its whitewashed hull had no windows and bore no insignia but was peppered with exotic sensors. The beast lifted off and banked overhead in a graceful arc as it gained altitude, angling off across the water and up into the palatial cloudscape of bulging cumuli.

As much as Zia wished she could escape as easily, she forced herself to return to Earth. Behind the pocket of coastal development, virgin jungle carpeted steep slopes and branching valleys that led up to a central peak cloaked in a halo of fog. No other land was visible from this angle, which meant she was either at the tip of a long peninsula or, more likely, stranded on a volcanic island. That meant the only way to get on or off the island was by air or sea, which in turn meant she had to infiltrate the airfield or the harbor and stow away. Zia chastised herself for not paying more attention during that damn security training. She had... approximately zero relevant skills and her only relevant experience was sneaking out of the chateau with her friends so that they could bluff their way into sketchy nightclubs. Oh, Zia could schmooze and navigate social intrigue like a champ, but clandestine operations were not her forte.

But hold on, there might be another way. Even if it wasn't a way out, it might give her more to work with than a needle. If she could get her hands on a phone, a computer, or any kind of communications device, she could call for help, let people know she was here. They could track her location, call in the cavalry. At the very least, knowing that people were out there looking for her might give her some leverage over her captors if they caught her again.

Zia peered out from her perch, thinking. No matter what, she'd have to skirt around the villas to get to the industrial facility. She squinted. Yes, someone was swimming laps in the pool and a group of kids were splashing in the shallow end. And where there were people, there were phones.

Going down was even worse than climbing up, and Zia's descent was only slightly less disastrous than her recent encounter with the banana tree. When she finally slithered down to the blessed ground, she vowed never to climb another tree if she could help it.

Holding back burgeoning dread, Zia focused on wayfinding. She had memorized the topography and noted key landmarks, but a rainforest from within was far less legible than a rainforest from above. If only her mom were here to help her navigate this warren of green on green on green. So Zia tried to channel Miranda's ghost, tried to see this primeval tangle through her naturalist's eyes. It smelled like growth and rot and life and death and soil. Yes, there was the trailing end of that foothill, there was the sheer face of exposed rock, there was the stream that must be fed by the waterfall she'd glimpsed higher up.

Zia pushed her mind beyond thought, her heart beyond fear, her muscles beyond exhaustion. Everything hurt, a deep, pulsing hurt, but finally she was crouched in the undergrowth peeking out from behind a gigantic fern at the manicured landscaping of the villas. She counted them, tried to place herself on her mental map. The ocean was that way. The volcano was this way. That meant the tennis courts were over there and the pool should be up the path that snaked under the long pergola covered in verdant bougainvillea. Zia forced herself to wait there in the bushes for five minutes, but the guards must have already cleared this area and she couldn't see any drones, although she could hear their plaintive whines over toward the beach.

The minute she stepped out of the bushes, the risk of recapture would skyrocket. If a guard so much as glanced up the path, they'd see her. She'd be exposed to whatever surveillance systems oversaw this place. Whatever slim advantage her escape had earned would crumble away to nothing. But staying in the jungle only meant that she was safe enough to die alone, and maybe not even that. If they wanted her badly enough, she wouldn't be able to evade K9 search teams. No, her escape hadn't bought her cover, it had bought her time. She needed to invest that time wisely to have any chance of getting out of here alive. And any investment that could generate a real return meant taking real risks.

Zia glanced back and forth to confirm there was no one around, wiped the mud from her hands, and stood up. She stepped quickly out of the bushes but once her feet were on the path, she slowed to a nonchalant stroll as if she were just taking a walk around the neighborhood. After the muck of the forest, the flagstones were smooth and firm beneath her feet. The air was thick with the scent of jasmine. Birds twittered in the branches of manicured trees. The second she reached the cover of the pergola, Zia sprinted up its entire length. Inside, it was a different world, a floral wormhole lit by pinpricks of light that might just lead her a step closer to freedom. The passage curved up and to the left between two villas and Zia was panting by the time she reached the other end.

Zia paused before reemerging into sunlight. Pulling back a vine, she peered ahead. Yes, her mental map had been sufficiently accurate. There was the fork that led right to the tennis courts and left to the pool. Kids were still wading around the shallow end under the watchful gaze of their mother. The swimmer was pulling himself out, muscled skin glistening as water streamed off him.

A drone was working its way over the rooftops and the hum of its propellers sent a jolt of adrenaline through her system. Zia stepped out and walked purposefully up the path. Left. No lock on the gate to the pool. Quick turn into the small locker room before any of the residents noticed how muddy and bloody she was. The locker room was plush and smelled of chlorine and shampoo. Smooth jazz played at low volume. Zia stripped down quickly, folded her ruined clothes, and stuffed them into the trash, palming the needle. Then she snagged a thick robe and fluffy towel and hung them on hooks in one of the shower nooks. She dropped the needle into the pocket of the robe, turned on the shower, and stepped under the steaming water.

The water washed away blood, grit, and tension. Zia trembled and her teeth chattered despite the heat. What was *happening* to her? She couldn't keep this up. She was supposed to be sitting in a meeting coordinating the efforts of various local nonprofits right now, not escaping the clutches of mysterious kidnappers. This kind of stuff only happened in stories like *The Princess Bride*, which Zia had read and watched over and over again on long-haul flights so many times that she knew all the dialogue by heart. Westley, Inigo, Buttercup, they would know what to do in this kind of situation. They would use a combination of charm and expertly applied violence to escape and expose whatever secret lay at the dark heart of this facility in the process. Too bad watching adventure films didn't help you absorb the skills of the protagonists.

Now that Zia was out of the forest and in what could have been a spa, the idea that armed goons were out there looking for her seemed utterly ridiculous. Maybe her abduction was a theatrical stunt organized by well-meaning friends forcing her to take a vacation. She laughed at the prospect—*that's it, meet fear with silliness*—and water poured into her mouth, reminding her of how thirsty she was.

Shampoo. Soap. Rinse. Move.

Turning off the tap, Zia rubbed herself down with the towel and pulled on the robe. When she looked at herself in the mirror, she saw everyone she'd ever known staring back, one face flickering into the next too fast to be recognized until the apparitions collapsed under their own weight. Thick black hair, terracotta skin, graceful curved nose inherited from a Mayan ancestor, haunted eyes the color of smoky quartz, small scar along the cheekbone from when she'd taken a fall chasing a lob across a hard court. No matter how disassociated she might feel, that was her. She tried out a smile, summoning everything she'd learned about acting from playing at politics. A good smile was all about the eyes. She turned up the collar of the robe to cover her bruised neck. Then she snagged a fresh pair of slippers from the neat stack near the door, popped one of the breath mints from the basket on the counter into her mouth, and walked out onto the pool deck projecting the air of unassailable entitlement she had spent years shrugging off.

The family didn't give her a second glance as she rounded the corner of the pool and headed over to where the swimmer was finishing a post-workout stretch. He looked up as she approached and she donned an embarrassed grimace. Time to channel Daniela, who had once charmed her way into Beyoncé's greenroom at an arena show.

"Sorry to bug you," she said.

"No problem," he waved off the apology. "What's up?"

"It's just—" She bit her lower lip. "Oh my god, this is embarrassing." She shook her head and let color rise in her cheeks. "I forgot which locker I put my stuff in. I've checked a few and now I think I'm going crazy. Is there any chance I might be able to borrow your phone so I can call mine and figure out where I stashed it? I promise it won't take more than a couple minutes."

He grinned. "Sure," he said. "Let me just grab it for you."

"Thank you so much, I just feel so silly."

"Not at all," he said. "I don't want to admit how many times I lose my keys."

She laughed, and saw a guard walking up the path past the pool. She turned slightly so her back was to the guard and hoped that the swimmer wouldn't be able to hear her pounding heart.

"So, what program do you work on?" he asked as he collected his things from a chaise lounge.

"Oh, that's classified," she said, injecting enough flirtatiousness into her tone that she might or might not be joking.

He glanced at her over his shoulder and she winked.

He laughed. "Aren't they all?"

That gave her cover to treat his question as rhetorical. "I really appreciate you helping me out," she said. "I'm just having one of those days."

He stood, unlocked his phone, and offered it to her.

"I swear I've seen you around," he said, cocking his head to the side.

"Maybe," she said, hoping against hope that her captors hadn't sent out some kind of APB. Dissemble. Context was everything. "Small world, right? I'm Joanna."

"I'm Logan," he said. "Hey, it's not too often you meet new people around here. After you find your phone, any chance you'd be interested in grabbing a drink? Donny just got in a shipment of good scotch."

Zia cocked her head to the side and looked him up and down. "You know what?" she said, with a sly smile. "I'd like that."

She turned and walked back to the locker room, letting her hips sway in the way her mother had taught her to dance salsa. She hadn't even had to stab him in the eye with her needle. And then she was back in the locker room with a phone and could hardly believe her luck. Finally she had caught a break. Maybe she'd make it out of here after all.

She stared down at the screen and drew a blank. Her momentary glee collapsed into indecision. Who exactly was she supposed to call? She'd been so focused on getting her hands on a phone that she hadn't thought about what she would actually do with it. She couldn't very well call 911. She didn't even know where in the world she was, let alone what, if any, authorities existed out here. The guards chasing her might well be the highest authorities on this damn island.

Her location, at least, was a question that Zia could solve. She opened a map and zoomed out from her GPS pin for context. She reeled. Nowhere near India. A tiny island in the Indonesian archipelago, not too far from Borneo. Who could possibly want to hold her here? How long had she been unconscious?

She could call Himmat, but what could he possibly do from India except alert Jason? Galang might know what to do, but Galang might very well have been abducted himself. Zia's finger twitched. She wanted so desperately to sign onto their group chat and declare her emergency. She had friends in moderately high places, maybe they could do something. But they were also scattered all over the world, and what could she possibly say?

Zia was the rock. She was the person other people could rely on. She didn't need help and wouldn't be controlled. Her stomach tightened. She was down a set, ad-out, and tossing the ball to serve. She was basking in post-coital bliss when Tommy doused the afterglow by asking why she wasted her time with people like Galang and Kodjo. She was telling the president-elect that she would not serve as her new ambassador to Sri Lanka. She was savoring a mouthwatering croissant when she received the call about her mother and the world turned upside down. Her hand found the needle in her pocket, caressed its slender, menacing line. If only life were so simple, people purpose-built for whatever the world demanded from them.

It was obvious who she needed to call, so glaringly obvious that she had been trying not to see it, trying, despite everything, to avoid a conversation she'd spent nearly a decade not having. She was a fugitive holding a shard of beveled glass connected to the digital infinite via an invisible lattice as dense as the jungle that had concealed her, and she could no longer afford the indulgence of lying to herself. The needle bent in her grip. He had billions of dollars, a global satellite network, and would do whatever was necessary to find her. There was nothing she wanted less than his help. There was nothing she needed more.

Maybe she should just return the phone and surrender to the guards, end this stupid little game. Better to face torture than the shadows that were gathering inside her. Pandora should have left her box closed.

Tears splattered onto the screen as Zia typed in the number.

He picked up on the first ring.

"*Papi*?"

"Zia? Oh, thank god, *thank god*. Where *are* you, sweetie? I stepped out to take a call and when I got back to your room, you had disappeared. We've been trying to find you all afternoon."

+

13

HER FATHER'S VILLA WAS SMALLER THAN THE ONE Zia had woken up in. It was nestled all by itself up on the mountainside, surrounded by impenetrable rainforest. Instead of the beach, it looked out over the airfield where another of those colossal planes was taking off.

Santiago León met his daughter on the wide deck. He had always been thin, but the intervening years had eroded whatever fat had once softened the lines of his face, leaving him gaunt. Large rectangular glasses framed intense dark eyes, and his silver hair was combed back from his forehead. He wore his signature plain white t-shirt, blue jeans, and leather jackboots. The only time Zia had ever seen him wear anything else was on the last day they'd seen each other in person, the day of her mother's funeral.

He pulled Zia into a hug, voice cracking as he whispered "*mi hija*" into her ear over and over again. She hugged him back, feeling his protruding ribs, his beating heart, his ragged breath. The familiar musk of smoke, cinnamon, and sweat dredged up memories of staying up past her bedtime writing code together, going on family backpacking trips into remote alpine country, squeezing his hand as tight as she could as a real-life rocket rode an incandescent pillar of fire into the heavens. Relief, pain, confusion, joy, resentment, admiration, longing, nostalgia, comfort, regret, exhaustion, pride, and a dozen subtle and ineffable emotions washed over Zia in a violent cataract. Ten years. It had been ten years.

They disengaged, looking each other up and down.

"I'm just glad you're okay," he said, shaking his head. "I was so, so worried."

Anger coalesced within Zia like an image coming into crystal clear focus.

"What the *hell* is going on?" she asked, remembering the chirping crickets, shadows glimpsed through the tresses of a pepper tree. "You had me *kidnapped*? You could have called, you know."

"What?" A shadow flitted across his face. "No! Of course not."

"Okay," said Zia. "Then what happened?"

"We *rescued* you," he said, suddenly unsure whether he was supposed to be backpedaling or reassuring. "There were a number of red flags. People attempting to hack you. Sophisticated people. Attribution was impossible. Then my people on the ground spotted a surveillance team following you. At first they just ran counter surveillance but when the bogeys moved in, they had no choice but to take action. Just in time, too. If they hadn't..." He shivered. "Who knows where you might be? My worst nightmare come true... Anyway, they managed to get you out and bring you here to safety. I was sitting with you waiting for you to wake up and stepped out to take a call but when I got back you were gone and... Oh honey," he ran a hand through his hair. "I'm just so relieved that you're safe. *Gracias a Dios.*"

"And why were you monitoring my accounts?" she asked as certainty settled over her like a winter chill.

"Wait, what?" he shook his head in confusion.

"How did you notice these 'red flags' if you weren't monitoring me remotely? Did these 'sophisticated people' message you with a heads up? Or maybe they sent you a pretty postcard saying, 'we're trying to hack Zia'?"

"We– I– It's just that–"

"And your 'team on the ground'? The ones who so conveniently stepped in to 'save' me? Who are they exactly, pray tell? You have people *stalking* me?"

There it was. The inevitable friction that built up between them as their reactions to each other escalated. Knowing that it was happening made it worse, accelerated the perverse cycle. Her mother had been able to diffuse it with a single chuckle or channel it into something productive with a simple question, releasing the relentless pressure that they brought to bear on each other. *Mis alborotaditos*, she'd say with a rueful smile. *Simmer down, y'all.*

"They're *protecting* you, sweetheart," he said. "If it hadn't been for them–"

"You hire spooks to follow me around and don't even *mention* it to me?"

Santiago's Adam's apple bobbed up and down.

"Typical," she muttered. "I should have known."

"If I had told you, you would have refused."

"You're damn right I would have refused!"

"Exactly! You're my daughter. I'm not going to let–"

"I'm my own person, for fuck's sake. I can handle myself just fine, thank you very much."

They glared at each other so hard the air seemed to crackle and spit.

"They had you drugged in the back of a van," he said softly. "That's a tough spot to get out of all by yourself. You needed help. Isn't that why you called?"

Zia's eyes narrowed. "And why did these mysterious attackers try to kidnap me in the first place? Who are they?"

"I don't know," he said, frustrated. "The dead guys we were able to ID were contractors hired behind a maze of fronts. It's like they hired Kafka to write the articles of incorporation for a cornucopia of shell companies."

"But you must have had a reason to assign goons to me."

"The red flags on your accounts."

Evasion, evasion, evasion. Santiago had built a commercial empire on his ability to anticipate and act on questions other people hadn't even thought to ask yet. That he was beating around the bush meant he was hiding something. Zia had learned to read his tells and challenged him on the unlikely provenance of the tooth fairy when she was still in kindergarten. The only other person he couldn't fool had been her mom—which was why he'd come to rely on their judgement.

"And why were you monitoring them in the first place after I specifically asked you not to?" she asked.

Santiago shifted uncomfortably. "We've been having... Infosec issues," he said. "The usual stuff. Phishing attacks. Engineers getting asked to lunch by gorgeous consultants of ambiguous origin. Blackmail of senior execs. That sort of thing."

"If it's the usual stuff, then why would that change anything?"

"It's been... The pressure's been growing. More leaks. More problems. So I had our security teams bump up their alert level across the board. And I didn't want you to get caught up in anything, so—"

"Why?"

"Just a precaution. As I said, the pressure's been growing."

"No, what I mean is, *why* is the pressure growing? What are you doing that intelligence services want to know about? What would be worth kidnapping me for?"

"I don't know," he shrugged. "We work on so many programs at Interstice. It could be anything."

Zia leveled her gaze at him.

Santiago looked like he wished the Earth would open up beneath him.

"You must have *some* idea," she said. "You're hardly the kind of person to throw up your hands."

Santiago stared up into the clouds, as if seeking forgiveness. He sucked in a deep breath and let it hiss out through his teeth. Lowering his head, he looked straight at Zia and there was an unfamiliar irresolution behind his eyes, as if he were struggling to escape a thorny paradox.

When he finally spoke, the quality of his voice had shifted in a way she couldn't quite put her finger on.

"There's something I need to show you," he said.

+

14

THE SURFACE OF THE EARTH CURVED AWAY IN ALL directions. At twenty-five kilometers up, the planet's shape was clearly visible and distance yielded truths that proximity occluded. Zia became viscerally aware of the essential strangeness of the solar system, that life for all its wonders was confined to a hunk of rock hurtling through spacetime along trajectories that could be traced all the way back to the Big Bang. The sun blazed in all its naked glory, that most intimate of stars edging ever closer to the horizon's sickle edge. Clouds stretched out far below in a ruffled carpet of impossibly rich texture, ten thousand spires and hillocks furling and unfurling, ragged tufts transfigured by shafts of light into resplendent mythological fauna. Zia had a flash of an elementary school science class, the bow-tied teacher twirling a basketball on his finger, saying that if it were the

Earth, its atmosphere would be no thicker than a single layer of plastic wrap.

Santiago touched his fingertips to the glass. The drone flew itself and they were the only passengers in its small cabin, joeys riding in the pouch of an algorithmic kangaroo. Time had hardened her father into an amber cast of his former self. As scared and outraged as she was, Zia couldn't help but feel a twinge of curiosity about whatever it was he had gotten himself into. He drove her crazy, batshit crazy, but he was still her nothing-will-stand-in-the-way-of-progress dad.

"Once enough people started using the Interstice low-earth orbit satellite network to connect to the internet, we ran into a new problem," he said.

"Traditional ISPs fighting tooth and nail to stay in the game," said Zia, remembering the years when his brainchild was under a constant barrage of vicious corporate espionage from ailing cable companies desperate to maintain their oligopoly at any cost.

"Greedy laggards were certainly a bump in the road," he said, snorting at what were once arch nemeses. "But what I'm talking about happened after they were dead and buried. With so many people on Interstice, the network would get overloaded at peak times and connections would slow down."

"So put up more satellites," said Zia. Old conversations reverberated at the ghostly edges of this one, scenarios spun out over the dinner table, crises averted, puzzles solved. The León triumvirate at its ingenious, bickering best.

"Then we'd have too much capacity at off-peak times," he said. "We needed a way to make the network more adaptive, more resilient. So we built this fleet of high-altitude drones that provide regional signal boosts to even out the peaks and troughs." He patted the bulkhead. "This beauty is my little secret though—I had her outfitted to carry passengers and you're the first person besides me to ride her." He spun a finger in the air. "The fleet is loaded with every exotic sensor we can get our hands on, and we give the data to scientific and educational groups pro bono."

Selai's research depended on that data. "And sell it to governments and corporations at stupendous rates?"

He shrugged. "They get what they pay for. Nobody else collects even one percent of what we can because nobody else has a reason to put drones all the way up into the stratosphere every day. You've been to our Pacific base, and we have an Atlantic twin off the coast of Senegal. It's the single biggest bet Interstice has made in the past decade, and it worked."

So this project was the cave Santiago had retreated to after the funeral, the hole in which he had buried his grief. Zia struggled to draw breath under the weight of everything that had been left unsaid. There were some gaps you just couldn't fill.

Zia tried to collect herself. "I'm sure the board is over the moon, but I'm failing to see how a successful R&D initiative got me kidnapped." Last night, a doctor had come to Santiago's villa and bandaged Zia up. She had called Himmat to reassure him that despite the rumors flying around the village, everything was going to be okay. A quick exchange of messages with Galang had confirmed he had arrived safely in the Maldives, which was a relief and a disturbing confirmation that Zia was the real target of the raid. Then fourteen hours of beautiful, blank, exhausted sleep that ended when Zia woke screaming and thrashing from a dream she couldn't recall.

His face tightened. "That's because I just told you the same story I told shareholders."

The pregnant silence swelled. Her father was many things, but a liar wasn't one of them. The year he started

Interstice, he had published an essay mapping out his entire long-term strategy for the company. When his early investors had objected, he had responded that it wasn't the idea that counted, it was the execution, and if they weren't interested in coming along for the ride, he'd be happy to find alternative sources of capital. Over the subsequent years, his relentless execution had proven the essay right, and his investors had congratulated themselves on their prescience. Later, Santiago's blunt honesty had sometimes proven to be a liability. Numerous senior employees had quit in the wake of receiving some of his "direct feedback" and Miranda had constantly coached him to soften his public statements. His patent disgust with playing politics was part of what had inspired Zia to get into diplomacy. Tired of pulling out the shrapnel of his candor, she picked up a healthy respect for nuance and cooperation. She suspected he hadn't acquired a similar respect for her own choice of career path, and she didn't like to admit how big of a role defiance played in why she had pushed so hard to get that ambassadorial post before the Heat Wave hit.

"So..." Zia said in a low voice. "What bit did you leave out?"

"There!" he pressed a finger to the glass and the endlessly curious little boy shone through her father's aging face.

Zia looked where he was pointing. The churning prairie of cloud ended in a surprisingly even edge that stretched for hundreds of kilometers in either direction. Beyond the creamy fringe to the northwest, ocean stretched to the arcing horizon in a heterogenous gray and blue patchwork. To the northeast sat a peninsula, afternoon sunlight casting shadows that highlighted its topography, the coastline pocked by inlets.

"Okay," said Santiago. "This is Luzon. See that city way over there on the east side of that huge bay? That's Manila."

His voice turned husky. "And there, straight ahead, that mountain? That's Mount Pinatubo."

Ringed by jagged peaks, an aquamarine lake filled the gaping crater of a massive stratovolcano. Pinatubo dominated the landscape around it, its lush slopes overlooking the surrounding farmland like a fickle geological deity. From this high up, it appeared simultaneously epic and domesticated, as if Zia could summon a mountain from the crust of the Earth with the ease of a game designer assembling a virgin world from scraps of code.

"In 1991, Pinatubo erupted," said her dad in an awestruck tone. "Lava shot thirty-five kilometers into the sky, forming a cloud four hundred kilometers across. Debris flows decimated the surrounding countryside. The high-pressure gas building up in the magma chamber shot billions of tons of molten rock straight up the center of the expanding tower of ash and ejecta. Some of that gas was sulfur dioxide, which oxidized to produce sulfate ions that combined with water vapor to create teeny tiny droplets of sulfuric acid that spread out across the planet's stratosphere in a thin mist with a combined surface area approximating that of every grain of sand in the Sahara Desert." He looked up from Pinatubo to the glowing turmeric coal of the setting sun. "When sunlight reached Earth, some of it reflected off that fine aerosol mist, backscattering off into space instead of reaching the surface of the planet. As a result, global temperature dropped by half a degree Celsius for the subsequent two years, despite the fact that humanity was burning fossil fuel and releasing greenhouse gas like a hormone-addled teenager." He sketched a circle with his hands. "Until those droplets finally fell back to Earth, Pinatubo's particulate haze was a veil that cooled the planet, protecting us from ourselves."

Humanity was burning fossil fuel and releasing greenhouse gas like a hormone-addled teenager. Hairs raised on the back of Zia's neck. That was a line from her mother's unfinished manuscript, the rough-cut masterpiece that Galang had helped Zia compile and publish after her death—against Santiago's wishes. It was part of the introduction, concluding a section detailing the ecosystem collapse, environmental degradation, and mass extinction brought on by anthropogenic climate change. The sentence had stuck with Zia because, as an only child, she couldn't help but wonder if it alluded to her own teenage transgressions.

Zia jumped from reverie to speculation. *There's something I need to show you.* Her father was not one for idle chitchat. He hadn't brought her up here on a lark. Leaning forward, she caught a last glimpse of Pinatubo as it passed beneath the long wing of this strange aircraft. Her blood ran cold. She could feel rough bark under her hands, hear insects chattering, see the fog-shrouded volcano rising up behind the villas through a gap in the foliage. What had he just said? *Protecting us from ourselves.*

"Please don't tell me you're planning to blow up the volcano on your island base in order to slow down global warming," she said.

"What?" Santiago's genuine confusion was the sweetest salve. He shook his head. "Oh, no, no, no. Nothing like that. I mean, sulfur dioxide isn't even that good of an aerosol. Plus, it accelerates ozone depletion and causes acid rain. And that's not even mentioning all the other toxic gases and lava and ejecta and all the rest that wreak havoc when volcanoes erupt. No. That would be like treating a broken wrist by amputating the arm."

"Okay, gross," she said. Her relief quickly curdled into frustration. She had been torn from her life to joyride twenty-five kilometers above the ground. She should be back in Chhattisgarh with Himmat, doing things that actually mattered. "So, why are we here?"

"The dangers of climate change require serious immediate action but eliminating the industrial economy's greenhouse gas emissions is extremely hard," he said, sobering. "The UN failed to accomplish much of anything. National governments failed to accomplish much of anything. The private sector failed to accomplish much of anything. The scientific community failed to accomplish much of anything. Environmental activists failed to accomplish much of anything. Those failures mean business-as-usual continues and business-as-usual means condemning future generations to climate hell."

Zia frowned, remembering Selai's graphs. "But global temperature has stabilized. As a matter of fact, it's even dropped slightly over the past few years. Selai tells me it's the big mystery in climatology right now. Reality is defying all the models."

Santiago's shit-eating grin was terrifying. He patted the armrest affectionately.

"Mystery solved," he said. "I call it: Project Svalinn."

15

+

TURBULENCE THRUMMED AS THEY DESCENDED INTO the capricious troposphere with its dramatic and changeable weather. Clouds whipped past, turning the windows into blank panes displaying nothing but the fact that they were in a machine flown by a machine, two humans huddled in the center of a matryoshka of generations of technology lacquered onto itself. Zia tried to ignore the butterflies in her stomach, tried not to wonder whether her vertigo stemmed from the bumps and jolts of the drone or her father's words.

"This fleet doesn't just boost Interstice bandwidth and hoover data," he said with the nervous enthusiasm of a child giving a tour of a newly constructed bedroom fort. "They spray a mist of purpose-engineered inert aerosols into the stratosphere, cloaking the planet in an envelope that reflects just enough sunlight to offset global warming. It's not perfect.

It doesn't do anything to solve ocean acidification from the buildup of carbon dioxide, for example. But the most disastrous effects of climate change stem from the direct impacts of rising temperature. This program buys us time by adjusting the thermostat." Santiago's monologue accelerated into a breathless manifesto. "It gives us room to adapt, to transition the energy system away from carbon. It heads off the positive feedback loop of melting permafrost that would otherwise accelerate warming. It saves countless species from the brink of extinction. It's a hedge against our inborn shortsightedness. It's shelter from a storm of our own creation. And it works."

Her father's eyes shone in the reflected light of the instrument panel. This was just the kind of silver bullet he would latch onto: a straightforward technical fix to an otherwise intractable problem. But Zia had lived with him long enough to see how such technical fixes were rarely straightforward and often produced new generations of intractable problems. Scientific progress was an escalating game of cat and mouse.

"Hold on," said Zia. "Global temperatures started stabilizing years ago."

Santiago rubbed his hands together. "Yep," he said. "I started working on the problem a decade ago and the first drones started flying three years later. Since they went up, we haven't set a temperature record, Arctic sea ice has advanced, some glaciers have started growing again, sea levels are holding, aggregate wildfire coverage is decreasing, and that's not even counting reductions in human suffering."

If that was true... "How do I not *know* about this?"

"*Nobody* knows about this," said Santiago. "Actually, to be precise, one other person besides the two of us knows about this: Ben Munroe, the chief scientist on the project. He lives over at the Atlantic base and manages all the modeling. But nobody else knows. I keep the entire engineering side of the project carefully sequestered in need-to-know teams distributed throughout Interstice and outside contractors. Ben does the same thing on the climatology side. The entire program is run remotely through a backdoor system I hacked personally and that only I can access, which annoys Ben sometimes." He chuckled. "Honestly, it's not that different from high-profile product development."

"Oh, come on," said Zia. "You're saying nobody suspects what you're up to?"

He shrugged. "We're Interstice," he said. "We have a good reason to be in the stratosphere."

"But—" Zia's train of thought caught up with her. Selai's research. The annotated papers. The broken models. *The fleet is loaded with every exotic sensor we can get our hands on, and we give the data to scientific and educational groups pro bono.* "You're— You're fleecing the data." Zia could hardly believe it, could hardly bring herself to say it. That was how she knew it must be true. "You're scrubbing any evidence of the—what do you call them? Aerosols?—from the feed you sell to governments and research groups." *No scientist I've interviewed has been able to fully explain it,* Galang had said. *Lots of handwaving.* "That's why the climatologists can't figure out what's going on, why their models don't work, why SaudExxon PR is having an extended field day. They're all operating on a false premise. You're lying to them."

Santiago's face hardened. "You've read your mother's books. The world knew about the risks of unmitigated global warming for decades, and did jack shit about it."

Her fingers dug into the armrests. "So you hijacked the climate."

He stared at the cloud-blank window. "I'm saving them from themselves."

Something unspooled inside Zia. Years of strict tennis training. Being shipped off to boarding school against her will. The unrelenting questions. The quiet and not-so-quiet judgements. The living-under-my-roof rules. Rationing of allowances. Condescension toward friends and lovers who didn't meet an unwritten standard. This wasn't an aberration. This was her father mercilessly pursuing his definition of what was best for the world. With such a starkly precise vision for what constituted the right thing, nothing would do except absolute control.

Scraps of cloud whipped past the window and then the drone dropped out of the bank and the view opened up like a time-lapse flower. There was the island poking up above the waves like the tip of a spear, its shaft obscured by the briny depths. Another long-winged drone was taxiing for takeoff, preparing to replace their own shuddering craft in a carefully choreographed high-altitude dance that stretched the sheerest of veils around this tumbling rock that life called home in an effort to make that home a little more hospitable for certain residents who couldn't be bothered to clean up after themselves. The last crimson slice of sun dipped below the horizon, smearing bloody fingers across the arching dome of sky.

"What are the side effects?" Zia asked softly.

"It makes sunsets redder, for one," said Santiago. "More light gets diffused coming through the atmosphere."

"And for two? And three? And four?" If there was one thing Zia had learned from her mother, it was that the Earth system was hellishly complicated. No model came close to capturing its entirety. One small change could cascade into ten thousand unforeseen consequences.

Santiago shifted in his chair. "Uptick in biomass accumulation," he said. "Many plants seem to prefer diffuse light so they tend to grow a little faster."

She let silence expand to fill every nook and cranny of the cabin, then asked, "What is it you're trying so hard not to tell me?"

Santiago stilled, retracting into himself like a pill bug.

The drone banked, lining up for landing.

Zia held her breath.

"When Tambora erupted in 1815, it created a stratospheric veil twice as thick as Pinatubo's, cooling the entire planet for years," he said. "As a result, the Indian subcontinent didn't warm up enough to suck in moist air from the surrounding ocean, and the monsoon failed."

Ice flowed down Zia's spine and seeped out to her extremities. The bitter taste of soil on every breath. The petty viciousness of the BSF officer. The brittle don't-fuck-with-me eyes of the fourteen-year-old girl who was selling herself for ration chits. The measured indifference of the mid-level government official who was diverting water intended for agricultural irrigation to an industrial facility rich enough to pay him off. The skyrocketing rates of alcohol and drug addiction.

A nation, crippled.

"Are you telling me that your pet project caused the drought in Chhattisgarh?" she asked.

Her father forced himself to meet her eye.

"I'm telling you it's not impossible," he said.

Touchdown.

+

16

"STOP," SAID ZIA, SPLAYING HER HANDS OUT ON the polished cement countertop in the open-plan kitchen of her father's villa as if the smooth, cool surface might help douse the rage blazing in her chest.

"Oh, grow up," said Santiago, running his finger around the rim of his tumbler of sparkling water. She'd never seen him drink a drop of alcohol lest the liquor dull the keen edge of his sober intellect even for a moment.

Implications reproduced like hungry bacteria in the rich substrate of Zia's mind.

"We're talking about the lives and livelihoods of more than one and a half billion people," she said. "It's not just India, it's the whole subcontinent—plus Sri Lanka. It's been three years since the last real monsoon. That's three years of crop failures, malnutrition, and economic stagnation. The poorest people are the worst hit, as always. And they're just some footnote in your scheme, not even worth mentioning. It's environmental colonialism."

"Look," he said, taking a sip in a failed effort to hide a wince. "I know you're close to—"

"What about the hurricanes hitting the Caribbean and US?" interrupted Zia. "Or the Ukrainian cold snap? How do you know your precious little drones aren't causing those?"

"The models—"

"You're the one who always told me that even the best models break when they hit the real world," she snapped. "That the problems with academics is that they need to get out of the lab and into the field. This is spray and pray—in dust we trust."

Santiago stood abruptly and his stool crashed to the floor. "What would the world look like without Project Svalinn? You really think unabated global warming would have been *better*? Yes, people in India are suffering. No, I can't prove beyond a doubt that I haven't contributed in some indirect way to hurricanes or cold snaps, although I can make some very educated guesses. But how many more would have died, how many more would be suffering, if I hadn't intervened? You want to see everyone totally fucked? You want to go post-apocalyptic? Storm surges. Resource wars. Nationwide wildfires. Look at Central America and sub-Saharan Africa, five years of consistent regional growth and increased life expectancy. What would those places look like if they hadn't had a respite from global warming? Imagine a world without my program and tell me, *tell me*, that you'd do a single thing differently." He paused, cheeks flushed, breath coming in sharp pants. "Humans started engineering the climate the minute we began burning fossil fuels in earnest, we just didn't realize it yet. But ignorance is no excuse. The only difference now is that I'm doing it *intentionally*. I thought you'd be thrilled. I'm trying to dodge the blows that you try to soften."

"Oh, so you want to argue net benefit, do you?" Zia stood to face him across the counter. The conversation was falling into the practiced, belligerent rhythm of a war drum. She knew he knew she could feel it too. Worn ruts diverging. No Miranda to coax them back onto the same page. "India suffers so that Africa thrives, but overall more people are better off? What gives *you* the right to make those calls?" She stabbed a finger into his chest. "Who are you, Captain Planet cum Stalin? Nobody else gets a say? *Nobody even gets to know it's happening?* What a staggering load of godforsaken bullshit."

"And who exactly would you trust with this? The UN?"

"Pull the plug," she said, shaking her head. "Call a halt. Shut it down."

"I can't."

"Stop, or I'll blow the whistle," she said. "And boy, will I blow it loud."

And then she'd take the opportunity to sever every remaining tie she possibly could. Order the lawyers to disband the trust. Change her name. Get a restraining order. Whatever it took.

"No, you don't understand," he said. "Even if I wanted to, I can't stop it now. At least, not right away."

"I thought you were the fucking circus master."

In one smooth motion Santiago swept up his glass and hurled it across the room like a pitcher throwing a fastball. The glass smashed against the French doors to the front deck, shards of tumbler scattering, cracks spiderwebbing out across the pane, drops of flying water fragmenting light into rainbows that lived and died in the space of a blink.

"For fuck's sake, Papi," said Zia, her shock tinged by a grim, guilty satisfaction.

"Sorry, I—" he looked around, suddenly lost, grasping for words. "Sorry."

The sparkling water pooling on the floor fizzed in the ensuing silence.

They both stared at it for a moment, then he shook his head as if to clear it.

"The aerosols are keeping the planet artificially cool, despite the fact that people keep burning fossil fuels," he said. "But take away my drones, and temperatures will jack right up commensurate with the actual levels of greenhouse gas in the atmosphere. Nobody really knows what that kind of a termination shock would look like, but we don't want to find out. So even if I were to discontinue the program, and I'm not, it would take years to ramp things down safely."

"Unbelievable," she said, grasping the counter for support. Human ingenuity was a gift and a trap, and for a shimmering moment all of scientific history coalesced before Zia in an interlocking chain of intensifying cause and effect. "You're not just hijacking the climate, you're holding it hostage."

"The people holding the climate hostage are the US, Europe, and every other country that got rich burning carbon and refuses to face the consequences. They're not just fucking over their own grandchildren, they're fucking over everyone who's not privileged enough to win the birth lottery and grows up somewhere else, somewhere poor, somewhere that doesn't have the luxury of centuries of fossil-fueled economic development. Poor people can't afford to 'just move' or to build fancy 'resilient infrastructure' or any of the rest of it, so their lives fall apart, if they're lucky enough to escape with them. This program gives them a fighting chance. It saves hundreds of millions of people from becoming climate refugees. It gives poor countries space to raise their populations out of poverty without being hammered by mega-storms." He gave her a look that was at once sharp and somehow vulnerable. "I thought that of all people, you would understand."

"When was the last time you actually talked to a poor person?" Zia was suddenly tired. So very tired.

"What?"

"All these people you say you want to help, when was the last time you met one of them?"

"Look, I'm running Interstice and this program simultaneously," he said. "I don't have time to tour around for enlightening chats."

"That's what I thought," said Zia, halfway transported to a dozen separate but identical beige conference rooms, playing nice with well-meaning donors and foreign aid project managers who salved their consciences with charity from a comfortable remove. "Well, let me pass something along. One of the most disempowering aspects of poverty is that your entire life is shaped by forces that you don't understand and that are totally out of your control. When everything happens to you, it's hard to learn that you can happen to things. And what I see here is another system in which the powerless have no representation, another system that's a mechanism of external control, another system built right on top of all the rest. If you care so much about protecting other people, why is this program secret? Why are you so afraid of sharing it, of letting other people participate in making decisions that impact their lives?"

"Because people suck at making collective decisions! Climate change won't wait for a bunch of miserable humans to squabble into a halfway workable solution. It just happens and we're fucked." His face tightened into an ugly, unfamiliar, wrenched expression. "Zia, I'm telling you, this program is the reason we haven't had another Heat Wave."

That hit harder than a thrown tumbler ever could.

Zia turned away and stalked out the door.

17

+

ZIA DESCENDED THE PEDESTRIAN PATH LEADING down from the house. Her shoes rasped against the flagstones. Low energy red lights lining the sides of the path provided just enough illumination to walk safely. Jungle encroached on all sides, buzzing with life. The Milky Way hung high above like a rent in the black velvet of the universe.

She had woken from drug-induced slumber a day and a half ago but it felt like she had been on this remote outpost of Indonesia for years. That was the thing about her father. His ideas were clockwork universes with internal symmetry that sucked in everyone they touched as they ratcheted themselves forward, ever forward. The inescapable gravity his visions generated was what had made him such a successful entrepreneur. If you weren't paying attention, they would sweep you up, claim your allegiance, and dictate the shape of your future.

Growing up, Zia had been enamored with her father's indefatigable sense of purpose and the breadth of his perspective. It took years for her to start to pay attention, really pay attention. Only then did she begin to notice that his worldview was not the world, that the grand architecture of his ideas had chinks and gaps and infinite loops, that their elegance was a product of their limitations, their internal consistency a feature of their imperfect reflection of reality.

That was when Zia finally began to appreciate her mother's books for the first time. Zia had always loved the hikes, the overgrown chaos of the untended garden, the bottomless well of naturalist lore. It took time and experience, but she finally began to make out the shadow of a slippery message that swam beneath the surface of her mother's words like a literary eel. A reader could follow breadcrumbs through the moving anecdotes and more easily imagine that reality far exceeded human comprehension, that truth was often messy and ineffable. That was why her mother's stories struck a chord that resonated with the zeitgeist. After putting down one of her books, you couldn't help but notice new shades of meaning brushed onto your world like glaze on clay. It was the depth of her mother's humility that had been the counterweight to the breadth of her father's hubris.

Zia reached an unmarked fork in the path and chose a direction at random. She could taste the sea. Leaves shushed each other in the surrounding darkness. She slapped away a mosquito and felt how stiff and sore her body was in the wake of fights, escapes, climbs, falls, and abduction. Her broken toenail ached. The creamy sweetness of the chai she'd enjoyed with Galang reverberated through the karmic medium from some previous incarnation.

The path turned a corner and suddenly she was back amongst the villas, their windows dark, their residents sleeping or absent. She wandered through them like a stray dog through a ghost town. The scent of jasmine hung in the air. She had a sudden urge, quickly suppressed, to track down Logan's villa and fuck her worries away. Underwater lights turned the abandoned pool into an aquatic gem. The tennis courts were empty. Like an illustrator assessing a blank sheet of paper, Zia took in the net, the lines, and unbidden and intermingled flashes from tournaments long past flitted through her mind. Bounce. Toss. Serve. Return. Volley. Point. Game. Set. Match. Zia had been good. Had she genuinely liked it, she might have been great. But tennis had been a discipline to her, not a game. It had taught her about concentration, about mastery, not joie de vivre.

Not that joie de vivre was something she had a lot of right now.

The path widened and she emerged onto the beach. Zia kicked off her shoes and relished the feeling of sand beneath her feet, sinking under her weight and grinding up between her toes. She walked through the gentle, wild-sculpted hillocks and down to the water. A wave crashed, collapsing into itself. Spray kissed her face and whitewater churned up around her ankles, salt stinging her scratches and blisters with a sharp, cleansing pain. She let another wave crash, and another. Then she retreated just beyond their reach. She sat down in the sand and crossed her legs. The surf washed away every vestige of her footprints.

Moonlight transmuted the ocean into quicksilver. The wet smack of froth hitting the beach was a metronome loyal to the rhythm of whatever distant storm had churned up these waves and sent them rippling across the Pacific. Zia picked up a handful of sand, let it dribble out grain by grain. *...a thin mist with a combined surface area approximating that of every grain of sand in the Sahara Desert.* She lay back on the beach and stared up at the stars. Did they twinkle more because photons reaching the end of their millennia-long journey across vast tracts of space had to find gaps in the fabric of her father's stratospheric veil in order to reach her eyes? What did it mean to try to fix the planet like it was a machine in need of maintenance? What did it mean to know that such a fix might indeed be possible, but demur?

Pulling out the new phone her father's people had supplied, Zia retreated into the comforting embrace of the group chat, scrolling through an endless feed of photos, anecdotes, video clips, teasing, emojis, discussion, and inside jokes that had ballooned into Escher-esque architectures of irony and self-reference. Aafreen and Galang posted a selfie drinking tea together in the floating capital of the Maldives. Selai had an extremely detailed breakdown of every Easter egg hidden in the new Pixar movie. Kodjo was asking for advice on navigating the fraught emotional straits of his divorce proceedings. Daniela, no surprise, had uncovered yet another unknown band that was sure to top the charts within a year. Li Jie's parents had been cleaning out his basement and discovered a forgotten stash of old clothes from high school, which he'd somehow managed to squeeze into, sharing ridiculous, nostalgia-inducing pictures of the results. This was why Zia's closest friends were still those she'd made in boarding school. The digital epoxy of the group chat had held them together over the subsequent years and across thousands of miles. It was the collaborative narrative of their lives, the stories they told themselves about themselves that made them who they were.

You won't believe this, typed Zia. She paused, searching for words, then retracted the message. No. She wasn't ready for that just yet. Even dropping a hint about what she was going through right now would attract a flurry of concern and offers of help, support she didn't want to invite and wouldn't know how to channel. Frustrated, she stashed her phone.

Zia wanted to return to Chhattisgarh. She wanted to brainstorm negotiation tactics with Himmat. She wanted to send off the quarterly report to Jason. She wanted to find her way to the airfield, commandeer one of those long-winged drones, set a course for India, and forget this ever happened. She and her father would go back to not speaking to one another and she would lose herself in a workload that built up as steadily as silt in a river delta.

But prying herself out of this mess wouldn't be as easy as hopping on the next flight out. Santiago's schemes weren't easy to extricate oneself from, no matter how desperate or practiced the fugitive. How could Zia hope to do her job with a full security escort following her around day and night? As much as she wanted to, how could she refuse an escort while her kidnappers were still at large?

It was still possible that her abductors had just wanted to hold Zia for ransom. It was still possible that they might have been hired by Governor Rao or some other grudge-holding Delhi powerbroker looking to pluck a thorn from his side. Anything was possible. But as Zia had learned working on President Kim's campaign, intrigue flocked to secrets like moths to a flame. Despite the fact Zia had known nothing about it at the time, it was difficult to imagine that her kidnapping and her father's geoengineering program were mere coincidences.

Which left her... Where, exactly?

Zia blinked. Something had blotted out the stars, a clotted mass of darkness devouring the sky. Panic seized her for a moment, a blind terror that the shadows might wrap her in long articulated fingers and squeeze out every drop of soul. She felt a sharp tap on her forehead. Reaching up, she discovered beads of water trembling on her skin. Then, tap. Tap, tap, tap. Fat raindrops fell in an accelerating rhythm. Zia sat up, heard the distinctive murmur of rain on sea. The rain pitter-pattered on her scalp, saturated her hair, poured down her face, dribbled along her spine and between her breasts, soaked her clothes. Leaning her head back, she opened her mouth and tasted the storm, each drop planting a cool kiss on her tongue.

"Zia, mija, is that you?"

She stared out at the sea.

Santiago hurried across the beach holding an umbrella against the driving rain. He sank down into the wet sand at her side. The umbrella formed a roof over them both. Rain hammered at it like a drummer's palm onto the skin of a conga, the water sloughing off and enclosing their little column of dry air in a sheath of waterfall.

Her father put his free arm around Zia's shoulder. She could feel his every breath, heavy from exertion, the sharpness of his ribs. Heat came off him in waves, and only because of his steadiness did Zia realize that she was shivering all over. She glanced over at him and was shocked to see silent tears streaming down the hard lines of his face.

Lightning flashed, momentarily illuminating the seething wall of water that encircled them. *This program is the reason we haven't had another Heat Wave.* It was all *so* like her father. An orthogonal solution to a problem everyone assumed was insoluble. Making global scale and universal application prerequisites. Never stopping to ask for permission or outside input. Assuming that unintended consequences could be tackled as they developed. Centralizing control to maximize individual efficacy and accelerate iteration. Cultivating various sources of value stemming from a single, technologically sophisticated operation such that the whole thing somehow managed to rake in outsized profits. Thunder growled in the distance. Yes, this godforsaken geoengineering project had Santiago's name written all over it.

He had begun ten years ago, in the wake of her mother's death. Just as Zia had thrown herself into humanitarian aid, Santiago had devoted himself to a secret skunkworks, both of them attempting to assuage their consciences by committing every ounce of their beings to subduing the demon that had murdered Miranda. Maybe if Zia could help enough people, she could save other families from the tragedy that had ruptured hers. Maybe if Santiago could wrangle the climate with his hack, he could avert future disasters of the magnitude of the one that had taken his wife. In the absence of other outlets, their respective endeavors were the tortured language of their grief.

Life is pain, Highness. Anyone who says differently is selling something.

Zia reached over and squeezed her father's knee.

18

+

ZIA SLICED THE BLOOD ORANGE IN HALF AND CRIMSON juice leaked out across the cutting board. The meat was striated cherry and hot pink and the sharp tang of citrus suffused the kitchen. Her father sat across the counter from her, finger tapping out the beat of the Cuban salsa playing at low volume. She remembered hearing the same song playing at the hole-in-the-wall where they'd pick up fried sweet plantains after tennis when she was little—how much she'd loved laughing with her dad as she licked residual sugar from sticky fingers. Beyond the wall-to-wall window, morning sun burned off clouds scuttling along in the wake of last night's storm and rising mist caught and scattered the light like gaseous prisms.

"You said that this program is a hedge against human shortsightedness," said Zia carefully. She was a general marshaling arguments instead of troops, anticipating traps and orchestrating flanking maneuvers. If she was going to get out of this mess, she had to be more than angry—she had to be as relentless as Santiago himself.

Santiago nodded. "Transitioning the world's entire energy system off of carbon is hard. Doing it quickly enough to avoid disastrous global warming is that much harder. Harder still to do it without undercutting the ability of poor countries to develop economies strong enough to raise their populations out of poverty. This gives us a buffer." He gestured out at the drone lifting off from the airfield, long wings glinting as it banked up and out over the ocean. "I'm buying us time."

Zia sliced open another orange. "You've always bet on the long run."

"There's no easier way to differentiate yourself from the mob."

Differentiating himself from the mob. Yes. Santiago wanted to be the best. Always the best. Anyone who wanted to win that badly would all too easily forget the full humanity of each and every person that made up the mob that they so desperately wanted to rise above. "And what's the point of short-term thinking if you want to make a long-term impact?"

"*Eso.*"

"So what's your long-term PR strategy?"

Santiago frowned. There weren't many words he hated more than "public" and "relations" strung together. Outside of her father's irregular, celebrated essays, Interstice was famously tight-lipped. Teams were broken up into strict communication silos. NDAs were ironclad. There was no logo. The service aesthetic was of seamless invisibility. The company itself was named for the small intervening spaces incidentally formed by interlocking structures.

"Silence," he said shortly.

Slice. Slice. Slice. Zia wanted to go after him with the knife. Instead, she let the word hang in the air, forcing it to endure their rapt attention like a model on a catwalk.

"I see," she said at last. "And how long do you expect to keep your secret?"

"Nobody's caught on yet."

"That's not an answer," she said. "And I thought the whole reason you assigned a clandestine security team to me, the whole reason I'm here and not rotting in a cell, is because you've been having infosec issues. You told me that Interstice is under increasing pressure from corporate espionage."

"They're fishing," he said, his tone thorny. "That's all it is."

"You hope," she said.

"There's no way—"

Zia scooped up an orange half and pressed it down onto the juicer. The electric motor interrupted her father and thick juice poured into a waiting glass.

"Meanwhile," said Zia, as if puzzling through a particularly circuitous brainteaser, "the rest of the world is less worried about climate change than ever because global temperatures have leveled off. Confined to their diet of Interstice data falsified to hide your operation, the scientific community loses more credibility by the day because they can't figure out what's really going on. SaudExxon's propaganda machine amplifies the confusion as their masters snap up new concessions and distribution contracts. And if I understood your explanation correctly, the more carbon gets pumped into the atmosphere, the worse the termination shock were your drones ever to be grounded." She paused to juice another orange. "So while your program may buy us time, the world, in its ignorance, appears to be using that time to make everything worse. And why shouldn't it? After all, nobody knows that they're squandering your precious buffer."

"I'm holding off disaster. Can you imagine where we'd be without the program?"

"Oh, I agree," said Zia. "It's a tremendous short-term plan."

"Hold on—"

She juiced an orange, ignoring his scowl. The scope and consequences of Santiago's endeavor meant she couldn't run back to Chhattisgarh and pretend this had never happened, no matter how badly she wanted to. And if there was one thing she'd learned from subverting her parents' wills as a teenager, it was that running away played right into her father's hands. No. The way to beat Santiago at his own game was to start with first principles and build up a vision of your own with enough momentum to displace his. And despite his many faults, Zia admired his intellectual honesty. No matter how much he hated it, Santiago wasn't afraid to be proven wrong.

"You know what I really don't want to imagine?" asked Zia. "What might happen when the world finds out what you're up to." She shook her head. "I mean, *maybe* you'll get lucky and everyone will come together and sing Kumbaya and reform their wicked ways and stop emitting carbon and shower you with roses. But you yourself pointed out how the international community has failed to take meaningful action to address climate change despite decades of evidence. I'd hate to see your cynicism applied to this scenario."

"Look," he said. "Obviously, we'll have to announce it eventually. We just—"

Zia juiced another orange and Santiago looked like he wanted to smash the whining machine onto the floor.

"Oof, and what do you think India will do when they find out you've crippled them by killing the monsoon?" she asked, wincing.

"The way attribution works with the models, it's impossible to know—"

Zia leveled the knife at him. "You're not going to win anyone over with that kind of nuanced logic. They'll turn you into a scapegoat, shoot your drones out of the sky, and score points with impassioned manifestos."

"That would be idiotic! The termination—"

"Weren't you just accusing politicians of being idiots? But you're probably right, some countries would see the light and intervene. Given the heterogenous regional effects of your meddling, I bet Russia and Canada and Fiji and loads of other nations will be thrilled at the results of your program. So they'll step in and deploy their own militaries to protect the program, or even better, build domestic programs of their own. But of course they'll disagree with each other about how it should be done, which will escalate everything further." She tilted her head to the side. "Come to think of it, you might just start a war. Now, wouldn't *that* be exciting?"

"Don't be ridiculous," he growled.

"You can't keep this secret forever, *Papi*," said Zia. "When I was campaigning for President Kim, she called the team together and told us she'd had an abortion while she was in college at UCR." Zia remembered the packed conference room, the nervous interns, the smell of stale coffee and sweat. "We all knew how that would play with the fundamentalist demo, and our coms guy jumped in with a plan for how we could keep it on the DL. But Kim said flat out that she was going to give a speech about it at a clinic in San Jose and turn the whole thing into a campaign issue. The other side's oppo research would dig it up eventually. She knew that it was better to get out in front and control the narrative. If she didn't, someone else would. And the way these things go, the someone else most likely to do it is usually the worst possible person, the one with the biggest bets staked against you."

Zia slid the glass of orange juice across the table to her father.

"Kim won because of that speech," she said. "All the analysts shit their pants."

Santiago's fingers weren't tapping out the *clave* any longer. His hands were pressed down on the countertop so hard that tendons stood out on his forearms. Accompanied by a trumpet riff, the vocalist sang about the murder of escaped slaves in an incongruously upbeat tenor.

Zia wiped the knife on the edge of the cutting board. Picking up one of the juiced orange halves, she squeezed the pebbled skin to extract one last drop from its pithy flesh. They both watched the scarlet jewel soak into the wood grain of the cutting board. Then she looked up and met his eye with the remembered force of his stern pep talks.

"You're a León," she said.

19

+

"SO, I'VE MET WITH AAFREEN'S SECOND COUSIN twice," said Galang, Zia's phone rendering his voice slightly tinny. "The first time was at this dive bar that smelled like the morning after a hyena sex party. The second time was on a docked fishing trawler that made me seasick. Both times he gives me this look and says *no phones* and it took everything I had not to scream *really? Oh, I never would have imagined we need to be careful about surveillance. I'm just a silly little investigative reporter, after all. Oh, and by the way, well done scheduling both our conversations for midnight. Not on-the-nose at all.*" Galang rolled his eyes. "I mean, I might not be Lynn Chevalier, but I'm not fucking clueless. Aafreen warned me that the guy's a total dick. Oh, his intel is good. There absolutely is a ring of government officials auctioning resettlement visas on the black market. It's just that it's obvious that he's *part* of the damn ring and hopes that by being the first to blow the whistle, he'll keep his name out of the headlines and then swoop in to give outraged speeches, oust his former co-conspirators, and catapult up the political hierarchy. So I help one asshole by taking down a bunch of other assholes and the world just keeps turning."

"Reminds me of Selai with her physics-cum-philosophy about quantum entanglement and there being no such thing as an independent observer," said Zia, leaning back in the hammock. More than anything, she wanted to call Selai and explain that the discrepancies Selai had identified in the climate models weren't a product of faulty algorithms but of Santiago meddling with the raw data. So, BTW, my dad is flying drones into the stratosphere to spray dust that makes the Earth shinier, reflecting more incoming sunlight back into space, thus reducing the amount of energy entering the Earth system and cooling the planet. Oh, and he's lying to everyone about it. But Zia couldn't just tell Selai everything. Project Svalinn was a secret sensitive enough to start a war over, and Selai was working on behalf of her uncles in the Fijian cabinet. If she found out what Santiago was doing, she'd have no choice but to inform them immediately, even if it might lead to disaster. They in turn would be honor bound to act in Fiji's national interest, whatever they interpreted it to be. Zia couldn't put her in such an impossible situation. Galang was different. His entire job was to reveal sensitive secrets for public benefit. "By telling people's stories, you become a participant."

"In practice, it definitely feels like my sources and I are both using each other. Makes me almost miss those heady days of 'objective journalism' that old-timers yammer on about, but I'm convinced they're just mythologizing a past that never really existed in the first place. Playing word games to disguise your point of view isn't objectivity. Better to explain your perspective to the audience and let them draw their own conclusions. Unfortunately, *my source is a total fuckwad who's leveraging his own misdeeds for personal gain which this story enables* is not the kind of delectable morsel that'll make it past Bonnie."

A butterfly drew Zia's eyes away from the phone, fluttering across her father's wide deck on an inscrutable mission all its own. She thought of fragile chrysalises hanging vacant, their papery walls hinting at life forever becoming life.

"What does it mean if friends use each other?" asked Zia.

"Umm, been to therapy lately?" asked Galang. "You're going to have to unpack that one for me."

"I was the target of an attempted kidnapping," said Zia.

"Uh huh, right," said Galang, then his face froze when Zia didn't respond. "Wait, *what*?" His expression crumbled into shock so dramatically that Zia couldn't help but laugh. "Get the fuck out! You were *kidnapped*? Are you okay? Where are you right now? What can I do? Oh my god, I can't believe I've just been blabbing on about my work when— How did you not tell me this already? What have I taught you about burying the lede, girl?"

Her view shook as he moved his phone closer to his face, the better to see her.

"I'm safe now," she said. "It's okay. It happened right after we met for chai in Chhattisgarh. Armed professionals, a team of them. The Zachary's delivery came in handy though. Turns out frozen pizza is quite a formidable weapon." She recounted the abduction, waking up on the island, and her aborted escape attempt. Galang was an appreciative audience, ohh-ing and ahh-ing in all the right places, demanding additional details, and uttering unrepeatable profanities in disbelief. Though she wanted more than anything to share it with someone, to get a second opinion, Zia demurred when she got to the part about the geoengineering project. That wasn't intel she could trust to even the most secure digital network.

"See?" said Galang. "I told you they need to turn your life into a movie. This is blockbuster material."

"Is it embarrassing to admit that I was thinking about that as I fell out of the window in the least photogenic way possible? It was as far from graceful as it's possible to get."

"So embarrassing," said Galang. "And so exquisite."

Zia laughed. "You're too much."

"You know what's too much? This story." Galang narrowed his eyes. "I do this for a living, love, and the little puzzle you just laid out is missing some big pieces. Who sent those men after you? Why? For that matter, why did Daddio have a secret team of bodyguards watching over you in the first place? WTF are you going to do now? I know you pretty darn well, Zia-san, and I don't believe for a minute that you didn't immediately start asking the same questions yourself. So, what aren't you telling me?"

Zia looked up at the blue sky arching over her. Thousands of feet up, sprinkled throughout the thin haze of the stratosphere, was the biggest story of Galang's career. An Interstice drone soared out from behind the volcano and lined up for landing. Maybe it was providing the signal boost that connected her call to Galang right now, their voices slurped up by microphones, digested into packets, and ferried through convoluted digital intestines before being reconstituted at the other end. Industrialists often dabbled in philanthropy, but usually they worked hard to publicize their efforts. What her father saw as clandestine charity was unlikely to draw charitable attention from others. Galang would tell the whole story, and tell it well. He wouldn't take shortcuts. He wouldn't give Santiago special treatment. He wouldn't stop until he had shone a comprehensive light on the skein of threats and promises that converged on those damn drones. And once he did, she could finally go home and get back to work, if she was even allowed back into India once the world found out about her father.

She looked back down to find Galang's eyes steady on her, his forehead furrowed. Zia was kidding herself, wasn't she? The secret had to come out, and it would make her already delicate position in Chhattisgarh totally untenable.

"How much longer do you need to stay in the Maldives?" she asked.

"Well, I have meetings scheduled with a couple more sources, there are a few places I want to visit just to get the context right, and I promised Aafreen I'd go drinking with her," said Galang. "But my tenure here depends primarily on the urgency of business I might have elsewhere."

"What if we could have a plane pick you up tomorrow?"

"Then I'd tell Aafreen I love her, tell her cousin to go fuck himself, and jump ship. Assuming, of course, that this enigmatic invitation might lead somewhere juicy."

"Aren't the juiciest leads always enigmatic?"

"It's taken almost twenty years, but you're finally starting to grok this whole journalism thing," said Galang. "Let me know if you're ever in the market for an unpaid internship."

"And work for you? God forbid."

"Always the slacker, this one."

A lump rose in Zia's throat. She was a dust mote carried on an unseasonable breeze through a shaft of afternoon light. "Hey, Galang?"

"Yes, Zia?"
"Thank you. I promise this'll be worth it."
"Oh hush, darling. I'm already packing."

+

20

ZIA SWALLOWED TO EQUALIZE THE PRESSURE IN her ears and peered out the window. Turquoise sea stretched from horizon to horizon, encroaching on a string of atolls that barely kept their palm-tufted heads above the surf. Speedboats, fishing trawlers, yachts, and cargo ships plied the waves. The plane descended toward the Maldivian capital.

New Malé was a miracle of marine engineering, a floating city built atop the flooded ruins of its namesake. Unable to avoid the pitiless irony of history, it had been designed and constructed by SaudExxon contractors. They were, after all, the premier experts on offshore platforms. New Malé was made up of thousands of adjacent platforms linked together in an urban chessboard anchored to the seamount below. The shoreline shape and platform heights varied to imply natural topography. Seagulls wheeled through the skyscrapers and cranes played Tetris with shipping containers at the port. Zia remembered visiting Aafreen during summer break in high school. Back then, high tides sloshed over Malé's seawalls and the city's technological reincarnation as New Malé had seemed little more than a pipe dream. That dream had been realized, and remained insufficient. A life raft too small for a nation.

The plane touched down and braked hard, the safety belt cutting into Zia's waist. Long runways were a mainland luxury. They taxied to the private terminal and memories of her stint here as a relief director flashed through Zia's head. Blinking ocean spray out of her face. Mopping up the savory remains of a plate of *mas riha* with fresh-made *roshi*. The devastation left in the wake of the last storm surge. Without Santiago's meddling, would Maldivians be even worse off than they were now? Had Project Svalinn spared them crucial centimeters of sea level rise? Or was it just yet another way for the outside world to encroach on the Dhivehi way of life?

Zia shook her head. Distance magnified the instinctual implausibility of Santiago's scheme. Everything about it sounded so *unlikely*, almost ridiculous. But wouldn't electrical lights have sounded unlikely to a medieval peasant? How would a nineteenth century scientific establishment that still believed in aether have reacted to the idea of splitting an atom? Reality was implausible. Santiago's project was positively banal compared to those heady frontiers.

"Ms. León?"

Her newly assigned bodyguard, Dembe, was a compact special forces veteran with braided kinky hair and striking amber eyes who spoke like a soldier and moved like a dancer. She wore a dapper suit with an orange pocket square over her fitted ballistic vest. Was this who Zia was now? One of those people who couldn't go anywhere without impeccably dressed, consummately professional, heavily armed minders? It was profoundly embarrassing in a way that resonated with Zia's irrepressible shame at being born into privilege.

"Please, call me Zia."

"Of course, ma'am—Zia." Was that a smile tugging at the corners of her lips? "We've cleared the perimeter and are ready when you are."

Zia unbuckled her seatbelt and followed Dembe.

A cool onshore wind buffeted Zia as they disembarked, welcome in the tropical heat. Sunlight glared off the tarmac and the smell of jet fuel cut through the ocean tang. Head tracking back and forth, Dembe murmured through the radio to her two colleagues as she led Zia across to the small private terminal. Inside, the building was a posh lounge. High ceilings arched overhead, indirect skylights funneling in mirrored sunlight. A long mahogany bar covered one side of the big room, glass containers of myriad tea varietals shelved behind it where a traditional bar might feature liquor. The walls were covered in luminescent abstract shapes that shifted like tectonic plates, drifting so slowly that their movement was almost imperceptible. Dembe stayed with Zia as the two other officers covered the doors to the tarmac and the air-train stop respectively.

Zia checked the time. Galang would meet them here in thirty minutes, just enough time for the plane to refuel for the return trip. Zia simultaneously couldn't wait and couldn't bear to see him. She desperately wanted to share everything she'd experienced in the last couple days but knew that sharing it would somehow make it more real, like a spotlight throwing a shadowy stage into sharp relief. As long as she kept it to herself, she could almost pretend nothing had happened. But pretending that nothing was really happening was exactly the attitude she'd had to grapple with day in and day out as a relief worker liaising with local and international elites who preferred to stifle problems with the silk blindfold of comforting ideology.

No. Inaction was action. Zia had lit the fuse. Santiago had reluctantly capitulated. Galang was on the way. There was no turning back. For better or worse, the secret would come out. She ordered a pot of top-shelf Ceylon tea at the bar and carried it back to one of the nooks tucked into every corner of the lounge—all the while trying to remember the joke Vachan's cousin had taught her during a visit to the family estate for memorizing the industry acronym denoting the highest grade of tea. Far Too Good For Ordinary People. That was it: FTGFOP. What Zia would give to be an ordinary person who didn't need a bodyguard. She sat down and looked up. Large broadleaf tropical plants formed screens between the sparsely populated seating areas and Dembe stood a few meters distant, eyes strafing the room in a practiced staccato pattern.

"Sit with me," said Zia.

Dembe pressed her lips together into a firm line. "On duty, ma'am."

"It's Zia," said Zia as she poured tea into two delicate porcelain cups. "And as your principal, I need your protection from the indignity of drinking alone. Cream, sugar, lemon?"

Dembe's face was hard but her eyes were smiling.

"Come on," said Zia. "I would ask *what's the worst that could happen* but I know you've already thought of whatever it is and prepared contingencies."

"Cream, sugar, no lemon." Dembe sat.

Zia obliged. "As a kid, I always loved pouring the cream," she said. "I'd watch it swirl into the tea and imagine I was summoning a djinn. It always struck me as odd that people read tea leaves to tell the future. Cream always seemed to be more fruitful material for prognostication."

"There was a woman in the village where I grew up who all the kids thought was a witch," said Dembe. "If you paid her, she'd tell your future. My friends would save up just to hear her spin a riddle. I never did. Why would I want to know my future? If she's right, I can't change anything anyway. If she's wrong, I just wasted my coin. The best part about the future is that it's unknowable. I wouldn't have a job otherwise."

"Personal protection as divination."

"I constrain downside risk," said Dembe.

Looking at Dembe, something clicked inside Zia—raising goosebumps. Those eyes. Those striking amber eyes.

"I've seen you before," said Zia, frowning as memory churned. A mother pushing twins in a stroller. The incomprehensible chatter of Japanese bankers. "You followed me in Zürich."

"Guilty as charged," said Dembe, calmly holding Zia's gaze. "I was assigned to your detail."

You hire spooks to follow me around and don't even mention *it to me?* Santiago's Adam's apple had bobbed up and down in mute admission. What did she have to do to get out from under him, to find the space to be her own person? Was independence too much to ask for? It felt like Zia had been trying to escape his ubiquitous, inexorable influence her whole life. Santiago applied his being on the world as a forcing function. Dembe was his tool, a weapon in his bandolier. That's how anyone ended up who spent enough time around him. That's what Zia was now too, in a way. She was doing what needed to be done for him, wasn't she? Even if it was against her will and, ostensibly, his.

"Were you there in Chhattisgarh?" asked Zia.

Dembe sipped her tea, examined Zia, nodded.

"What is it like," asked Zia, remembering the half-imagined fireworks show that accompanied her descent into drug-induced oblivion, "to kill someone?"

"It's hard—until it's not," said Dembe, eyes luminous. "The better question is: what is it like to save someone?"

"Thank you," said Zia, voice suddenly hoarse.

"Just doing my job," said Dembe, taking another sip of tea. "You messed that guy up pretty good with the pizza. I've seen a lot, but never that."

"Zachary's is better pizza than he deserved," said Zia.

Dembe laughed a bright, sparkling laugh that counterbalanced her gruff manner, then cut off abruptly and touched her earpiece. She listened intently for a moment, then met Zia's eye.

"Someone's here for you," she said.

Zia smiled. "Galang's arrived early," she said. "He can help us finish the pot."

"Not Galang," said Dembe. "Aafreen Solih."

21

+

EVERY TIME ZIA SAW AAFREEN, SHE WAS STRUCK by her friend's undeniable beauty. There were good looking people, there were people who worked hard to fine tune their appearance, and then there were unselfconsciously beautiful people, people who caught and held the eye like magnets without even meaning to. With her delicate features, radiant skin, and fierce sense of presence, Aafreen was one of these rare creatures, a falcon goddess in human form. No wonder Li Jie had had such a crush on her in high school—the awkward mix of infatuation and veneration dooming it from the beginning.

Even from across the lounge, Zia could see the coiled energy in Aafreen's posture, her gorgeously embroidered headscarf, the way that even the carefully managed attention of Zia's security team couldn't help but skirt Aafreen's event horizon. After Zia had dumped Tommy when he'd made his intentions clear, he'd pursued Aafreen in an unrequited campaign that had made Zia jealous despite herself—which had probably been his ultimate goal anyway. Years later, once he'd taken his rightful place in the SaudExxon corporoyal court, he had spearheaded the New Malé contract in what Zia suspected was an effort to win over Aafreen and benefit his career at the same time. But Aafreen had politely dismissed his advances and was now the Maldivian minister of foreign affairs, traveling with bodyguards of her own.

Zia walked over to greet her friend.

"I didn't think we were going to get to see each other!" Zia pulled Aafreen into a tight hug. "Weren't you supposed to be in a meeting with the prime minister? This is fabulous. You have to have some tea with me while we wait for Galang. We can take a selfie of the three of us for the group chat. Sorry to be stealing him away, I promise you can have him back."

Aafreen squeezed Zia hard, holding on as if she were a life raft.

"I've missed you, sister," said Zia.

"You too," whispered Aafreen, voice cracking.

"Look at you, getting all emotional," said Zia, heart swelling. "Be careful, it's contagious."

Aafreen heaved a deep sigh on Zia's shoulder.

"Hey," said Zia, taking a half step back to get a real look at Aafreen. Her friend's face bore the carefully neutral expression of someone accustomed to public scrutiny, but there was something feral in Aafreen's eyes. Zia's chest ratcheted tight like cable under a lever winch. "What's going on? What's wrong?"

Aafreen swallowed.

"Let's sit down," she said.

As they walked over to the table, Zia noticed Dembe conferring with Aafreen's security team out of the corner of her eye, spurring Zia herself to check that nobody was within earshot of their nook. They sat in front of the half-empty cups and Zia wondered what she had failed to glimpse in the swirling eddies of cream.

"I don't know how to say this," said Aafreen.

"Just say it then," said Zia, palms sweating.

Aafreen bit the corner of her lip, let out a breath, and met Zia's insistent gaze.

"Galang's dead."

"What?" asked Zia flatly.

"He's dead." A flurry of micro expressions stormed across Aafreen's face like a gale. "Galang is dead."

Cold, numb disbelief. That couldn't be. Galang was going to fly back to Santiago's island with Zia. He was going to break the story of the century. He was going to walk through the door in a few minutes with a dirty grin on his face and reveal that this was all some big misunderstanding, or maybe a prank to tease out just how much they cared about him.

"How?"

Aafreen took a deep breath. "They found his body in a brothel early this morning. Single gunshot to the back of the head. Execution style."

"A brothel?" That wasn't like Galang at all. He could wrap a man around his finger in a heartbeat. Paying for sex wasn't his style.

"I know," said Aafreen. "Maybe he was there to solicit a source or something, I'm not sure. Nobody's sure of anything yet, forensics is still on site."

"Murdered," said Zia weakly.

"Certainly appears that way," said Aafreen with forced

calm. "Hard to shoot yourself in the back of the head."

"Fuck," said Zia.

"Fuck," agreed Aafreen.

You're an angel, he'd told her in Chhattisgarh. *And you're the best kind of devil,* she'd responded. Vertigo swept Zia away. The amorphous paintings surged off the walls and into three dimensions. The potted plants grew impossibly fast, filled the cavernous room with desperate, grasping tendrils. The skylights blazed like the magnifying glass with which Zia had ignited an ant as a child. Galang. Sweet, sly, cantankerous, gossipy Galang. Zia sucked in a shaky breath and tried to ignore the kaleidoscopic barrage of color on the inside of her eyelids. Aafreen was leaning forward, had taken Zia's hands in hers.

"I know, honey," murmured Aafreen. "I know."

Zia took a deep breath, bundled up her heart like a parent swaddling a child, and opened her eyes. There were shadows under Aafreen's eyes and tight lines around her mouth. Her hands were dry but cold around Zia's.

"I'm sorry," said Zia, squeezing back. "You're going through hell. What can we do? How can I help?"

"Not a lot at the moment," said Aafreen. "The police are investigating but the case is so fresh I don't expect to hear much for a while yet. What I'm trying to figure out is who might have done this and why. Galang is too savvy to have gotten himself randomly murdered and we both know he wasn't there for a quickie. Can you think of anything that might be relevant?"

Zia frowned. "He told me he was working on the black market resettlement story, using your second cousin as a primary lead. What if someone in the ring found out he was digging?"

Aafreen's gaze sharpened. "That's exactly what I'm afraid of," she said. "Who knows what people are capable of when they think their back's to a wall? I'm having my people look into it, officially and unofficially. If there's so much as a peep, I'm going on the warpath."

Galang's Pulitzer-winning headlines cycled through Zia's head like a newsreel. "He's made a lot of enemies over the years, hasn't he?"

"That he has," said Aafreen. "Motive doesn't narrow the field much." She glanced over at Dembe who was still consulting with Aafreen's security team. "He said you were coming to pick him up for a story?"

Everything came rushing back like air into an airlock. The island. Santiago's secret geoengineering program. Could whoever have kidnapped Zia somehow be involved with Galang's murder? Had her father's hubris killed her friend?

"Yes," said Zia. "It's complicated, and—it makes me enough of a target that I need suits." She nodded to Dembe. "But Galang didn't know any of the details."

Aafreen gave her a long look that exerted gentle pressure in the way only a longtime friend could. "Want to talk about it?"

The secret filled Zia up like water behind a dam, currents seething as they reached for the crest. Aafreen was a minister in the cabinet of a country that had been literally flooded by climate change, a brutal reality Zia had seen up close. The Maldives were a poster child for the future Santiago wanted to avert, and it was likely thanks to his project that anyone still managed to eke out a living on these remote atolls. More importantly, Aafreen was a friend. A patient, brilliant friend who would at least give the program a fair hearing before passing judgement. Zia had been impressed by the careful machinations of Aafreen's analytical mind since they were Latin study buddies.

But as a friend, Zia could see that Aafreen was already pushing herself to the limit. And it wasn't just being woken up in the middle of the night by a crisis. It wasn't even the vicious infighting to come. It was that Aafreen had invited Galang here, passed along whispers of corruption, and introduced him to her cousin. She had set him on a course that might very well have led to his killing.

Just like Zia.

It was better to get out in front and control the narrative. That was the moral of the story Zia had told her father. What would President Kim do in this situation? Acknowledge that this wasn't the right place or time. You didn't broach a geopolitical scandal to people who had just become embroiled in a homicide investigation. There were too many variables, too many conflating factors. And with the nightmare her friend was already facing, unloading on Aafreen under these circumstances wouldn't just be imprudent, but cruel.

Zia let out a long breath. "Thank you," she said, "but no. At least, not yet." She paused, and Aafreen waited her out. "It's not impossible that there is some connection to whatever happened here. I'm going to need to do some digging of my own."

Aafreen gave her a curt nod, equal to equal, and Zia was absurdly grateful for her friend's unconditional trust.

"I'll keep you apprised," said Zia. "You'll be the first to know if I find anything."

"I'll do the same," said Aafreen.

Thoughts stampeded, impossible to corral. From nothing, you could extrapolate anything. If she hoped to make sense of any of this, she needed more data, and the place to find data wasn't in the whorls of her own mind, but right in front of her.

"What about the newsroom? Do his bosses know?" asked Zia. "Maybe they're aware of something else he was working on that would make him a target."

"My staff is talking to them now," said Aafreen. "I came straight here after notifying the family."

"Oh, Aafreen, I'm sorry," said Zia. The family. Galang had always had a tortured relationship with his parents, but he and his sister Kemala were close. Zia couldn't imagine what it must have been like telling them what had happened. Thank heaven she hadn't further burdened Aafreen with her own confession.

"It's okay," said Aafreen with a tired half-smile. "For better or worse, this job has given me practice at breaking hard news. It doesn't get easier. But you do get used to how difficult it is."

"Fuck," said Zia.

"That's about the size of it," said Aafreen, pain moving behind her face like kelp under a shifting sea. Zia wanted to spare her, to break down in tears, to scream denial at a deaf cosmos. She remembered the minty smell of her mother's body wash and the way Miranda would sing along to old *cumbia* songs under her breath. Why did fate take the good ones?

"Look, Zia," said Aafreen. "I know you want to help, but—"

"No, I get it," said Zia, shaking her head. "You don't need a close friend of the deceased barging in to interfere with the details of a police investigation without any intuition for local politics. Don't worry, I won't be the bull in your china shop. The windmills I need to tilt at aren't on New Malé anyway. The best way for me to help is to go back and tease out any clues of a connection to the reason I'm here in the first place."

Sorrow and relief suffused Aafreen's voice. "Thank you," she said, her voice raw. "Of anyone, I hoped you'd understand. You remember how it was during the storm."

Zia nodded, wishing those memories didn't poison her dreams. "The only thing that matters is finding out what really happened," she said. "I'll get right back on that plane and get out of your hair. But promise me that when you find out who these bastards are, we take them down together."

Zia had never seen anything as beautiful or terrifying as the sublime expression that crossed her old friend's face.

"You have my word," said Aafreen.

One of the Interstice drones circled high above the island, long wings glinting, giving them a landing window. Their plane touched down and they disembarked. It was a clear day and the peak of the volcano rose jagged and alone into blue sky. Steam evaporated off the hot tarmac. As they crossed it, Zia pulled Dembe aside.

"I'm worried that the people who tried to kidnap me killed Galang," said Zia after a moment's hesitation. "I know it's a long shot. But can you think of anything that might test that hypothesis?"

Dembe ran a hand over her braids. "Sorry, boss. That isn't really my area. I'm a tactics gal."

"Then what can you tell me about their respective tactics?"

They walked in silence for a few moments. Seabirds cackled overhead.

"They had a four person team for the kidnapping in India," said Dembe. "Professionals. They knew what they were doing. If we hadn't already been shadowing you, or if they knew we were, you would've been toast."

+

22

ZIA COULD SEE MOVEMENT THROUGH THE PEPPER tree, hear footsteps coming up the alley toward her hiding spot, feel the arm lock around her neck.

"The New Malé hit though..." Dembe shook her head. "I was talking to your friend's security team and—well, it wasn't squeaky clean."

"What does that mean?" asked Zia, trying to suppress nausea as she imagined Galang crumpled on the floor of a cum-stained brothel love nest, eyes empty, limbs at odd angles.

"Well, for one thing, if you decide to off someone, why make it obvious?" Dembe shrugged. "Like, if you just want them dead, you invite a lot less suspicion if you make it look like a suicide or an accident. Or you make them disappear altogether."

Zia shivered. "So if you make murder look like murder, you do it to send a message."

"Exactly," said Dembe.

"But what message?" asked Zia. "And to whom?"

"That's above my pay grade," said Dembe.

They parted ways at the edge of the tarmac, Dembe to report to security headquarters and Zia to climb the hill to Santiago's redoubt.

"Hey, thanks," said Zia.

"No problem," said Dembe. "I'm sorry about your friend."

Zia started up the pedestrian path, crossing a threshold from the industrial sprawl of the airfield into the embrace of encroaching jungle. Insects buzzed. Light dappled the flagstones. Sweat dripped down Zia's spine as she ascended the winding steps.

Maybe one of the corrupt Maldivian officials was trying to intimidate anyone who might blow the whistle on the ring. Maybe the people behind Zia's kidnapping were escalating to assassination to prove their seriousness. Maybe a powerbroker from the long list Galang had disgraced was exacting revenge.

Her friend was dead. They would never talk again, never trade gossip, never tease each other about their love lives, never question what they had been put here to do. A familiar void opened inside Zia. Death didn't destroy the past, it stole the future. It snatched away all the could-have-beens, all the we-should-definitelys, all the next-times. It made you realize all the things you wanted to say to someone, wanted to thank them for, and then gagged you.

It was too late.

It was already too late.

It was always too late.

Zia climbed faster, relished the acid burn in her muscles, the ache of her swollen throat. When her mother had passed,

Galang had been there for Zia. He had helped her obsessively excavate her mother's files like a deranged archeologist who studied fossils in a secret attempt to resurrect them. He never pressed Zia to talk about her grief, never asked why she wasn't talking to her father, never encouraged her to see a therapist. Instead, he was just there for her. Side by side, they'd compiled Miranda's interviews and field observations, reconstructed her shorthand, and posthumously published the annotated rough draft of her manuscript. By immersing herself in Miranda's world and helping to share her story, Zia had felt closer to her mother than she ever had in life. When the book finally hit shelves, earned critical acclaim, and leapt to the top of bestseller lists, it felt like losing her all over again. Now Galang was gone and Zia did not know what to do with the sucking vacuum inside her.

Her father's villa appeared—a sleek human artifact pushing back against teeming green.

Zia stepped through the door and heard him shouting.

"For the last time, Ben, I'm not giving you admin access. Why the hell do you—"

Zia couldn't hear the other side of the call.

"For fuck's sake, I give you all the data your models can eat. When have I not implemented your suggestions? Name a single goddamn time."

Santiago's interlocutor must be Ben Munroe, the chief scientist on Project Svalinn who was stationed at the Atlantic base that mirrored this one. It made Zia think guiltily of Himmat. She needed to let him know she'd be gone for a while yet. Selai was right: it really was time to promote him.

"Don't pretend you're a product designer, we don't need faster iteration. The timescales here are nothing like consumer software, so stop spouting bullshit at me. I'm already stuck dealing with the fallout from Cory Doctorow's latest digital rights manifesto and I'm not in the mood to coddle you."

It sounded like their relationship was about as functional as most of Santiago's.

"No, I said *no*. We have protocols for a reason and I think that funding this entire fucking program, including *you* I might add, gives me the right to make some executive decisions."

Appealing to your own authority was never a good look.

"Seriously, this isn't the time to throw another of your fits. The board ripped me a new one this morning. They haven't been this uppity in years. I suspect there might be some activist hedge fund vipers angling for something. So don't act mutinous unless you're ready to crawl back to academia. Now, fuck off."

Santiago ripped out his earbuds and tossed them on the counter in disgust.

"Tough day at the office?" asked Zia.

He spun. "Zia, sorry you had to hear that. I—" He took three long steps toward her and reached out his arms, then hesitated for a vertiginous moment and dropped them uncertainly.

"I'm so sorry about Galang," he said. "I know you were close."

Zia saw her own pain and confusion reflected in his eyes, and hated him for it, hated him for not wrapping her in his arms, for his conviction in everything but connection, hated herself for feeling all of that and more and doing nothing about it. Memory and twisted logic piled up until Zia felt like she and her father were peering at each other through spyglasses from the ramparts of doppelgänger emotional fortresses. This was the moment when Miranda would step in and bridge the gap between them, which made everything worse. Their mutual awareness of her absence was a call to arms.

"Yeah," she said, more harshly than she meant to. "We were."

"I—I don't know what to say," he fumbled, color rising in frustration.

"Maybe start with 'I will never be able to live with the guilt of Galang being killed because of me, so I am endowing a foundation in his name and have already started ramping down Project Svalinn.'"

"Oh come on," said Santiago. "What makes you think his death had anything to do with us?"

Us landed like a gut punch. "You think it's a coincidence that someone assassinated him the night before I was going to tell him everything?" asked Zia. "For all your bullshit about owning your mistakes, you can't accept responsibility for anything, can you?"

"I'm just saying that given the stories he writes, he must have a lot of people gunning for him."

Zia swept the earbuds off the counter. "And you're making a new enemy right now."

Santiago's eyes followed the earbuds to where they skittered to a stop on the floor.

"You're overreacting," he said.

Anger blazed so bright in Zia that it vaporized any response she might have thrown back in his face, leaving a shell-shocked clarity in its wake. Miranda had always said that there weren't enough china shops in the world for her two bulls. Feuding with her father wouldn't bring Galang back. Nothing could. What mattered was bringing his killers to justice.

"Look," said Santiago. "Maybe we need to call this whole publicity thing off, keep quiet until things calm down."

"That's the *last* thing we should do," said Zia.

Was it possible that her father had had Galang assassinated, that by pretending to accede to her plan and then killing him, he could keep his secret a little longer? No. That was crazy. Santiago could be an asshole, but he wouldn't call a hit. Zia was spiraling. She tamped down burgeoning paranoia and forced her thoughts into line like a carriage driver reining in spooked horses.

"What have your people dug up on my kidnappers?" asked Zia stiffly—trying valiantly but unsuccessfully to channel Dembe's indefatigable calm.

Santiago shook his head. "Skilled operators with good infosec. We haven't been able to determine attribution, but their sophistication means they're a major player. China, Google, South Korea, Amazon, Chile, Disney, SaudExxon, Ethiopia, maybe the US."

"That's a long list, not even considering factions within them," she said. Far less consequential secrets had led to war. The greatest danger of this geoengineering program was the number of unknowns. People with competing agendas would interpret uncertainty in the way that best served their vested interests. She could only pray that future historians wouldn't dub Galang the 21st century Franz Ferdinand.

"We're chipping away at it," said Santiago.

"Let's cross reference with anything we can find that relates to Galang's murder."

He nodded. "I put our analysts on it as soon as I heard."

A knot formed in Zia's stomach. "In the meantime, we need to share your secret as quickly as possible. Making it public destroys its value as clandestine intel. It's the only way to clear the deck."

Santiago sucked in a breath. "Look, I'm under a lot of pressure at the moment."

"*You're* under a lot of pressure?"

"The board—"

"I was nearly kidnapped. I still can't go home to India without Dembe glued to my hip. Galang is dead. Odds are you set off this chain of events by deciding to become an eco megalomaniac. So you may want to reconsider whatever complaint you were about to lodge about your precious board."

"Oh, please. You're calling me a megalomaniac because I'm trying to solve a big problem, rather than traipsing around the world handing out ration packs?"

"You're right," said Zia, sarcasm corroding her words like acid. "Of course, you're right. Instead of actually helping people, we should just commandeer the forces that control their lives. Granting them any agency of their own just gives them an opportunity to fuck things up. I imagine you wouldn't mind one bit if some stranger started making major decisions on your behalf without your knowledge."

"Meanwhile, all of your charitable efforts have led to such sustainable social change that when disaster strikes again, people will be able to help themselves, eh? Get down off your high horse. The world is made in the mud."

"We're breaking the story." Rage simmered beneath her words. "If you want your pet project to work, people need to know. I didn't ask for this. I don't want to be here. But your little secret puts a bullseye on your back, and mine by association. You want to get in the mud, play at pragmatism? I'll back off the minute I see a credible plan that isn't doomed to fail because it depends on pulling the wool over everyone's eyes. I'm not going to let you screw over the entire planet with your pipe dream. I never thought daughters were supposed to say this to their dads, but grow the fuck up."

"And how do you plan to break the story without Galang?"

The question stopped Zia in her tracks. Galang had the expertise and the platform required to tell the world about what her father had been up to in a way that encouraged thoughtful debate, that gave this program a chance to be the beginning of a conversation instead of leading to a violent end. If Santiago called a press conference and announced it directly, nobody would trust him or the data he presented. If she approached the wrong journalist, they might seek to milk the situation for every ounce of inflated drama, cultivating outrage that would sabotage any attempt at earnest collaboration. Galang was the only person Zia trusted to do it right who also had the credentials required to be seen as independent. He would have been curious but skeptical. He would have seen that this story did not need to be exaggerated to be compelling, that breaking it was an opportunity to bring people together instead of fracturing them along established ideological lines. With sufficient nuance, perhaps something aside from disaster could be fashioned from Santiago's preliminary efforts. But with Galang under the coroner's knife, who could Zia trust to tell such an explosive story with sufficient nuance? To whom would she hand a casus belli on a silver platter? Zia was trapped between risking world war by speaking out, or risking the same by staying silent. She was trapped on this godforsaken island, ensnared in the sticky web of her father's plans. Vachan had once told her that nobody survives childhood, they just keep going. Zia wasn't so sure she'd managed to go very far at all.

"That's what I thought," said Santiago. "You—"

Zia's phone rang. Aafreen. "I need to take this."

She stepped out onto the deck to take the call, not wanting to admit to herself just how much she relished cutting

Santiago off. No matter how much he deserved it, lashing out at her father wasn't going to get Zia out of this. The only real way to take back the reins of her life was to clean up this mess as quickly as possible. She would do what needed to be done, and then do her best to forget he had ever existed.

"Yes?"

"Nothing significant yet," said Aafreen. "They're running the bullet through ballistic analysis and trying to crack an encrypted drive they found in his pocket."

"At least that's something," said Zia. "Let me know if you need Interstice support cracking it."

"I will," said Aafreen. "But that's not what I'm calling about."

Zia gazed out over the richly textured rainforest canopy.

"What is it?" she asked.

Aafreen let out a breath. "His sister is arranging a small funeral in New York next week," she said. "Kemala asked if you would say a few words."

A flock of colorful birds burst from a stand of rubber trees, wheeling and screeching as they took wing toward the volcano. Miranda would have been able to name them, no matter how obscure the species. She would have been able to distinguish the males from the females and deduce volumes about their lives from this briefest of glimpses. As it was, Zia could see only birds, and remember her mother's gleeful explanation that birds were living dinosaurs, refugees across epochs.

"A few words," murmured Zia, "is the best any of us can hope for."

23

+

ZIA'S PREPARED REMARKS VANISHED LIKE SMOKE IN the wind as she looked out at the array of assembled faces. Galang's colleagues from the newsroom. Friends Zia had never met. His sister Kemala, fierce and hollow-eyed, steeled against their parents' refusal to attend. The group chat incarnate, Kodjo and Aafreen and Selai and the rest, the follow-on reunion Galang had wanted realized by his passing. Dembe was stationed in the back by the door alongside bodyguards for the others in this airy Manhattan loft who constituted high value targets. What a strange thing, to live in the sights of unknown enemies.

Panic emerged like a bear out of hibernation—thickheaded and ravenous. There was nothing Zia could possibly say that could capture who Galang was, what he had meant to her, to all of them. People could not be reduced to less than themselves. The only thing she could do was share small, hopelessly inadequate moments that might help coax his soul to surface, and shine a light upon it.

Zia took a shaky breath, felt the Earth beneath her feet, heard the wail of distant sirens, and began to speak. She spoke about shared intimacies, insatiable curiosity, and Galang's long running passion for pistachio gelato. She spoke about big plans, little jokes, and unrealized dreams. She spoke about boarding school, rules flagrantly violated, and how family wasn't something inscribed in blood, but forged in life. *Oh hush, darling. I'm already packing.* Refusing to wipe away the silent tears, she spoke about friendship, loss, and journeys that could only be taken alone.

And then there were all the things left unsaid. How Galang had seen through the masks behind which people hid their true selves, and yet somehow managed never to lose his affection for humanity. Squeezing Galang's shaking hands as he confessed how after he came out to his parents, they had sent him to boarding school to keep him away from his little sister. How Zia had lost Galang when she needed him most, how much she feared that his death might herald countless others, how much of an imposter she was standing up here eulogizing a friend she might well have condemned.

Like the last grains of sand in an hourglass, Zia's final words tumbled out and she was done and standing up there by herself in front of the solemn crowd and she was as lost as she'd ever been and had no idea where to go or who to turn to and half-suspected she might just fade into the aether but then Kemala, who looked so like Galang and yet so different, was standing and pulling Zia into a hug that was infinitely more articulate than any speech, that grounded her in reality, that illuminated the tentative, silly, profound bonds that they all shared, and that the pain of severance stemmed from the joy that Galang had brought to the world, the love he had showered upon them all.

A hand touched her arm as Zia made her way back to her friends. She did a double take. "Tommy?"

"That was beautiful," he said, voice husky.

With his sandy hair, tan skin, piercing blue eyes, and impeccably cut suit, Tommy looked like the Platonic ideal of the man his high school self had been destined to become. She remembered sneaking up to the roof of the chateau to hook up under the glittering alpine stars and how basking in his undivided attention had made her feel like her life meant something, that she was special, that she mattered. He told her stories about hawk hunting with his uncles and playing football under the famous air-conditioned domes that surrounded Riyadh like a string of pearls. They spun out elaborate fantasies of shared futures that ranged from pioneering nuclear fusion to seeking enlightenment in hidden monasteries to pulling off art heists of unprecedented ambition. And then there was the moment that shattered those sugar-glass visions, when he had propped his head up on his elbow and asked her why she was friends with those plebs, told her that she shouldn't waste time with losers who came from powerless families in weak countries, that they weren't worthy of her.

The fact that he had meant it as a supportive intervention was the worst part. His arrogance was so unselfconscious. She hadn't wanted to shake off the afterglow of sex, hadn't wanted to wrap herself in the sweaty, sticky sheet, hadn't wanted to ask him to leave, to demand it when he protested, to threaten to scream when she saw a shadow that might be violence in his eyes.

"We're all going to miss him," said Tommy with a sad smile that made Zia despise herself for harboring decades-old resentment. She wasn't the same person she'd been in high school. Surely, Tommy wasn't either. They'd all been selfish, generous, kind, cruel, confused, coddled, tortured teenagers. They'd all acted like jerks at one point or another. And it was hard to imagine anything more soul-sucking than being born into the SaudExxon aristocracy. Holding a grudge was exactly the kind of behavior she was apparently still judging Tommy for. And who was Zia to monopolize grief at Galang's untimely passing? How shamelessly petty. Old bitterness washed away in a cathartic rush. What was death, if not an opportunity to forgive?

"Thanks," said Zia. "We will."

It had been a very long time since Zia had included Tommy in any kind of *we*, a semantic embrace that Galang would have underscored in the script of her life, scribbling feverish notes in the margin about every ending being a new beginning.

+

24

DURING THE RECEPTION, THE CROWD BROKE UP into groups, sipped pinot noir, and recounted memories of Galang in hushed voices. Kodjo told them about how Galang had been there to listen and provide counsel when his wife sued for sole custody. Selai laughed at how Galang would always go cross-eyed when she talked about physics too much. Daniela reminisced about going clubbing together and seducing the prettiest boys with theatrical ploys. Li Jie reminded them of Galang's absurdly overzealous deployment of exclamation points in text conversations. Zia shared how much he'd helped her with Miranda's manuscript, how it would never have been published without his support. Tommy joined the circle and Aafreen shot Zia a significant look but he told them how Galang had been the first openly gay person he'd ever met, and how it had felt to befriend someone who made you question the way you'd been raised.

Then again, Aafreen's glance might well have been about Galang, not Tommy. Without the emotional intensity of standing up and speaking in front of everyone, guilt filled the void of Zia's grief. This wasn't some freak accident. Galang had been killed for a reason. Odds were, Aafreen or Zia was that reason. They as good as killed him and here they both were, swapping sob stories.

Vachan was describing how Galang had sent him twenty-seven uniquely disguised glitter bombs on his twenty-seventh birthday and how Vachan was still finding glitter in his pockets all these years later. Zia wanted to be present, to be there for her friends, to fully inhabit the shared ache, but her attention was split. She eavesdropped on nearby conversations, glanced at passersby, and mentally reviewed the layout of the space. *In practice, it definitely feels like my sources and I are both using each other*, Galang had said in their last conversation. Now, Zia was attending his funeral with her own ulterior motive.

There, over by the bar.

"I need a refill," she said, leaving her friends and approaching the small, elegant woman with a shock of gray hair and horn-rimmed glasses who was pouring herself a neat Scotch. Zia found it all too easy to imagine her presiding over a hectic newsroom.

"Bonnie?" she held out a hand. "I'm Zia. Galang told me a lot about you."

Bonnie Hillenbrand looked up and something dark and nebulous seethed behind her eyes for the briefest of moments before the older woman gave Zia a hard smile and shook her hand.

"Not too much, I hope," said Bonnie in a precise, clipped tone.

"Only good things," said Zia.

"How uncharacteristically dishonest of him."

"Well, he did mention that your mentorship involved telling him to come to terms with the fact that 'journalism is and always has been a Sisyphean task suited only for workaholic attention seekers with guilt issues.' So I guess that tough but fair would be a more accurate descriptor than good for how he talked about you."

"I'll take that," said Bonnie.

"Look," said Zia. "Could I steal you away for a moment? There's something I really think you should know."

Bonnie looked like she was about to decline, then reconsidered.

"Okay," she said flatly.

Zia led her out onto the wide balcony. Manhattan rose up around them, a forest of glass and steel and brick. Late afternoon light angled down the avenues and the nonstop rumble of urban life enveloped them. Zia loved New York for its admixture of old and new, class and grunge. There was something overwrought and self-consuming about it, like the superheroes chronicled in the classic comics it had birthed. Maybe Superman would burst from a nearby window and rocket up, cape flapping, to tear one of Santiago's drones from the stratosphere. Or maybe Clark Kent would studiously run the numbers and conclude that the only way to defeat his new arch nemesis, climate change, was through teamwork, not brawn, and break the story that should have been Galang's in the *Daily Planet*. Perhaps it would take an alien from Krypton to bring the appropriate perspective to a plot that implicated the entire earth system.

But Clark Kent wasn't here. Bonnie was.

Zia looked over the railing. People scurried like ants along the sidewalk below. Cyclists maneuvered between honking vehicles. The leaves of the street trees were turning brilliant shades of yellow, orange, and red. A vision dropped into Zia's mind fully formed. Handing Bonnie her glass of cabernet franc and vaulting over the railing. Wind roaring, stomach rising, everything around her stretching out into a vertical blur. A scream born not of fear, but of rapturous delight. Time distending into singularity at the moment of impact, every fiber of her soul resonating at the same frequency before shattering like a crystal champagne flute under the ringing soprano of an opera singer.

"Ms. León, you said there was something you wanted to discuss?"

Bonnie's cool voice swept Zia up from her imaginary leap as surely as Superman could have. She took a sip of wine to cover her fugue and tore her gaze away from the street.

Sun glinted off Bonnie's glasses and Zia couldn't quite see the other woman's eyes. Her suit was stylish but conservative. A cashmere scarf was wrapped around her neck. She held herself with the cultivated intensity of someone who'd had to fight for every centimeter.

Was this Zia's best opportunity or greatest mistake? Santiago had demanded they keep the program quiet until things settled down, but things might never settle down. If Zia brought in someone like Bonnie, he couldn't very well refuse to talk. Doing so would invite scrutiny he couldn't handle, and raise the stakes when the truth finally came out. Whether he liked it or not, Zia could force his hand. But she was painfully aware of the scale and range of unforeseen consequences. Could she trust Bonnie to approach the situation with the requisite rigor and care? Bonnie was a veteran editor, but would she cultivate the patience necessary to dissect and communicate the complexities of the science involved? Would she illuminate nuance or pass snap judgements?

This whole geoengineering mess combined so much uncertainty with so little time. You could call for more research forever while the planet became less hospitable to humans with every passing season. And yet, without the results of that research, you wouldn't know how to gauge your interventions. Zia had torn into her father for making such momentous unilateral decisions with imperfect information, and yet that was precisely the position she herself was in with respect to Bonnie.

At a certain point, you just had to make a call.

"I think I might know why Galang was killed." Zia glanced around to make sure they were alone and lowered her voice. "He was meeting me about a story that someone doesn't want told."

"And who exactly is that someone?" There was an edge to Bonnie's voice that might or might not have been sarcasm.

"I'm not sure," said Zia. "But I'm trying to find out."

"Are you now?" asked Bonnie. "A veritable Nancy Drew. And what, pray tell, is this story that needs so badly to be hushed up?"

Zia was put off by Bonnie's poorly concealed antagonism. How had Zia managed to get off on the wrong foot so quickly? Should she beat a quick retreat or forge ahead?

"It's complicated," she said.

"Conspiracies always are," said Bonnie.

Even as Zia was trying to formulate a response, the other woman turned away and stalked back inside, leaving Zia to stare at her retreating back and wonder what had just happened, and what to do next.

25 +

ZIA TURNED BACK TO FACE THE CITY. THEY HAD visited New York when she was a girl, Miranda, Santiago, and Zia, the three musketeers as her father liked to call them. They went to see *Hamilton* and even though she didn't fully understand the plot, the music transported Zia to a different time, a different place, a life that made sense and fit a narrative structure that imbued it with meaning in a way that made her own story feel disjointed and flat. She had listened to the soundtrack thousands of times, memorizing all the words and driving her parents crazy. But it was the good kind of crazy, the kind where they'd exchange a glance and roll their eyes and Zia would sing even louder.

They'd eaten greasy pizza and ridden on the crowded subway that roared like a mechanical dragon. They'd strolled atop the massive seawalls and watched the ferries chug across the bay to the Statue of Liberty. Miranda explained how Manhattan had once been a rich wetland, and Santiago described how it had been built into a rich city. Zia had made the mistake of believing that this was how life was going to be from then on. The three of them exploring a mysterious world, together.

But then the vacation came to an end. They flew back to Costa Rica. Santiago disappeared into Interstice, Miranda retreated into her next book project, and Zia wandered the backyard alone, finding hiding places in the brush where she could look out on the garden without being seen, singing *Hamilton* softly to herself. *There's a million things I haven't done, but just you wait.*

And what had she done? Excelled in school and tennis and every other activity in which her parents had enrolled her, all in a desperate attempt to earn their scarce attention, an effort that proved in vain when they announced she'd be attending boarding school in Switzerland as if it were something that should delight her. Zia had erected internal seawalls as thick as New York's to push back the fetid tide of betrayal and smiled when they explained how big of an opportunity it was for her. She had camouflaged her true motivations so well over the years that they seemed to believe she was driven to achieve for its own sake, as they were.

The other kids at the chateau had their own stories. Some curled up in their bunks and cried for hours on end without explanation. Some despised their families and were thrilled to escape them. Some were excited at the prospect of a new adventure. All were terrified the first time they set foot in that mountain redoubt fashioned from ancient stones, though most refused to admit it. In the midst of the subsequent studies and squabbles and teenage folly, Zia had realized that

Vachan and Aafreen and Selai and the rest had become a new kind of outcast family, a little gang of adolescents abandoned by their parents in the most luxurious possible way, who were also socially excluded from their primly exclusive classmates who came from families that had enjoyed generations of wealth and power down which they'd sent all of their progeny to this remote corner of the Alps as a rite of passage. There were few bonds as strange or as strong as a shared inability to fit in.

Someone had shattered that bond by murdering Galang. And now... what? *Conspiracies always are*. Why had Bonnie reacted the way she did? Could she somehow already know about Santiago's stratospheric aerosol injection program? Did she suspect that Zia was responsible for Galang's death? Or was Bonnie understandably in shock at the death of a friend and colleague, temper shortened by grief? Maybe it would have been better for Zia to have set up an appointment with her later this week, rather than get straight to it. But Galang had always said that Bonnie didn't suffer fools lightly and was ruthless about not burying the lede.

Zia pushed away all the could haves and should haves. You could drown in the past while the future passed you by. Next steps were the only thing that mattered. Bonnie's hostility changed nothing. But if she wasn't the person to break the story, who was? Zia could take it to President Kim, who had been reelected for a nonconsecutive second term, but Kim would be obliged to notify the UN, and the situation would immediately escalate to a game of chicken between the great powers. No. This kind of story needed to come from an independent source so that people could try to make sense of the implications without immediately attributing everything to self-reinforcing geopolitical power plays. That was the only way to provide an opening that wouldn't lead to retrenchment, that might turn what would otherwise be a divisive threat into an opportunity to come together. All of which meant that Zia was back to square one.

"There you are." Tommy leaned against the railing, an updraft from the street scattering his blond hair. "You begged off for a refill and disappeared."

Zia sighed. "I needed some fresh air."

Tommy inhaled deeply and exhaled slowly. "It tastes good," he said. "Fresh air. Even Manhattan's version of it. In Riyadh, everything is indoors and underground, sumptuous but enclosed." He didn't have to explain that frequently fatal daytime temperatures made outdoor living impossible in most of the Gulf. "Filtered air just isn't the same. You get used to it, until being outside somewhere else reminds you how artificial it all is."

"Not quite the Alps?"

He chuckled. "Not quite the Alps."

There was a moment of silence as they both grappled with time-weathered memories. Tommy had been anything but a social outcast in boarding school, his slot guaranteed from birth as a member of the corporoyal court. Perhaps that was why his affections had so enticed Zia at the time, they gave her a taste of the acceptance she so craved. Until, of course, she realized how membership in a club defined by inbred superiority wasn't the golden ticket she'd imagined it to be. Even so, she couldn't deny the good times they'd shared. *Being with you makes me feel invincible*, he'd told her once, his words—ardent and earnest enough to be contagious—sparking the same of sense of burgeoning immortality in Zia.

"How is it, over there?" she asked.

"At SaudExxon, you mean?" Although he smiled easily, his eyes hardened in a way that reminded Zia of Aafreen. "It's... Well, it's probably what you expect, only more so. When you control assets worth trillions of dollars, competition at the top is fierce."

"Sounds like an environment where you'd thrive," said Zia, trying not to sound passive aggressive.

He snorted. "I'm doing alright," he said. "Irons in the fire and all that."

"Was there going to be a 'but'?"

"Oh, there are many 'buts,'" he said. "*But* the old timers still hold the reins decades past their prime. *But* the idiots trying to seize power have no vision for what to *do* with it. *But* the accelerating growth of solar and nuclear threatens our powerbase. *But* SaudExxon is a ship navigating treacherous waters with an obsolete chart. But. But. But. But. But."

"And you know better?"

"Of course I do," he said. "It's obvious. We need to bridge our oil wealth into something new. The present can't operate without us. We need to ensure the future won't be able to either."

"What a heartwarming thought," she said.

"Reality isn't heartwarming."

"And certainly won't become so if people assume it can't be."

"Maybe once I'm in charge, I'll be able to afford to update my assumptions."

"Doesn't being at the top mean you'll have the most to lose?"

Tommy golf clapped. "See?" he said. "I miss this. If there's one thing that court life lacks, it's spirited banter. Everyone's so dour all the time."

"Not like at a funeral."

His grin faded and Zia couldn't help but feel a little guilty. Tommy was here after all, that was more than could be said for Galang's parents.

"Sorry," she said.

He held up a hand. "No, you're right," he said. "I'm the one who should be apologizing."

They stared out at the city. The last rays of sun illuminated the low hanging ceiling of clouds from below, painting their underbellies orange and yellow to match the autumn leaves. Birds darted through the skyscraper canyons. A trumpet player busked at the nearest subway entrance. Everything felt alive in a way that highlighted Galang's absence. This was a world in which he would never again set foot.

"Don't take this the wrong way," said Zia. "But I hope you're not here to pitch me again. I said I would consider your offer, and I am." She'd had much, much more urgent things to think about lately. Jason might get antsy, but this could wait.

"Of course not," said Tommy. "As I said in Zürich, I wouldn't consider making a grant without your blessing."

"Why, then? You and Galang were never close."

"Not like us, once," said Tommy.

If this was bait, Zia wouldn't take it.

"Honestly," said Tommy, his voice dropping an octave, "I was hoping to see you."

"Grief isn't the aphrodisiac you seem to think it is."

"Not like that," said Tommy. "It's just... Look, back in school I was a jerk and you dumped me. But I always liked you, and I really do miss the banter. So I just wanted to ask you, as a friend, whether your dad could be convinced to sell Interstice."

Because the casual inflection in Tommy's voice didn't change, it took a moment for his non sequitur to register. Could

Santiago be convinced to sell Interstice? Had Tommy flown halfway around the world to attend Galang's funeral just to ask her that question? Was that any less believable than his flying halfway around the world to mourn a high school acquaintance? Rage, curiosity, recrimination, sadness, and disgust flared in quick succession like oncoming headlights on a highway, but Zia reined them in. Whatever Tommy's intentions, she wouldn't give him the satisfaction of provoking her.

"That sounds like a question you should ask him," said Zia evenly. The funding offer must have been a way to butter her up for this question. That it was so predictable made it even more sad.

"Of course," said Tommy. "It's just that we've been hearing rumors for a while now that he's ignoring his duties as CEO and that shareholders and even some senior executives don't know what he's really spending his time on. The board is up in arms."

"I can't speak to any of that," said Zia, remembering her father's shouting match with Ben, his admission that the board was giving him trouble. If Tommy was hearing rumors, Santiago wasn't being nearly as careful with his skunkworks as Zia had assumed. That made it even more urgent that she break the story before someone else did. On the other hand, Tommy might just be fishing. By gauging her reactions, he might be hoping to sniff out intel his army of analysts couldn't. "But what does it have to do with you anyway?"

"Like I said," said Tommy. "SaudExxon needs to evolve. Right now, it powers the world. I think it should connect the world to itself."

"This is your big move? Acquire the satellite network that stitches the internet together? Use it to climb to the top of the pile of princelings?"

Tommy raised his hands. "Oil isn't going to last forever. We need to start thinking like Huian Li and Rachel Liebovitz. Do you think he'd be open to it?"

"My father and I aren't close," said Zia, shrugging. "I have no idea."

But she knew. Of course she knew. Santiago had grown up in a rural village outside of Limón, Costa Rica. He'd worked in a pizzeria and spent every minute of his free time devouring computer science papers and discussing their implications on obscure forums. Unable to afford a high-bandwidth connection, he'd hacked together an illegal tap to the nearest fiber optic line, then expanded the tap to connect his neighbors. In a few short years, the ramshackle pirate network became a legitimate wireless internet service provider which displaced domestic and then international competitors and grew like wildfire until Interstice satellites strung the globe in a brilliant necklace, gems hurtling through their orbits and coating the planet in an invisible membrane that transformed every square meter of Earth into a threshold to the digital. Sometimes Zia suspected that Interstice was more of a child to Santiago than she was. There wasn't a chance in hell that he'd sell, no matter how exorbitant the price.

"Come on, now," said Tommy. "The minute our bankers whisper anything about this, it'll turn into a thing. I know how mercurial Santiago can be and so I'm here as a friend trying to float something, hoping for your advice on whether it might stick."

"When people preface something with 'as a friend,' they really aren't," said Zia.

"Fine," said Tommy, and something subtle shifted in his voice. "But when things get ugly, remember that I asked nicely first."

Zia looked up at him, more astonished than scared. "Are you threatening me?"

"Naw," said Tommy with a lopsided grin. "I'm just reporting the facts, like Galang."

+

26

ZIA STROLLED THROUGH CENTRAL PARK, TRYING TO digest what had happened at the funeral yesterday.

The cloudless sky was baby blue. The sun shone. The air was crisp. It was one of those magical autumn days that made New York irresistible, as if the city glowed from within. Office workers sat out on the grass eating lunch. Tourists rode in horse drawn carriages and toddlers clambered around on the play structures. The whole scene was so idyllic that Zia could almost forget that Dembe and her team were shadowing her at a respectful distance, guardian angels throwing furtive glances back and forth instead of frisbees.

I'm just reporting the facts, like Galang. Had Tommy meant that like Galang had done for many years, he was reporting facts? Or that one of the facts that he was reporting was Galang's demise? Knowing Tommy, it was probably both, the delivery intentionally enigmatic. If so, was it possible that Tommy himself had ordered the hit? He had led the construction of New Malé, so it was entirely possible he held enough sway in the Maldives to pull something like that off. Maybe he'd bribed some of the officials in the black-market ring in order to win the project for SaudExxon and didn't want that coming to light if Galang exposed them.

But then why would he have attended the funeral? Why would he have hinted at it to Zia, even enigmatically? No. She was missing something.

She knelt down and picked up a fallen trident maple leaf. Veins branched into smaller and smaller capillaries and the edges were uneven, serrated. It was deep red, almost brown, the color of rust, of drying blood. She'd helped Li Jie back to his hotel room after he got too drunk at the funeral and started weeping inconsolably. It had reminded her how her own tears had refused to come at her mother's funeral—a fact that still left Zia feeling confused and vaguely guilty. The leaf crackled when Zia crushed it in her fist.

What if Tommy knew? What if SaudExxon was behind the increase in ambient corporate espionage Santiago had reported? What if Tommy's "rumors" weren't a fishing expedition, but coded communication alluding to the geoengineering program? For a brief paranoid moment, Zia had asked herself whether Santiago might have ordered Galang's killing in order to keep his secret safe. She had immediately dismissed the notion, but maybe Santiago wasn't the only one who wanted his program to stay under the radar.

Intelligence services from half a dozen countries might already know. They might be using it as leverage for other intel or it might have gotten stuck halfway through their bureaucratic intestines, never reaching political leadership because the scheme was too complex, too technical, too abstract. They might be starting up clandestine geoengineering programs of their own and didn't want to attract public scrutiny to the stratosphere.

Her phone buzzed. *Forensics decrypted the drive they found on Galang,* texted Aafreen, *but they won't tell my people anything about it. I'm pressing, but so far I've come up dry.*

Interagency rivalry or something else? asked Zia.

Not sure yet, but it's pissing me off, texted Aafreen.

Go get 'em, tiger. And let me know if there's anything I can do to help.

You bet. This particular tiger will eat their careers for breakfast. Any luck on your end?

Zia thought for a moment before responding. *Maybe,* she texted, *too early to say.*

Pocketing her phone, Zia looked up to find herself at a wooden gate opening onto a narrow dirt path that led up a forested hill. The second she crossed the threshold, she seemed to have stepped from a crowded public park into a tiny pocket of wilderness. Dembe appeared beside Zia and sent one of her henchmen up ahead, then retreated with the other to shadow from behind.

Zia climbed through thick foliage. The path switched back up the hill, and once she'd turned the first corner, she was alone, having left all sights and sounds of the joggers and strollers and dog walkers and tourists behind. It was a relief to escape the pressure of all those eyes, all those other lives, but despite her guardian angels hovering just out of earshot, Zia couldn't help but wonder whether camouflaged attackers lurked in the shadows behind that rotting stump or in that tangle of brambles or behind that hulking boulder. Her pulse leapt when she heard a squirrel scrambling across the boughs above.

She had pressed her father to consider who would have the most to gain from outing the program. Would India, citing the devastation of the failed monsoons, descend on his islands with swarms of fighter jets to shut him down and get their rain back? Would environmental activists launch massive campaigns to stop him meddling with the climate? Would Ghana celebrate him as a hero for saving them from further destruction that global warming would have brought without the program? Or maybe an Interstice competitor would use it to discredit the company, or a short seller would make billions by betting against the stock, or an intrepid young journalist would make a name for themselves by breaking the story.

But maybe the real question was who had the most to gain from keeping the program secret. Zia herself had pointed out to Santiago that his program undermined public climate science by feeding labs fraudulent stratospheric data that couldn't explain the stabilization of global temperature. SaudExxon had been spending billions on propaganda campaigns designed to sow doubt and misinformation about climate change since well before the corporoyal consolidation. Santiago might be trying to offset the biggest threats of global warming, but in doing so he was inadvertently advancing the cause of its progenitors. The longer the program stayed secret, the more it would corrode the credibility of climatology. Moreover, the direct effect of limiting the worst impacts of warming could be used to justify unabated burning of fossil fuels. If climate change wasn't that bad after all, why bother reforming the global economy's energy infrastructure? If you pumped more carbon into the atmosphere, you could just spray more aerosols into the stratosphere.

It was a perfect short term salve that would create a much larger disaster over the long run as carbon and aerosol buildup escalated until the termination shock became an existential threat for humanity—any break in the program over the subsequent centuries leading to climate catastrophe. That's why Santiago saw the program as simply a way to buy time, not a solution in its own right.

But the value of SaudExxon's oil reserves depended on maintaining the status quo. The faster the world transitioned off of fossil fuels, the faster SaudExxon descended into obsolescence. From a certain perspective, Santiago's program was a stay of execution for SaudExxon. It sabotaged their scientific adversaries in public debate and slapped a bandage over the worst side effects of their operations. It meant they could keep up business as usual for decades to come.

Zia's foot slipped on a root and she put her hand out to catch herself on a tree. She looked at her hand splayed against the trunk, brown-red skin against the variegated grays and greens of moss and lichen growing over the dark ridges of the oak's bark. The textures were dense and lavish and the soft, diffuse light rendered every shade more itself. For a fleeting moment, Zia could feel the ghostly presence of her mother, as if some fragment of Miranda's soul had migrated into the living wood of this ancient oak. Her mother had always been so quick to see how human systems interlocked to create perverse side effects. Where others glimpsed only gears and cogs, her view took in the whole machine, and her prose rendered it legible to everyone, a literary cutaway diagram. The annotated manuscript Zia and Galang had posthumously published held a special appeal in part because its very roughness revealed Miranda's creative process in a new way—a cutaway diagram of a cutaway diagram.

Zia remembered the breeze ruffling Tommy's hair, his kooky lopsided grin, the steel beneath his teasing tone. He had attended that funeral for a reason that certainly wasn't mourning. He had sought out Zia to deliver a message, however enigmatic. What had been a runaway thought experiment collapsed into certainty.

Pulling back her hand, Zia hurried up the path but couldn't escape the dark silhouette coalescing behind her thoughts. In boarding school, Tommy had treated every relationship as a chip in a vast game. The black hole of his raw ambition pressed him to scramble to the top of the social hierarchy at any cost, lest the howling void of self-awareness rip away the thin veneer of an identity pegged to what other people thought of him. Zia tried to put herself in his shoes, returning to Riyadh after years spent studying abroad, tossed around by warring factions, desperate to make a mark, unable to ignore the circling hyenas that were his peers and cousins, trusting no one, knowing that the only way to control his own destiny was to bring the entire corporoyal court under his sway, that his fragile, conflicted ego depended on it. Alone and afraid, his first big gambit had been to orchestrate the construction of New Malé. What if this was his next move, the kind of risky, ambitious play that might catapult him to the very top?

She remembered his string of buts. But *the old timers still hold the reins decades past their prime*. But *the idiots trying to seize power have no vision for what to* do *with it*. But *SaudExxon is a ship navigating treacherous waters with an obsolete chart*. He had claimed that his offer to buy Interstice represented a pivot from oil to the internet, but maybe it was more than that, maybe he could have his cake and eat it too. He could pretend to be after Interstice's satellite network when what he was really after was Santiago's fleet of drones. Then it wouldn't be a pivot at all, but a self-reinforcing engine that would expand SaudExxon's reach even as it consolidated their power base. It had a tragic elegance Miranda would have intuitively grasped, an intuition Tommy shared for precisely opposite reasons: one to lament, the other to harness.

Zia's breath came in shallow gasps, the incline and the knot in her chest conspiring to steal the air from her lungs. She was back in the chateau, locked in a room alone for an entire weekend as punishment for curfew violation. She was drinking cheap beer with Daniela in Guatemala, both of them trying to drown their frustration at international aid organizations who spent millions delivering emergency rations in the wake of the earthquake but wouldn't spend a dime improving building codes to make the next one less deadly. She was tearing apart her hotel room, smashing glass on tile and ripping linens from the bed before collapsing onto the bare mattress to curl up in fetal position and try to come to terms with the fact that she would never see her mother again. What was it about humans that made them rain misery down on each other? When death was certain to rob you of everything, what possible prize was worth causing others to suffer?

As Zia crested the hill, she glimpsed skyscrapers through the canopy, geometric steel and glass edifices overlaid by gnarled branches, hanging moss, and a panoply of leaves. She paused, calves burning, chest heaving. Like when abrupt silence reveals that music had indeed been playing, Zia was suddenly aware of being thrust between two imperfectly aligned worlds, standing at the center of a hastily sketched cosmographic Venn diagram.

"Ma'am?"

Zia startled. She hadn't heard Dembe come up behind her.

"Sorry to bother you, ma'am, but I need your phone," said Dembe.

"What?"

"Your phone, ma'am."

Confused, Zia dug out her phone and placed it in Dembe's outstretched hand.

Without even a moment of hesitation, Dembe hurled the device off into the undergrowth like a pitcher throwing a fast ball.

"Hey," said Zia, more confused than angry.

Dembe turned back to face Zia.

"We need to go," she said in a calm, commanding voice. She rocked on the balls of her feet and her amber eyes glowed like embers in the dappled light. "Right now."

+ 27

THEY DIDN'T STAY ON THE MEANDERING PATH BUT blazed a trail straight through the forest down the other side of the hill. Fallen leaves crunched underfoot. Spiderwebs clung to their faces. Zia hopped over a fallen log and batted away a low hanging branch. She accelerated, trying to keep Dembe in view. Mud sucked at her shoes and she almost slipped on a section of glacially polished stone, desperately pumping her legs to keep up with gravity as she sprinted down the striated mass of exposed rock.

Then they plunged back into forest again, roots reaching up to trip Zia and brush hemming her in on all sides. Ahead, she could hear Dembe barking orders over the radio as she danced through the landscape like a wood nymph, Zia crashing along behind. Who were they running from? What was so urgent that they couldn't afford to follow the path back down the hill? Could this have something to do with the texts she was trading with Aafreen? Surely not even grizzled ex-special forces contractors would attempt to kidnap a principal with three professional bodyguards in the middle of Central Park. Zia knew she should be scared, but there was something exhilarating about leaving the manicured path to chase Dembe through the trees.

They burst out onto a wide, paved walkway crowded with pedestrians who looked up in surprise at the two women emerging from the undergrowth. Zia dodged around a stroller and followed Dembe across an open lawn, onto another walkway, and over a bridge. Kids were feeding the ducks and a solo tenor was singing an aria. A carriage driver swore at them as they darted across the street, spooking the horses. They skirted a mass of European tourists and pounded up the pavement. Out of the corner of her eye, Zia could see Dembe's two colleagues flanking them a hundred meters back, ties flapping and mud-spattered suits soaked with sweat.

Before Zia realized what was happening, they'd reached the edge of Central Park. They leapt up a flight of stone stairs three at a time, pushed their way across the crowded sidewalk, dodged between two shawarma stands, and dashed out into traffic, Dembe smacking the hood of a car that honked at her as she cut it off. Just as they reached the far curb, sirens blared, cutting a wedge in the traffic like Moses parting the Red Sea. Zia looked up the street and saw a line of black SUVs roaring through the opening, lights flashing.

The curb beneath her feet felt suddenly like the edge of a cliff, as if Zia might rock back and tumble off the brink, falling thousands of meters, wind roaring past and stomach doing somersaults in weightless free fall, before smashing into the very asphalt that she had just stepped off of.

"Ma'am?"

The two other bodyguards had arrived. Zia looked ahead. Dembe was beckoning from the top of the stairs that led to the entrance of a soaring tower that was just one of thousands in the engineered forest of Manhattan. Zia mounted the stairs, keenly aware of her aching muscles, her sucking, desperate breathing, the sour burn of bile in the back of her throat. If only she had the discipline to train for marathons like Vachan. Ouch. She had tweaked her left ankle somewhere along the way. Her walk in the park hadn't been a walk in the park.

As they hurried through the wide glass doors into a spacious atrium, Zia threw a glance back over her shoulder. The SUVs had pulled up onto the opposite sidewalk and serious men in dark suits and glasses poured out, assembled into teams, touched earpieces, and set off at a brisk jog into the park, civilians scattering out of their way like animals before a wildfire.

Ahead, Dembe was touching her own earpiece and the building's concierge was waving them through to the elevator bank. Zia's shoes squeaked on the gleaming marble floor. The other denizens of the lobby shot them strange looks and steered clear. Zia imagined how they must look: red in the face, wild-eyed, and covered in mud and brambles.

One of the bodyguards cleared the elevator bank area, the concierge placating tenants. Dembe called two elevators which arrived with a soft ding. She sent the other bodyguards up in one and pulled Zia into the other alongside her. As soon as they were in, she pressed the button that held the doors closed and counted to seven under her breath before directing it to take them to the roof access level.

The elevator rose, acceleration pushing them down, compressing their spines, rooting them in place. The interior of the elevator was lined with mirrors and the cascading infinity of women with dilated pupils, bruised necks, and flushed cheeks who stared back at Zia felt less like herself than a string of strangers glimpsing each other through a slender tear in the delicate membrane that separated parallel realities from one another. In a bid to escape the cognitive dissonance, Zia turned to Dembe.

"What"—inhale—"the"—exhale—"fuck?" she asked.

Dembe, who to Zia's chagrin wasn't even breathing hard, quirked her lip into a humorless half-smile. "We got a tip from inside the bureau that FBI was running a sting."

"Who are they after?"

Dembe raised her eyebrows. "You," she said.

Zia imagined teams of agents scouring the forest for her phone. She tried to catch her breath. "Me? Why would they want to arrest me?"

"The situation is evolving," said Dembe. "For now, my only priority is getting you outside of US jurisdiction."

The elevator slowed and Zia's stomach rose into her throat. Had Washington discovered Santiago's scheme? Did they assume she was party to it? Knowing that she'd attend Galang's funeral, had they planned to snatch her up and charge her with crimes for which there was no precedent? Could the CIA have been behind the botched kidnapping attempt in Chhattisgarh? When Zia had been preparing for her ambassadorial post, she'd learned more than she necessarily wanted to know about the tense relationship between diplomatic and intelligence services, and the sordid history of clandestine operations gone wrong.

The elevator doors opened onto a small but well-appointed waiting area. One of the officers who Dembe had sent ahead was standing across the room at the exit, sidearm at his side.

"Clear," he said.

Dembe nodded and they jogged past him and out onto the roof. Zia blinked in the sunlight. A helicopter perched on a raised landing pad in front of them, rotors spinning. Zia leaned into the blast of downwash as she ran up the stairs and across the platform. Dembe hopped up into the open cabin, then reached back to pull Zia in after her. The second they were both inside, the engine howled and the chopper leapt off the roof like a scalded cat. Zia stumbled and fell to her knees, grasping for purchase, but Dembe maneuvered across the bucking floor like a bull rider, slamming the door closed, hoisting Zia into a jump seat, getting her buckled in, and then sitting down across from her.

The chopper banked and Central Park spread out below them, a swath of green hemmed in on all sides by steel and concrete. Zia craned her neck to see if she could pick out the FBI agents, but while she managed to spot the line of parked SUVs, the people swarming around them were the size of ants and indistinguishable from one another. Then the nose of the aircraft dipped and they roared off across the hungry, grasping New York City skyline.

28

+

ZIA READ THE EXPOSÉ IN STUNNED DISBELIEF, TRYING to ignore her father screaming into his phone out on the deck. Zia was sitting at the counter where she'd sliced the oranges, and surreality crept into her mind like the crimson juice that had leaked across the cutting board, a sense that the world was not what it seemed, that there was no underlying truth, just illusions stacked one atop the other forever.

Bonnie had written the story herself and as Zia read, it was as if Bonnie were reading the article aloud in her precise, clipped tone—glasses glinting in the afternoon sunlight, scarf arranged just so.

Only instead of journalism, she was narrating a fairytale.

It started out true enough, profiling Zia and her parents, describing the tragedy of her mother's passing and how Zia had embarked on a career in humanitarian aid while

Santiago had forged ahead with Interstice. That was where things went off the rails. The drive the Maldivian detectives had found on Galang's body had been decrypted. It contained reams of evidence from an ongoing investigation: financial records, video clips, interview transcripts, message archives, photographs, and on and on and on.

The evidence painted a disturbing picture. Using Zia's disaster response work as a cover, she and Santiago had sold Interstice data to terrorist groups and rogue regimes the world over, violating seventeen different international laws and secreting billions into anonymous Swiss bank accounts. There was video footage of Zia in meetings she had never attended, messages she had never written, audio recordings of words she had never uttered, receipts for purchases she had never made, GPS breadcrumbs leading to locations she'd never been, corroborating confessions from people she'd never met.

This fantastical patchwork was woven together with threads of truth. Zia had been in the general areas detailed in the articles during those times. She had been responding to hurricanes, fires, earthquakes, floods, epidemics, and famines. She just hadn't snuck away for excursions to sell sensitive data on the black market. They even had an annotated transcript of her meeting with Galang in Chhattisgarh, supposedly gleaned from a secret recording device he'd brought along. But instead of recollections, friendly needling, and career woes, the transcript had Galang pressing Zia for information about her clandestine activities to which she responded with defensive misdirection, counteraccusations, and veiled threats. Even though she could sense the impending conclusion, it still blindsided her.

Zia and her father had called a hit on Galang to stop his investigation. The only reason the truth was coming out at all was because the assassin had been sloppy and missed the drive in his rush to escape the scene. Maldivian analysts had cracked it and immediately shared the contents through international counterterrorism channels, and with Bonnie's newsroom. Zia had confirmed her guilt in the public eye by fleeing arrest in New York. Bonnie even quoted from Zia's eulogy at the funeral, painting a disturbing picture of a deranged, supremely confident sociopath determined to bask in the aftermath of her misdeeds.

By the time she reached the end, Zia was clinging to the counter for support, as if the smooth, cool granite was a life raft that might buoy her away from this whirlpool of disinformation that threatened to suck her down into schizophrenia. The story was so disturbing, so detailed, so utterly convincing. Did Zia not even know herself? Did she harbor a split personality in some dark corner of her mind that seized control and ferried Interstice data for blood money? Had she slipped into one of the parallel realities she'd glimpsed in the elevator, a universe in which she was, in fact, a hardened criminal?

Contradictory futures spooled out before her. Going on the run and living out the rest of her days as a fugitive from a vindictive system that could see through every camera, gaze down from every satellite, listen through every microphone. Sitting on a concrete floor in solitary confinement, biting her nails to the quick as repressed memories of her misadventures flickered back to life like flames up dry wood tossed atop dying embers. Discovering some hole in Bonnie's article that, if extended to its logical conclusion, would bring the whole mountain of accusations crashing down on itself. Tearfully admitting her guilt in front of the International Criminal Court and throwing herself on its mercy. Buying her way into organized crime as a vehicle to escape false accusations of involvement with organized crime.

The new phone they'd assigned to her rang, vibrating through her like an electrical shock.

It was Himmat. Himmat with his soft eyes, formal manner, and organized mind. Himmat whom she had abandoned in Chhattisgarh to direct operations when her life had taken an unexpected and unwelcome turn. How she wished she could be there with him right now, sipping on chai and debating dryland farming best practices.

She retreated into the back corner of the kitchen. "Yes?"

"Zia," his voice quavered, uncertain. "A man from the government came here this morning. Military or CBI or something. He said that your visa has been revoked and you have been banned from entering the country. Then he demanded to search your room." She remembered how morning light would slant in through the window to illuminate her sparsely decorated cell in Chhattisgarh, her heavily dog-eared signed first edition of William Goldman's *The Princess Bride* sitting on the floor where a nightstand should be, the variegated purple flowers of the orchid that curved back on itself like a sickle. "I tried to stop him, but... Well, I didn't know what to do. He bagged up your things and left. He told me—"

He paused and she swallowed, forcing herself not to interrupt.

"He told me that if I heard from you, I should report it to him personally, that"—he faltered—"that you're wanted for terrorism." His voice faded into a whisper and trended up at the end, only partially transforming the statement into a question.

Zia squeezed her eyes shut and scrunched up her face, trying to disembark from the carousel of horrors spinning inside her. That Himmat was trying to defend and warn her was a miracle in itself. Given that she had mysteriously disappeared from Chhattisgarh a few weeks ago, he had more reason than most to suspect her. Then again, maybe this call was a setup. Maybe the CBI man was hovering over Himmat's shoulder, egging him on as they tried to tease out a confession while tracing the connection.

"He kept pressing me about a few dates back in May," said Himmat. "Asking where you'd been. I checked back in my journal and it was the weekend we did a field visit to Patan together. I told him I was with you the whole time, that we were meeting with families and training survey teams. But he said it was impossible and when I showed him the dates in my diary and confirmed it in my message history he called me an idiot and said I must be mistaken. Then he confiscated my diary!"

"Thank you, Himmat," said Zia thickly. "I can't tell you how much I appreciate it."

"There's no need to thank me for being honest," said Himmat indignantly. "The guy was a jerk. But Zia, I'm worried about you. Is it..."

The question was no less clear for trailing off.

"No," said Zia with more conviction than she felt. "It's not true." Saying it felt like planting a flag. "I'm still trying to figure out what's going on, whether I'm being framed or this is all some elaborate mistake, but I'm not a spy or a terrorist."

"I know," said Himmat. "Of course not. I just– It's scary, right? What's going to happen?"

"I don't know," said Zia, wishing more than anything that she did, that through force of will she could magic her life back into normalcy.

"Well, I've already filed complaints with the chief minister's office," said Himmat. "I doubt it'll go anywhere, especially because Governor Rao is already crowing about it, but I know how important it is to be diligent with these things. Is there anything else I can do to help?"

"You've already done more than enough," said Zia. "Please just keep your head down and don't make a fuss. I don't want you getting caught up in all this."

"Making a fuss is what friends are for."

Himmat's indefatigable calm was a lifeline that reeled Zia back from despair into fury. Only a few weeks prior she had admitted to Galang that years of leading humanitarian aid missions had convinced her that there was no such thing as a natural disaster, only human disasters revealed by nature. And with his signature insight, Galang had pointed out that Zia had *got out of politics only to realize that the real challenge of humanitarian aid was, in fact, politics.* But now that some apparatchik had officially revoked her visa and her job, Zia's ambivalence about her work vanished. There was satisfaction in helping people in need, even if your help didn't prevent future instances of need. For all the systemic frustrations of disaster response, she'd been doing her very best to better the fortunes of the least fortunate rather than extending the fortunes of the most fortunate, which was the vast river into which society's watershed guided the efforts of the privileged. That Zia's desire to return to Chhattisgarh was waxing in no small part because her ability to do so had just been abrogated laced her burgeoning resentment with guilt.

"Just stay safe, okay?" she pleaded.

"Don't you dare act as if this is goodbye."

Zia hadn't realized that was exactly what she was doing until Himmat pointed it out.

+

29

SANTIAGO STORMED BACK INTO THE VILLA, EYES bloodshot, hair mussed, face livid. When Zia was a child, she had woken up one night, climbed down from her raised bed, and wandered out to get a glass of water from the kitchen. There had been a wedge of light spilling into the hall from her father's study, and she'd tiptoed up to investigate. Peering in, she'd seen Santiago hunched over a keyboard, screen aglow, typing with so much pent up, manic energy that it could only be bled off into whatever digital missives he was sending into the night like ballistic missiles. Terrified that disturbing him would be like sticking a fork into a power outlet, Zia had fled back up the hallway, making sure to avoid the squeaky floorboard near the bathroom, and returned to bed sans water.

Now, her father joined her in the kitchen and poured himself a coffee. Whether his hand was trembling from that same surplus of internal vim or simple over-caffeination, Zia couldn't tell. He stirred in cream and sugar and took a sip, then placed the mug on the counter.

"There are warrants out for our arrest in seventeen countries," he said. "The US government has frozen my assets, our stock is crashing, and the board is calling for my resignation. You spend decades building something and the minute someone paints a bullshit target on you, everyone jumps ship. The hyenas are circling, and they smell blood. That... *shit*"—he gestured to her phone, indicating the article she'd been reading—"is a goddamn telenovela. I'm being taken down by vaporware."

"*You're* being taken down?" A lit fuse, hissing. "I didn't ask for any of this." She stabbed a finger at his chest. "You started it all with your secrets and your monumental ego. It took a kidnapping for you to even loop me the fuck in, and by then it was too late to do anything but damage control, which was the last thing in the goddamn universe I wanted to do, but how could I not?" Santiago was right about one thing: you couldn't trust anyone but yourself. Just because it broke your heart didn't make it any less true. "You stopped the monsoon. You undermined the entire scientific community. You're a spider. You weave people into your plans regardless of their own." The spark ran down the fuse toward the detonator. Closer. Closer. Ignition. "All I wanted was to get *away* from you. To live my own life."

He stiffened, his back going ramrod straight. Pain flashed behind his eyes in the instant before they froze over and Zia was filled with a regret she wanted to, but couldn't quite, deny.

"Go, then," he growled. "Just go."

"And where exactly am I supposed to run?" But ambivalence dulled the sarcastic edge of her question and it came out sounding like she was addressing it to herself instead of her father.

"I don't know," he said, his voice sounding as if it came from a great distance. "I hardly know what truth means anymore."

They sized each other up for a moment, each searching for an answer to the question neither could bring themselves to ask the other: *was there a seed of truth buried in the false allegations? Had father or daughter committed any of the crimes Bonnie described, without the other's knowledge?* Their eyes met, the mutual suspicion and guilt filling an invisible crucible that forced them to recognize the same doubts mirrored in the other, doubts that recognition quelled.

"It's not about truth, it's about optics," said Zia, forcing herself to rise above the fray, consider next steps. She tried to channel Vachan's preternatural ability to game theory his way through any crisis—a side effect of growing up under his grandmother's tutelage. "Nobody's going to blame anyone for jumping on a bandwagon and a lot of people have a lot to gain from your downfall."

"And who has so much to gain that they'd concoct this farce?"

In her mind's eye, Zia could see the skyscraper through the canopy, rustling leaves over gleaming metal. She could smell the loam of Central Park, hear birds twittering in counterpoint to the barely perceptible hum of distant traffic. Something uncoiled in her chest, tendrils spreading through her to pull pieces into place.

But just as Zia opened her mouth to answer, her phone rang again, then cut off abruptly. She looked down at the screen. Kodjo. But why had he called and then hung up? Frowning, she unlocked the phone and noticed the anomalous symbol in the top left corner of the screen.

"Papi, why is there no service?"

Santiago cocked his head to the side. "What do you mean? Of course there's service. We have persistent global coverage."

Zia raised her eyebrows and held out her phone to him. He accepted it and lines creased his forehead. Then he dug out his phone and checked it.

"Hijueputa," he said and leapt up to grab his laptop from the side table.

"*Hijueputa,*" he repeated, and snatched up a tablet that was charging in the corner.

Then he dashed down the corridor that led behind the kitchen and Zia hurried after him. He threw open a door to the small workshop that housed his shortwave radio set. He slid into the seat and began working the controls like a pianist on a keyboard. The chorus of "We Are the Champions" blared out in an infinite loop. No matter how many frequencies he tried, there was only Queen. He threw down the headphones and spun to face Zia, his face pale and pinched.

"We're being jammed," he said. "Wide frequency transmitter on ultrahigh power. No signal in or out. We're deaf, dumb, and blind."

A vise tightened around Zia's chest.

Dembe ducked her head in through the open door. "We have a problem," she snapped. "There are—"

A sonic boom shook the villa to its foundation. Pain lanced through their eardrums. Plates rattled in cupboards. The shortwave headphones skittered off the desk and fell to the floor. Zia and Santiago cringed.

They stumbled out past the kitchen and onto the deck to see a squadron of attack drones coming around for another pass, schooling like fish in a formation far too tight for any human pilot. Dembe pointed and they dropped their gazes to the matte black frigate cutting through the aquamarine sea toward the island. The angular, hulking form was hopelessly out of place in this tropical paradise, a tiger in a pet shop.

"It has some kind of stealth shielding, which is why we didn't pick it up on radar," Dembe had to shout to be heard above the ringing in their ears. "Definitely military, but it's not flying a flag or displaying an insignia."

Zia had taken a statistics class at Berkeley. The professor was obsessed with puzzles, as if life was a vast crossword waiting to be decoded. Selai would have loved it. Every question on the final exam was a labyrinth unto itself, riddled with misdirection, red herrings, and dead ends. Zia grappled with the last question like a Sumo wrestler, but kept getting pushed out of the ring. Drained and frustrated, she had looked up at the winter light slanting down into the high-ceilinged hall. Staring at the revolving motes of dust, she'd glimpsed the answer. But just as she picked up her pen to jot it down, the professor called time. The bittersweet memory echoed in her heart—she had reached the solution, but too late.

The drones roared overhead again, a glistening mass of sleek airborne predators that were simultaneously omniscient and heedless with their sensor arrays and silicon minds. One of them peeled off from the flock and decelerated to circle the Interstice compound, a banner unfolding from its tail. Zia tasted the crisp air of a clear Swiss night, smelled the sweaty funk of sex, recognized the searing brand of self-recrimination. She knew who the author was before she could so much as read the text printed on the rippling fabric.

Meet me on the beach.

30

+

THEY MET TOMMY IN A CABANA.

Zia and Santiago waited in the shade, watching the Zodiac approach on a churning bow wave. Gulls bickered over a half-eaten crab carcass and heat radiated off the sun-drenched sand. Dembe had assembled as many security officers as she could spare to take up stations at various points along the beach, a show of strength that so paled in comparison to the sleek monster anchored offshore that Zia feared the exercise might prove counterproductive.

How strange it was to see an armed standoff on a remote island between a multinational telecommunications company and a corpomonarchy vying for control of a fulcrum that no one else was even aware existed. All the twentieth century statecraft case studies Zia had read in preparation for her ambassadorial appointment rang false. There were echoes of earlier times, the vicious forays of the British East India Company for example, but something was different here too: the suggestion of a new thread in the tapestry of history.

The driver gunned the engine at the last minute and the Zodiac ran up onto the beach, disgorging commandos who fingered assault rifles as they and Dembe's team stared each other down through the requisite dark sunglasses. Zia remembered her desperate flight through Chhattisgarh, her escape from the villa she thought was a cell, the all-too-recent footrace with the FBI in Central Park. These were people for whom such extraordinary circumstances were ordinary. They specialized in violence, in emergency, in operating on the razor's edge until its very keenness became banal. What constituted extremity for them? A lover's quarrel? An afternoon curled up with a book? A life that acquired a regular, predictable rhythm?

Tommy leapt over the gray buoyancy tube of the Zodiac, landing in the sand with easy grace. He wore an ivory linen suit and leather boat shoes without socks. He grinned as he walked up the sand toward them, waving away the two commandos hurrying to escort him. Every movement was infused with tense energy, as if he couldn't quite contain himself.

That was one of the qualities that had drawn Zia to him all those years ago. Even as a teenager, Tommy was always brimming with ideas, plans, opinions. He was constantly reaching beyond himself, attempting to lasso the ineffable. That striving was part of his charisma. It pulled people to him even as it warped them to serve his purposes. This situation was that self-consuming logic followed to its ultimate conclusion.

How to reconcile the brutal image of Galang's corpse on the sticky floor of a New Malé brothel with the winsome man whose eyes twinkled as he made his way across the beach?

Zia was surprised to discover that seeing Tommy here in front of her, she felt not hatred but an abiding sadness—regret that he had debased himself to such a profound extent that he was willing to kill.

"Zia!" he said brightly, as if they had just run into each other at a cocktail bar. "I'd say you look smashing, but"—he winced in false sympathy at her cuts and bruises—"to be honest, it's more like smashed."

"You look like the weird uncle who supplies cocaine to bored kids stuck in Cape Cod for the summer."

"Charming, as always." He turned to her father. "And Santiago, I've followed your work for many years. It's an honor to meet the genius behind Interstice."

For half a second, Zia thought her father might lash out and crush Tommy's windpipe, setting off a firefight on the open beach. But instead, Santiago simply ignored Tommy's extended hand and said, "And I hear you're a good-for-nothing princeling."

"I've taken quite a bit of initiative, believe it or not." Tommy winked. "There's nothing quite like the feeling of having a lot to lose and putting it all on the line. I mean, when you started out, you had nothing to lose, so I don't expect you to understand. You rags-to-riches folk are always so... blue collar, if you know what I mean. I don't blame you. You just don't understand that power is about making other people do the work, rather than doing all the work yourself. But don't think that I don't respect it, it's people like you who make shiny new things for people like me to use. I am in your debt for being in my debt."

"I don't owe you a thing, *comemierda*," snapped Santiago.

"It's okay," said Tommy, in a patronizing tone. "I know how stressful succession can be."

Santiago nearly exploded but Zia gave him a nudge. There was nothing to be gained by letting Tommy provoke him. They sat on the edges of twin chaise lounges, Tommy on one, Zia and her father on the other. The shade was a relief, but they were uncomfortably close, almost knee-to-knee. What had Tommy said to her in Zürich? *This conversation isn't for me to vet you. It's the reverse.* If only Zia had taken that to heart, unearthed the subtext she had coached Himmat to notice. There were worry lines on Tommy's face that hadn't been there in boarding school, and there was something sour about his smile that implied a sneer. If once he had lived with a light, sardonic touch, now maintaining that same impression seemed to cost him dearly, as if he were a paper airplane that required a rocket booster to stay airborne.

An awkward silence followed that none of them seemed able to break. Waves lapped at the shore. Fingers rested lightly on triggers. Time swelled and distended, sticky and elastic like rising dough. Finally, Zia couldn't take it any longer.

"How'd you find out about the geoengineering program?" she asked quietly.

Santiago tensed but Tommy looked nonplussed, as if she had just played an ace he'd been sure was up his sleeve. He recovered his composure and said, "Leadership isn't about money or intelligence or charisma, it's about people. Simple as that. Whenever things go right, it's because of the people behind them. And whenever things go wrong, it's for the same reason. Now, Santiago,"—his eyes flickered to her father—"I am your *biggest* fan, I assure you. But let's be honest, you're a total control freak. You make all these amazing things and drive people crazy doing it. You can't seem to learn that the best way to win other people's trust is to extend your own trust to them."

"I didn't ask for a therapy session," said Zia.

Tommy raised a finger. "Therapy," he said, "is something both of you could use a lot more of."

"Ben Munroe," said Zia.

"Ding, ding, ding!" said Tommy, delightedly. "You're as sharp as ever."

"That ungrateful mother*fucker*," growled Santiago.

"See? That's exactly what I'm talking about," said Tommy. "Your chief scientist was so sick of needing to ask you for permission to do any damn thing that it was all too easy to persuade him that a change was in order, that maybe he should be leading Project Svalinn himself. Turns out that much of the rest of your senior team and board of directors feel similarly. They're all powerful people who don't like to be put in their place, even when they're wrong. And while Ben knows what you've been doing out here, nobody else does and they've become pretty darn frustrated with a CEO who's spending an inordinate amount of time on a remote airbase instead of at Interstice HQ. Not a good look."

"It's my goddamn company!" said Santiago.

"Except it's not," said Tommy. "Not really anyway, certainly not anymore. Interstice is just a group of people working toward a common goal. So I've just gone ahead and adjusted the target a little. We've bought up a decent portion of your stock and with your reputation on the rocks and the market cap in free fall, it's time to swoop in for an outright acquisition."

Zia met his eye. "You murdered Galang and framed us," she said slowly, as if trying out the idea for the first time. It was a strange thing to say, more seal than statement. "The grant. The kidnapping. You wanted leverage. Hijack the program that had hijacked the climate, right?" Horror curdled at the center of Escher-esque spirals of logic. Zia didn't want to believe it, but she couldn't not believe it. "And when you failed, you killed Galang and drowned us in deep fakes all to keep Project Svalinn from going public."

"I play to win," said Tommy with forced nonchalance. "But offing Galang was just a lucky bonus. My contractors wouldn't have bungled the kidnapping, except that you rushed us with your sudden binge of climate model archive searches." Selai's naked skin against her own under alpine stars. *It starts, as all truly great stories do, on a dark and stormy night—better yet, it's about why we can't seem to make sense of how nights get all dark and stormy in the first place.* Of course. Tommy had been tracking Zia's Interstice accounts, surveilling the research Selai had inspired and setting off the red flags Santiago had noticed. "Getting your pretty face back would be quite a convincing reason for Santiago to sell his precious company, Project Svalinn included." He shook a finger at her and Zia's hands flexed as she remembered clutching the frozen pizza in that dark alley below laundry fluttering in the breeze. "But when you slipped away, I couldn't very well risk y'all deciding to tell the world about the program. So"—he shrugged—"here we are. Plan Bs usually aren't this magnificent, if I may say so myself."

"My lawyers are going to eat you alive," snarled Santiago. "They'll tear apart your case piece by piece. I'll expose every backstabbing asshole on the board for the scum that they are. You think they don't have skeletons in their closets that I know about? I'll hire every private investigator on earth to stalk you until the day you die. And once I kick your scrawny ass, I'll use every Interstice asset at my disposal to break up your incestuous corpokingdom and leave you to bleed out on the desert."

"Oh, do tell," said Tommy. "I am curious, though. How are you going to pay your attorneys with all your assets frozen? How will you be able to leverage Interstice once the board suspends you? And with this many warrants out for your arrest, do you plan on mounting your defense from prison or as a fugitive?"

It was a neat trap, she'd give him that. Tommy always had a way of working people around to his side. He'd lob questions and drop comments throughout a conversation and his interlocutor wouldn't realize what was happening until he leapt in at the very end to make a point that harvested all the seeds he'd planted. One fell swoop was the ideal he aspired to. This chaos was that aspiration, violently realized. Zia felt like she was in one of those dissociative dreams where you looked over your own shoulder.

Santiago laughed. "You think the fairytale you're spinning will stand up? It's easy to corral people who hold a grudge. But what happens when digital forensics reveals that those videos, photos, messages, all your precious 'evidence,' are nothing but forgery? Hard to prosecute on nothing but hot air, hotshot."

When Interstice was in the midst of displacing the traditional cable companies, Santiago had regaled Zia and Miranda with stories of his ongoing exploits. Zia hadn't been able to understand any of the jargon, but she understood that her father was a fierce commander who always managed to outmaneuver his enemies with consummate cleverness. That same angry confidence accented his words like a highlighter, but rather than presaging inevitable victory, Zia feared it was brittle armor hastily donned at the onset of a surprise attack.

"Yes, yes, *yes*," said Tommy. "This is one of those times when I wish we were recording this little tête-à-tête. I mean,

I don't *actually* wish that, but there are some real gems here. It's adorable how much you believe in the ability to win people over with facts. Very endearing. You think this will all disappear when some academic expert pronounces those videos doctored? As if the world cares about a he-said-she-said attribution dispute between two technical wizards nobody can understand anyway. You don't get it: *you've already lost*. Even if I were to wave my hand and make it all go away, you're stained by association. You might convince people that something fishy is going on, but they'll never stop suspecting you're connected to it in one way or another."

"You think I care what other people think?" asked Santiago.

"That's a lovely contrarian sentiment, really it is," said Tommy, and Zia wanted to shout in his face that none of this was necessary, that if *he* had cared a little less about what other people thought, this whole disaster could have been avoided. "But there's one thing you need that you don't have: time."

"The fuck is that supposed to mean?" demanded Santiago.

Tommy's smile had a touch of melancholy that terrified Zia more than any of his vainglory had. "The Indonesians have promised a signed extradition order by tomorrow morning. The minute we have that in hand, my marines will move in and arrest you, all by the book of course. The corpomonarchy is, after all, one of the victims of your illicit data dealing. Plus, we have treaties in place with the Maldives, which is where your hired killer did his dirty work. It's a short flight to Riyadh and I promise you, the SaudExxon criminal justice system isn't nearly as slow or bureaucratic as its Western counterparts. We won't burden you with endless appeals or astronomical attorney fees or anything along those lines. The trial will be quick and decisive. Which brings me to the real reason I'm here: to discuss the terms of your sentencing."

"That's a clear conflict of interest," said Santiago. "Nobody will stand for it."

"I'd say that the interests of the judicial and executive systems are, in fact, very aligned in this case," said Tommy. "Which will streamline the process further. And the rest of the world will thank us for cleaning up the mess."

It was at this point that Zia belatedly realized that Tommy was right. She was so accustomed to her father's endless contingencies and indefatigable drive that she'd mistaken his weak ripostes as strategic ploys intended to draw Tommy out, like a boxer pretending to favor a leg only to accelerate off it at the last minute with an uppercut for the knockout. But his defensiveness was all too real. Santiago had become so obsessed with this geoengineering project that he'd inadvertently lost control of Interstice. He thought he'd been keeping all the balls in the air when, in fact, another juggler had been snatching them away. Now that it was becoming apparent, he was reacting as he always had, with righteous anger, but there was no weight behind it, no map to which the future must conform, only an old man who didn't want to admit how tired he was.

Sun sparkled off the surf and the briny air tickled Zia's nose. She reached down and scooped up a handful of sand, letting it fall through her fingers, marveling at the simple fact that humans had harnessed the silicon embedded in these grains to invest objects with cognition. Humans had drilled thousands of feet into the earth to harvest corpses entombed in vast reservoirs, fueling civilization with the liquefied remains of prehistoric life. Humans had devised these miracles and more, and yet were still consumed by divisiveness, still betrayed, hurt, and killed each other over petty collective fictions of status, wealth, and power. It was as if God were indeed real, but spent all His time drinking cheap gin and playing penny slots.

"This is quite a coup for you," said Zia. "Publicly, you take SaudExxon in a bold new direction by taking over Interstice. Privately, you keep pumping aerosols into the stratosphere to sabotage any threats to your hydrocarbon empire. This could set you on a trajectory for the throne."

"Co-option is the highest form of flattery," said Tommy, and she believed him, knew that underneath his piracy was a twisted kind of awe, the jealous obsession of a fan stalking their favored creator. Tommy acted as if he looked down on Santiago precisely because he looked up to him.

"Do that," said Santiago, color draining from his face, "and the risks of a termination shock skyrocket. We don't understand the earth system well enough to set the stakes that high. This program buys time to transition away from fossil fuels. Once we take carbon out of the energy equation, we ramp down aerosol injection. It's a stopgap measure."

"No need to complicate things," said Tommy. "It lowers global temperature, which means we can burn all the oil we want and keep global warming in check."

Zia had been aghast when her father admitted the program might have contributed to India's failed monsoon. Volcanic eruptions cooled the planet and decimated human settlements. Tampering with the global climate created regional effects that were hard to predict or even explain, and that was when the people doing it pretended to care. SaudExxon wouldn't take the fates of subsistence farmers or endangered species into account. They would optimize Project Svalinn to maximize the value of their oil and gas reserves, which meant throttling it up to accommodate emissions growth and keeping it secret to disarm scientific adversaries.

What had she told Galang? *There's no such thing as a natural disaster. There are only human disasters revealed by nature.* Vindication had never been so abhorrent.

"You're dumping all the risk on future generations," said Santiago, voice hollow. "You could set off an ice age."

"Look how clever this very solution is to a problem so many claimed was impossible," said Tommy. "Future generations will figure things out, or they won't, which means they didn't deserve to. Evolution at work."

Tommy was enjoying this, reveling in his nihilistic savvy.

Zia brushed off her pants, repressed the terrors lurking in her heart, yawned dramatically, and stretched like a cat. "Well, this has been horrifying," she said. "But your extradition order doesn't come through until tomorrow, and I've had quite enough of listening to you mansplain your big plans. Great to see you've so impressed yourself, Tommy boy."

"This isn't about me, it's about you," snapped Tommy, and his voice lost its affected humor. "Do you want to be tortured to death in front of each other or live out your lives in the isolated luxury of your own compound in Riyadh? I have the company. I have the both of you. But Santiago has the access codes for the Project Svalinn command module that runs the clandestine injection and pulls the data. Ben needs them. I need them. We can do this the easy way or the hard way. Either you give up the codes to me of your own volition and the judge goes lenient on you both, or I let my interrogators rip them out of you, fingernail by fingernail." He stood abruptly. "Think about it. When we arrest you tomorrow morning, I expect a decision. In the meantime, we'll be jamming all transmissions and shooting down anything that isn't one of your gorgeous little drones. Nothing like a little quiet time to sharpen the mind."

Tommy strode off across the beach, kicking up sand. He stopped a few meters away, and half-turned back toward them. "Oh," he said. "And Zia? Fuck you and your little cabal. I'm glad Galang's dead. He was a mouthy little fag. You, Aafreen, Kodjo, all of you deserve each other."

Zia stared at him, speechless. A shadow of self-recrimination passed over Tommy's face, as if he wanted to take back what he'd just said, but stubborn pride replaced it and he spun and stalked over to the Zodiac. The commandos piled into the boat behind him and they backed off the beach, reversed direction, and roared out into the oncoming waves.

The surf eroded their wake, distorting the spreading V, and Zia marveled that Tommy might resent exclusion from a group he disdained, that he envied their lot as outcasts even as he cast them out, that for all his talk of the primacy of relationships, he so misunderstood friendship that he believed it to be a right, not a privilege. When you held yourself above reproach, the whole world was to blame.

+ 31

ZIA AND SANTIAGO STARED OUT TO SEA LONG AFTER the Zodiac had disappeared from view. Waves crashed and crumbled and shushed up onto shore, leaving behind gleaming crescents of wet sand when the water sucked back out to rise into another break. The sky was a blue dome overhead and Zia could feel the volcano rising up behind them, imagine its slope extending down, down, down to the ocean floor. Standing on an island meant standing on the exposed peak of a seamount. Tommy's ship was so large, so solid, that it appeared unaffected by the rolling groundswell, a manmade island untethered from the Earth's mantle.

Father and daughter wordlessly began to trudge back up the beach. All color seemed to have been washed out of the world, faded by the strength of the afternoon sun. The sand shifted under every step. The heat thickened the air and left them listless.

Vivid sensory impressions flickered through Zia's mind. The sickeningly sweet taste of a date plucked from a finely wrought bowl in the hermetically sealed Riyadh mansion where she and Santiago would live out their lives reading and arguing, forgotten by the wider world and visited by escorts when they pleased their jailers. The feeling of soft but immovable restraints on her wrists, neck, and ankles accompanied by the faint smell of ammonia and disinfectant in whatever theater of pain SaudExxon's professional sadists performed in. Sitting next to her father, their legs dangling in the pool, clinking champagne flutes in a final toast before swallowing a deadly cocktail cobbled together from the island's pharmacy, waiting for their souls to recede ever so slowly into the glorious tropical sunset.

"*Comemierdas*," said Santiago. "All of them."

Santiago had taken Zia to the US Open for her ninth birthday. She had been giddy with anticipation, excited to spend time with a father who always had people and business demanding his attention. They arrived in time for the hotly anticipated Walsh vs. Ye quarterfinals, but at the beginning of the second game Santiago took a work call. The attendant asked him to be quiet, Santiago argued with him hotly and then disappeared into a corridor to continue the conversation, leaving Zia to watch the match, mortified and alone. At the time, she'd believed that her father's unpredictable anger was the flip side of his genius, the keen edge of brilliance. Later, she realized that his rash outbursts weren't inevitable side effects of his creativity, discipline, and independent-mindedness. His short temper was nothing more than a short temper. People put up with it because of his success, cutting him slack he didn't deserve. Now, for the first time, seeing his clenched fists, tight shoulders, and how his gait stiffened, Zia recognized that the wrath he unleashed on others was displaced rage at a world that defied his efforts to tame it.

Zia herself wasn't angry. Despite everything, she wasn't even scared. She was empty, hollow, fragile, her soul a painted eggshell. She couldn't even bring herself to hate Tommy. He'd murdered Galang. He'd framed her and her father. He was hijacking Interstice and the geoengineering program to salvage a fading empire for personal gain. But the more he set himself up as her nemesis, the more tragic she found him. To care enough about hoarding power to be willing to kill, to repress your basic humanity to such an extent that this seemed a fair price to pay, a person who'd reached those extremes deserved pity more than anything.

Having nothing to look forward to, Zia looked back. Tommy had spent boarding school screening his privileged peers, leveraging those relationships later to advance his own cause. Why hadn't she suspected him earlier? How could she have allowed herself to fall for Tommy's act? *Fuck you and your little cabal.* There had been a strange hurt in the look Tommy had thrown her as he marched off across the beach, as if all his bluster, all his scheming, was nothing but a false front to cover up rejection. Zia remembered bouncing up off the bed, donning her clothes, and telling him "we're done" as soon as he'd judged her choice of friends. She hadn't wanted to realize that her lover was a social climber blinded by an insecurity that rendered every relationship a rung on a ladder up which he could never quite escape the gravity well of crippling self-doubt. In retrospect, the signs were obvious: the snide comments and dirty looks that stemmed from internalized privilege, the way that believing himself to be exceptional had been a way of degrading others, how desperately he cared what other people thought of him. In dumping

Tommy, Zia had felt so righteous, so sure of herself, so like her father when he tore apart someone else's idea with absolute precision.

What had seemed righteous then now looked petty and misguided. She had blamed Tommy for judging her friends and had responded by judging him even more harshly. She hadn't tried to change his mind, to flex her empathy to accommodate a boy born into corpomonarchy, to show him why treating friendships like realpolitik was ultimately self-defeating. Zia had indeed channeled Santiago, but instead of her father's courage, she'd tapped into his very worst quality: a capacity for capriciousness and the desire for absolute control. In doing so, she had reinforced the perverted beliefs that she so stridently claimed to oppose. She'd exorcised Tommy, and now here he was with that original kernel of rejection in full flower. A life worse than wasted walking a trail he'd chosen but she'd help blaze.

"*Comemierdas,*" Santiago repeated under his breath as they walked back through the villas and to Zia he seemed appallingly old and impossibly young all at once, as if age distanced you from childhood only to ferry you back.

Secrets. Power plays. Warships. Extradition. A planet wrapped in the sheerest of veils. Zia needed to find some purchase on reality in the midst of this madness. She focused on the rustle of palm fronds, the hawk riding thermals off the volcano's ridgeline, the white chalk lines against the dark red clay of the tennis court.

"Want to hit?" she asked.

"I—" A flurry of expressions passed across her father's face. "You know what, why not?"

If these were their last few hours of freedom, they might as well enjoy them.

They found rackets and balls in the little clubhouse and lined up on opposing baselines. Zia bounced the ball once, twice. On the third bounce, she stepped into it with a forehand shot straight down the middle. Santiago returned it and Zia sidestepped and responded with a crosscourt backhand. And then instinct took over and they were rallying, the ball rocketing back and forth across the net, rackets hissing through the air to find it, shoes skidding on clay. Slowly at first and then with burgeoning clarity a rhythm began to manifest. Like dancing partners feeling their way through a song, Zia and Santiago fell into sync with each other, every lob, volley, and slice contributing a piece to an emergent pattern.

Thought sublimated into presence.

Time dilated.

There was only the next stroke.

And then, like a screech of feedback interrupting the climax of a song, something broke the flow. At first, Zia didn't understand. Then she saw that Santiago was flagging. His clothes were soaked with sweat, his feet were almost but not quite getting him to where he needed to be, his grip was too tight—killing the little bird and torquing his shots. Zia tried to accommodate by slowing down her groundstrokes and hitting directly to him but she could see Santiago denying his own exhaustion and rather than falling into a new, slower tempo, he forced himself to keep the previous pace so that the rally advanced in jerks and hiccups, like a water strider across a pond.

Zia lobbed a shot into the corner and Santiago sliced the backhand return straight into the net. She reached for the extra ball in her pocket but her father sank to his knees, pressed his forehead against the strings of his racket, and began to rock back and forth, his gasps for breath interspersed with a high-pitched keening.

Startled out of her flow state, Zia hurried around the net to kneel beside him just as Dembe sprinted up from where she'd been stationed courtside. He was hyperventilating and his signature white t-shirt was sopping wet where Zia touched his shoulder. His hands were shaking from gripping the handle so hard and he never stopped moving—rocking back and forth like a bobblehead.

"Breathe," said Zia, injecting her voice with a calm that belied her inner terror. She had never seen him like this, never seen him so utterly out of control. "Breathe." This was her father. The rock. Caster of shadows she fought to get out from under. He didn't break down—he fixed other people's problems for them, whether they liked it or not. He had just lost the company he'd dedicated his life to, the secret project he'd pursued to honor his wife, his belief in his own infallibility. "Breathe." She remembered how outraged she'd been when she discovered Santiago had assigned her covert security, how maddening his supreme confidence always was. She'd always secretly wanted to see him break, to see his conviction collapse under its own weight. In the event, she wished he would regain his self-possession, once again become the father who might drive her crazy, but always had a plan. "It's going to be okay. Well, it probably won't be *okay*, but if you die on me, it'll be even less so."

He unclenched his grip and the racket fell to the ground. Empty hands shaking, he waved Dembe away and turned to Zia. The strings had pressed a grid of red indentations into his forehead like a waffle iron—bars of the cell of the mind.

"Mija." His voice was thick, words forced out between shallow sips of air. "I'm sorry I wasn't there for you. I'm sorry I didn't make the time. It's the only thing that mattered, and I messed it all up."

"Papi, *relájate,* I—"

"No." He clutched at her forearm, squeezed. "No. I'm the one who sent you away to boarding school. Your mom didn't want to, but I convinced her it was important for your future, so you wouldn't have to endure what we had to overcome. And all the time I've been telling you what to do, what to think, when I should have been telling you how proud I am of you for creating the life you wanted to live for yourself, how proud I am of who you are. And after your mom... afterward I should have been there for you. That's what she would have wanted. That's the only thing she really would have wanted. I even stood in the way of you and Galang publishing her manuscript, which was such a beautiful thing for you to do but which I couldn't bear because it reminded me that she was gone. I'm just—I'm sorry, mija. I'm so sorry."

Like a key into its lock, something slid home inside Zia. There were so many other things they should be worrying about, so many other things they should be doing, but she belatedly realized that the aspect of this surreal disaster that was the most insane was that she and her father had barely spoken to each other since her mother's death. Instead of coming together they had grown apart, shutting themselves away in their own private worlds to grapple with their own private loss. Zia had told herself that it was because Santiago was controlling, because their conversations so often ratcheted up tension instead of dissipating it. There was truth to that, but the kind of truth that only served as a convenient excuse smeared across something deeper and darker. Zia was scared, terrified of the magnitude of her grief and her inexplicable guilt, afraid to face a world without Miranda. Santiago was too. So they sought to evade the memories each evoked in the other even at the cost of their relationship.

Zia sat down heavily, then leaned back until she was lying directly on the clay. Santiago flopped down beside her. She sank into a churning mass of memory. The smell of Miranda's shampoo. The silvery glitter of moonlight off the still surface of an alpine lake. A few bars of an otherwise forgotten salsa tune. The taste of bone broth. Lying awake to the incessant, deafening rhythm of her own beating heart. The stories Zia told herself about herself loosened, the identity their scaffolding supported going all wonky, betraying how insubstantial it really was. The sun beat down from above. Heat radiated up from below. The Interstice satellites orbiting overhead would see their forms spread-eagled on red clay, ten thousand unthinking, unblinking eyes logging, tagging, and collating data to create a digital mirror world to which they were the bridge—a bridge Zia couldn't reach through the electromagnetic tempest of Tommy's jamming. Tomorrow Zia and Santiago would be at Tommy's mercy. With those satellites in hand, the rest of the world would be too.

"The aerosols," said Zia. "Do they change the color of the sky?"

"Not perceptibly," said Santiago, his voice slightly calmer. "Sunsets are a little redder, but the human eye wouldn't be able to distinguish the blue we're seeing from the blue we would be seeing without the program."

"But it *is* different, even if we can't see it."

"Any change in atmospheric chemistry affects refraction and scattering in one way or another," said Santiago. "So technically, yes."

The subtlest shift in the shade of blue heralding a different future.

"Remember when *Mami* took me to the Grand Canyon? She scooped up some water, let it dribble through her fingers, and told me how each of the tiny molecules in each of those little drops might seem insignificant, but that over time it was they and only they that had carved out the vast rock walls rising up on either side."

Santiago's hand found Zia's and squeezed. Grit bit into their sweaty palms.

"I once asked her why she wrote," said Santiago. "She told me how willows suck toxins and heavy metals from the soil. They're so effective at cleaning their environment that they're used for phytoremediation on lands we've polluted. She said their tresses do something special to the quality of the light when they hang over flowing water, create a permanent golden hour inside their embrace. Medicines like aspirin were derived from their bark. These beautiful trees aren't just growing up, they're giving back all the time in countless ways. That's what she wanted her writing to do, to *be*: a willow tree."

A cloud metamorphosed overhead, refusing to take a stable shape, driven across the heavens before a wind they could not feel.

"When I joined my first humanitarian aid mission, part of it was that I wanted to give back," she said. "But another part of it was that I just wanted to... disappear. I just couldn't even..."

Santiago's grip tightened and Zia squeezed back until it hurt. They had each buried themselves in the world to hide the ugliness of their pain.

"I'm sorry too," said Zia. "Sorry for all the horrible things I've said. For disap—"

"You have nothing to be sorry for. *Nothing*." His voice was raw, fierce.

"Some *leónes* we are," she managed. "Abandoning each other to the hyenas."

"Too fucking proud," he said.

"Too fucking proud," she echoed, the last word disintegrating into something between a laugh and a sob.

The cloud shifted, split, reformed. The heat was viscous and all-consuming, displacing thought, demanding everything for itself. The satellite footage that haunted Zia's dreams surfaced in her mind, Gilberto stumbling out of the jungle, the skinny guide barely able to keep his footing as he supported Miranda, half-carrying her across a barren patch of earth to the nearest cement-block building. They were visible for less than thirty seconds. Jungle. Stumble. Building. Jungle. Stumble. Building. Jungle. Stumble. Building. A thousand loops. A million. The loop of a lifetime. A lifetime of loops. Neither Zia nor Santiago had ever set foot in that cursed rainforest.

"I miss her *so* much," said Zia, the admission prompting a Gestalt switch that reversed the joy and pain of grief, foreground and background of the selfsame loss flipped so that she could no longer see it the way she had before.

"Me too," Santiago choked on the words. "Me too."

A flash of silver. One of Santiago's long-winged drones, circling lazily as it came in for landing. The kaleidoscopic rush of impending ruin. The SaudExxon machine rearing up to crush the world in its maw. She had initially fallen for Tommy's act at Galang's funeral because she wanted to believe that people could change. But he hadn't changed. He was the same old arrogant, terrified boy she'd known all those years ago.

When Zia was a child, Miranda had shaken her awake early one morning at the house in Guanacaste. *Come*, she'd said. Blinking the sleep from her eyes, Zia had followed her mother through the backyard and down to the stream. *Look*.

Miranda pointed. A traveling circus had performed in the village the night before and a raccoon, bandit-faced and bushy tailed, had gotten his hands on some cotton candy. He placed the pink pillow on the sand, ripped off a chunk, and dunked it into the stream, the spun sugar dissolving into the flowing water. He looked at his empty palms in consternation, tore off another chunk, and repeated the process. Zia looked up at her mom. *They wash their food before they eat it*, said Miranda. Visibly frustrated, the raccoon tried again. Then it sat back on its haunches and huffed. Its snout turned back and forth between its enigmatic prize and the stream. Then it buried its face in the cotton candy and didn't stop eating until its belly was round. *She learned*, exclaimed Zia. *Just like us*, said Miranda. *Learning is life.*

Tommy might not have changed. But Zia could.

Fuck you and your little cabal.

She squeezed her father's hand.

"I have an idea," she said.

+

32

RAIN LASHED AT THE WALL-TO-WALL WINDOWS OF Santiago's villa, gusts of wind smearing drops across the glass. Zia, Santiago, and Dembe had shemaghs wrapped around their faces. The surround sound system was pumping Kendrick Lamar's posthumous album at max volume, intricate lyrics tumbling into and over each other in a waterfall of words and beats. Any audiovisual bugs that had survived their sweep would have a hard time gleaning anything useful and couldn't transmit through the jamming anyway.

Dembe placed three small headlamps on the kitchen counter.

"Darkness is our friend," she said. "So don't use them at all if you can help it. And if you absolutely have to"—she clicked one on and it emitted a flat red glow—"you'll get low energy red light." She zipped up her jacket. Santiago opened his mouth to say something and Dembe silenced him with a hard look. "I don't need suggestions. I need obedience. We *will* get there. Just stay close. Ready? Good."

They snatched up their headlamps, cinched their hoods, and slipped out the back door into the storm. Dembe led them quickly across the flagstone path and into the forest. Zia followed and Santiago came behind. Raindrops clattered against their hoods, drowning out all other sound. Mud sucked at their boots, branches grasped at them through the pitch darkness, and every breath contained nearly as much water as air.

Dembe was nothing more than a shadow among shadows before Zia, who was desperately trying to keep up and just as desperately trying to make sure they didn't lose Santiago. They slid down a slick rock face and forded a swollen stream, the rocks on the bottom shifting underfoot. Zia's left ankle throbbed. Nerves screeched like electric guitar feedback through the studio of her mind. The storm and the jungle closed in around her, locking her off in a murky world of tropical deluge where the only hope was the grayscale shudder that might be Dembe's receding back.

Born alone. Suffer alone. Die alone. Life was a single player game where the only victory conditions were self-imposed. It was as if everyone were stuck in hermetically sealed bubbles, hands pressing against impenetrable glass as they tried but never quite managed to reach each other. That gap was what her mother had tried to bridge with prose, burying herself beneath the words for readers to excavate and recognize in themselves.

Zia sucked for air, coughed up water, and nearly lost her footing. She threw a look back over her shoulder. Nothing but trunks and vines shrouded in gloom. Panic wiped her mind blank. Where was her father? They had lost him in the forest, abandoned him to his own bubble. Electric tendrils fingered out from her gut. Anything might be lurking behind the inky mess of trees and undergrowth and falling water—anything but Santiago. Had he slipped and broken a leg? Had he returned to the villa on some misguided quest to provide a distraction to cover their escape? Had a clouded leopard survived on this remote island and decided to exact vengeance on the prime trespasser this very night? She turned to call out to Dembe for help and Zia's panic redoubled when she saw she had lost their guide. Black on black on black. Why hadn't she paid attention to *The Princess Bride*? Never enter the motherfucking Fire Swamp.

Calm down. Think. Reaching up, Zia switched on her headlamp. The light was red and soft and gritty, transforming the jungle into a surrealist hellscape, ferns reaching out of some adjacent, bloody dimension to brush her shoulder with a frond. And then the fronds parted and Santiago stumbled into her. Zia clutched his jacket to keep from falling over and they caught their balance. She looked back again, sweeping her cone of red light across the foliage and Dembe was standing right behind them.

"Almost there," hissed Dembe. "Just over the next rise."

Zia switched off her headlamp, plunging them back into darkness. Before anyone could move, she reached out and clasped Santiago and Dembe's hands. Santiago's was cold and slick with sweat. Dembe's palm was warm and surprisingly dry despite the downpour. They paused for the briefest of moments and then both squeezed without a word and Dembe led them out of the ferns and up a muddy slope.

Zia held Dembe back when Santiago was flagging and encouraged her father to speed up when terrain permitted.

The feeling of their hands in hers was so sharp, so present compared to peering into the surrounding darkness. She felt their every slip, change of balance, and moment of doubt. She knew when they found a solid foothold or sank ankle deep into a puddle. Urgency surged back and forth through their palms in tides of emotional osmosis.

And then they reached the top of the ridge and the lights of the airfield blazed up at them through the intervening trees, illuminating cascading sheets of rain and casting long twisted shadows across the forest floor. A few cars were parked between one of the hangars and the edge of the forest. Dembe approached one, popped the trunk, and tossed each of them a large, tightly packed backpack. Then they jogged across the slick tarmac to the drone taxiing for takeoff. Long wings trembled in the gusts of wind and light glittered off the rain-slick silver hull.

This elegant machine was one of the hundreds of peripherals through which Interstice's geoengineering system manipulated the stratosphere. The last thing Tommy wanted to do was disrupt the very drones he prized so highly, the fleet whose helm he would take as soon as he secured Santiago's access codes. What Tommy couldn't know, what not even Ben knew, was that Santiago had outfitted one very special drone to take passengers. All they'd had to do to slot it into the flight schedule was update the protocol via a hardwire connection.

A seam appeared across the belly of the metal beast and a narrow stairway lowered to the tarmac with a hiss of hydraulics. As they climbed, Zia flashed back to the first time she'd boarded this bird at Santiago's insistence, the aquamarine lake set like a jewel in the gaping crater of Pinatubo, her horror at the secret Santiago had been so hesitant and yet so eager to share. An inscription she hadn't noticed before greeted her as she squeezed into the cramped passenger cabin behind Dembe and her father:

In front of the sun
does Svalinn stand,
The shield for the shining god;
Mountains and sea
would be set in flames
If it fell from before the sun.
—Grímnismál, the Poetic Edda

Engines howling defiance at the raging storm, the drone accelerated up the runway, pressing them back into their seats before they had time to buckle their restraints.

33

+

AS THEY ASCENDED THROUGH THE STORM, ZIA WAS sure Tommy's destroyer would shoot them down. Their ploy had been discovered and their world was about to explode in a burst of anti-aircraft ordnance. Or maybe the carrier would launch a swarm of attack drones to force them down. Turbulence rocked their drone, pressing them up against each other in the tight cabin. Lightning flashed. Zia was convinced the wings would snap under the force of the wind. The excruciating beat stretched into an eternity and then they broke through the cloud layer and were engulfed in sudden, incomprehensible calm—purgatory fading in the dawning awareness that they were, at least for the moment, free.

Santiago checked his phone and shook his head.

"Nothing," he growled. "We're still within range of their jammer."

Not quite free, then. They might be off the island, but they were still inside the invisible bubble of chattering radio waves emanating from Tommy's transmitter, suffusing the spectrum with nonsense, just like his smear campaign had filled the headlines with so much scandal that there wasn't room left for truth.

They were airborne, and gagged.

Reaching into an inside pocket, Dembe produced a small bag of dark chocolate-covered almonds, popped a few in her mouth, and offered the bag to Zia who waved it away, nauseous.

"Eat," Dembe insisted, shaking a few almonds into Zia and Santiago's palms. "We all need to keep our blood sugar up. Right now you're running on nothing but adrenaline. Once that dries up, you can't afford to crash. I've lost good soldiers because they didn't eat their snacks." She gobbled a few more. "These have chocolate to perk you up and protein to keep you going."

Zia put one almond in her mouth and chewed, trying to ignore the urge to vomit. Dembe raised her eyebrows and Zia gave in and managed to swallow a few more.

After passing around a water bottle to wash down the nuts, Dembe rested a hand on the bulkhead and looked at Santiago.

"Let me in," she said, calling them back to themselves with her composure.

He nodded, retrieved a tablet from his backpack, and plugged it into a slot on the control panel. Opening a command line, he began to type, code spiraling ever inward toward the kernel. His singular focus was contagious and mesmerizing to watch. Then, like a canvas screen disappearing behind a projection, Interstice's digital skeleton vanished as he brought up a dashboard and handed the tablet to Dembe.

"Full admin access to this drone," he said.

Dembe gave Zia a questioning look.

"Fiji," said Zia, remembering the taste of fresh coconut juice, aquamarine tide pools, and coral reefs bleached white as bone. She'd deployed there for nine months in the wake of a typhoon that had wrecked the archipelago's infrastructure. "Aim for Nacula Village in the Yasawa Islands."

Dembe nodded. "I'll make the course corrections, delete the changes from the logs, and backfill the database with records from a previous flight."

"Fiji?" asked Santiago. "Why Fiji?"

"With any luck, Tommy will find it just as counter-intuitive a destination as you do," said Zia. "Plus, I have a friend there who might be able to help." She could only pray Selai hadn't already forsaken her as a terrorist on the basis of Tommy's lies. "Speaking of..." Zia checked her phone. "Still no service."

The drone dipped left and right, then evened out again.

"What was that?" asked Zia.

"I'm not sure." Dembe was frowning down at the tablet. "Unless—"

"Full bars!" shouted Santiago, holding up his phone. "We've breached their jamming perimeter. The autopilot must have recalibrated after syncing with the satellite."

There was a moment of unexpected silence, as if none of them had quite believed they'd make it this far. Then service bars appeared on Zia's phone. Dembe reacted first, swiped her tablet to deploy the routines she'd written to fabricate the satellite logs as she absentmindedly popped more almonds into her mouth. Santiago met his daughter's eye and the argument they'd had after her first drone ride over Pinatubo echoed in collective memory.

Stop, or I'll blow the whistle. And boy, will I blow it loud.

The moment of truth had finally come.

A full confession was the only way to unravel Tommy's plot. Revealing the geoengineering program would precipitate a geopolitical crisis. Scientists would rightfully condemn Project Svalinn. Tribunals would break up Interstice on the basis of its data falsification. Santiago would become the world's most hated man. India would demand to know whether or not the program had sabotaged the monsoon, and few would accept the answer that attribution was impossible in such complex models. Countries who believed they were being hurt by the program would call for an immediate ban while those that believed the program gave them a regional climactic advantage would fight for continuance. Powers great enough to mount their own efforts would do so, further complicating the picture. Strike forces would deploy. Tension would escalate, with no end in sight. It might even spark a world war.

But even that dreadful scenario was preferable to letting Tommy hijack the skunkworks. Increasing aerosol injection to mask the impact of burning more fossil fuels, he'd jack up the program until the risk of termination shock was apocalyptic. He'd protect the value of SaudExxon's holdings, take the throne, and run the planet into the ground from the safety of an air-conditioned palace. If anybody stumbled on the truth, the same scenario would play out, only worse because the stakes would be yet higher.

But if the world found out about the program a priori, Tommy's house of cards collapsed. SaudExxon could push for aggressive injection in the diplomatic scrum to come, but the chance at a clandestine flywheel of pure profit would be dashed. Only by blowing the whistle could Zia and Santiago hope to save themselves, and every minute they kept silent was a minute Tommy still had to silence them.

"I'll start prepping my statement," said Santiago, his tone at once meek and dreamy, as if dissociation was the only way he could bear to confess his long-held secret. The world might not believe it, coming from a suspected terrorist on the run from the law. Certainly, many would think it was a poor attempt at distraction from the accusations being levied at the Leóns. Breaking the news in such a charged environment would doubtless undermine anyone's ability to react thoughtfully, increasing the risk of violence. But by the very same token, it would attract enough attention to guarantee further investigation, investigation that would wreck Tommy's plans.

Zia unlocked her phone, held her breath, and signed in.

Data spooled across the screen. Photos of Zia and her family plastered all over social media. Headlines painting them as monsters. Articles peppered with quotes taken out of context. Threats and questions and fiery op-eds holding forth with unassailable conviction—righteousness at its most corrosive.

Only under the onslaught of notifications did Zia realize what a blessing it had been to have been involuntarily disconnected. She didn't want to see the news, open her overflowing inbox, triage the texts, or listen to the voicemails. She didn't want false sympathy or official summons or death threats. She didn't want to know what the world thought of her. She wanted to stay in this drone forever, cruising through the thin outer reaches of the atmosphere, beyond Tommy's reach.

Beyond *anyone*'s reach.

Zia had always run. At every turn, she had obsessively sought out opportunities to be of service, without acknowledging that she had needs of her own. She had gazed out at life from behind a one-way mirror, without letting anyone gaze back in. If she gave shelter without taking it, she'd be free to do whatever she wanted, to be fully herself. But maybe she couldn't be fully herself, maybe nobody could be fully themselves, except through connection. How had Galang phrased it? *We're like electrons, we only exist in relation to each other.* Maybe the freedom she'd been chasing wasn't freedom at all, but alienation.

It wasn't that she didn't love her friends and family. She loved them so much that she wanted to offer them everything, and never ask for anything in return. She was the host, the rock, the pillar they could lean on in times of need. She was always there for them, but would never expect them to be there for her. She had convinced herself that extreme self-reliance was a prerequisite to love, but it was actually just another kind of flight, another way to run from life's terrifying interdependence. It was time to run toward her fear, to embrace vulnerability as a source of strength, to stop pretending that she could rely only on herself. No matter how uncomfortable it made her feel, she needed to ask her friends for help.

As she opened the group chat, she steeled herself against recrimination. Santiago might be her father, but Aafreen, Selai, Kodjo, Daniela, Vachan, and Li Jie were Zia's found family. She would rather suffer the contempt of millions of strangers than endure her friends' judgement. With fictional tales of her imagined sins dominating the news cycle, what must they be thinking?

Zia froze when she saw the most recent messages.

She scrolled back, read, re-read. Scrolled back, read, re-read. Scrolled back, read, re-read. It was as if dawn was breaking inside her, thick slabs of cloud painted pink and orange, rays of light slanting across the sky, warmth kissing frost covered meadows. The glow started in her gut and swelled, filling her up to the brim, buoying her heart into her throat, raising goosebumps on her arms, and suffusing her with grace.

They weren't condemning her.

They were saving her.

When Bonnie's story broke, the group chat had erupted in outraged disbelief. But Zia's friends had immediately started poking holes in the article. Just as Himmat had checked his calendar and refuted the CBI agent's accusations, Kodjo had gone back through his personal diary and discovered that on the night the article claimed Zia had been meeting with a rebel leader from the Democratic Republic of Congo, Kodjo had in fact been confiding to Zia the details of his engagement to Lucy over a few too many bottles of rum in a remote Ghanian village where Zia was managing an anti-malaria program.

Kodjo shared his discovery with the group, setting off a flurry of cross referencing and fact checking. The article cited an audio recording of a negotiation between Zia and an Argentine general in charge of political kidnappings that was timestamped during a site visit she and Daniela had made to a blight-ravaged Bolivian agricultural region. When a fake video placed Zia on the yacht of a Kazakhstani oligarch, Aafreen and Zia had actually been pitching a foundation to extend their funding beyond immediate relief to support reconstruction with more resilient infrastructure.

Tommy had woven threads of truth through the web of lies he was spinning around Zia and Santiago in order to maximize verisimilitude. Using her humanitarian aid missions as a cover for subterfuge made it easy for outsiders like Bonnie to confirm circumstantial evidence that supported Tommy's fiction. Zia really had been in those places at those times. She just hadn't been meeting those people or doing those things.

With the full weight of SaudExxon's influence behind it, the sham evidence was enough to convince the FBI to issue a warrant and freeze León assets, especially when so many in power would benefit from Santiago's downfall. But as convincing as those tidbits of truth were to people who didn't know better, there were people who *did* know better.

Nobody was more ruthless in assessing and enforcing social standing than teenagers. At boarding school, Zia and her friends had bonded precisely because classmates like Tommy had shunned them for coming from poor countries with little geopolitical sway. Those same countries were most exposed to the ravages of a changing climate from which they had profited least, a perverse catastrophe that Miranda's death had inspired Zia to help mitigate. That was why Zia had ended up leading missions to each of her friend's home countries, and why each of those friends was now an alibi. They had already started contacting reporters, and stories that called Bonnie's article into question were trickling out, a trickle that with any luck might soon become a flood.

None of their efforts would matter if SaudExxon had Zia and Santiago in custody. They would be rushed through a sham trial and executed. But Zia and Santiago weren't waiting for Tommy's troops to arrest them. Instead, they were flying through the rarified reaches of the stratosphere in a drone running an unprecedented experiment in what could easily prove to be a misguided effort to tweak the entire energy system of the planet it was soaring over. Stars blazed above. Waves churned below. By attempting to set the perfect trap, Tommy had given Zia the slimmest of chances.

Vision blurring, Zia nudged Santiago.

He looked up from the trance in which he'd been composing his press release.

"What's wrong?" asked Santiago.

Dembe's hand was on Zia's forearm, quietly comforting.

Zia almost laughed as she wiped away her tears. There was so much wrong it was hard to know where to start, but she was crying because something was finally starting to go right. She would do everything in her power to keep things heading in that direction.

"Wait," said Zia.

"What do you mean?" asked Santiago.

Zia turned to Dembe. "How much time do we have?" she asked. "How long do you think it will take for Tommy to track us?"

Dembe waggled her head from side to side. "No way to know. It depends on how quickly he discovers exactly how we got out and on how well we've covered our tracks."

"But if you had to guess?"

"I'd give us a day," said Dembe. "Disembarking unconventionally will help throw him off."

A day.

A day wasn't nearly enough for what Zia had in mind.

A day would have to do.

Control the narrative.

That was what Zia had learned working on President Kim's campaign. That was what Galang and years of managing disaster response had taught her. That was the advice Zia had given to her father. That was exactly what Tommy had done. Scandal. Intrigue. Betrayal. He had harnessed the power of unbridled Schadenfreude at the prospect of a magnate, toppling.

Zia had tried to enlist Galang's help to tell this story properly, and Tommy had had him killed. She had tried to do the same with Bonnie, and Tommy had gotten to her first. But maybe the issue wasn't finding the right person to report the story, but changing the ending of the story itself.

Zia initiated a video call to the group chat.

As the phone rang, she asked her father, "How much sway do you still hold at Interstice?"

His expression darkened. "The board's dead set on ousting me. VPs are jockeying for position. It's a goddamn mutiny."

"But you're not out *yet*."

"I'm technically still CEO of a cage full of vultures."

"Scavengers are a crucial piece of any ecosystem."

"Are you calling me carrion?"

"Prove me wrong," she said. "Can you swing a covert asset sale?"

Santiago's gaze sharpened. "Depends," he said cautiously. "I need board approval for transactions over a certain size."

"What if the buyer paid only one dollar?"

Kodjo's face popped up on her screen. "Hello, Zia? Is that really you? We've been trying to contact you for ages. Are you alright?"

"Find out," Zia urged her father, then raised her phone.

More faces appeared on the screen, the digital ghosts of her closest friends channeled through Interstice's satellites, turning the slim shard of glass in her hand into a more powerful scrying glass than any sorcerer had ever managed to muster. *Fuck you and your little cabal.* Tommy was right. They were a cabal. And the thing about cabals were that they were just small enough to make decisions and just big enough to make an impact. If Zia was going to attempt the impossible, there was no one else she'd rather have at her side. There was Li Jie, boba tea close at hand. Aafreen looked like she hadn't slept in days, and somehow still seemed as radiant as ever. Vachan was chattering animatedly, not realizing his microphone was muted. Daniela was popping in earbuds. Selai was outside somewhere, wind hissing in the background. Everyone was talking at once.

Zia held up a hand, and they fell silent.

Her father had tried to singlehandedly save the world from itself. But true salvation could only come from the inside.

"What if I told you all the bullshit you're seeing on the news isn't even half the story?"

+

34

"BEIJING WILL GO ABSOLUTELY APE SHIT," SAID LI Jie. "I mean, they've been cloud seeding for years and there's nothing technocrats like better than the idea of Mother Nature doing the Party's bidding. Honestly, I'm surprised this is your dad's thing and not one of their secret military projects."

Zia muted herself and caught her breath. The air in the cockpit was stale and funky. They were three in a space meant for two and couldn't keep from jostling each other. Santiago had earbuds in and was rattling off a bunch of legal jargon Zia couldn't even attempt to decipher. Dembe was double-checking the emergency hatch release.

"Or a CIA initiative," added Daniela. "There aren't many countries the Yankees haven't fucked up with bungled intelligence operations since Langley got up and running. This seems like just the kind of thing that would appeal to the Beltway crowd." She mimed taking a sip from a cocktail. "'Well, we ran out of land, so we're taking our Manifest Destiny to the stratosphere.'"

Zia hadn't known where to begin when she started laying out the situation for her friends, so she just walked them through everything that had happened since the reunion. She remembered pulling her dress up and over her head on the shore of the alpine lake, the shock of sudden submersion, Selai describing her frustrating attempts to decode a puzzle to which only Santiago held the key—a revelation that Zia had only just now been able to share, and that Selai had accepted not with the shock Zia might have expected, but with the prim satisfaction of someone who knew that their calculus had been correct all along, that at least one aspect of life's indomitable obstinacy had an explanation after all.

Telling the whole story out loud made it feel like a ridiculous screenplay pitch for the melodramatic biopic Galang had proposed. That he had proved its first casualty was exactly the kind of irony he'd demand the director jazz up. Zia swallowed the lump rising in her throat. *We need to get the old gang back together more often.* When had life become so damn complicated? What had the world come to, what had they themselves come to, if it took catastrophe to bring them together? Zia returned her attention to the faces clustered on her screen as her hand instinctively grasped the absent tennis racket. She needed to show them that this was a catastrophe only they could avert.

Vachan was shaking his head. "If it really did throw off the monsoon... I've seen what it's done to our farmers here in Sri Lanka. And Delhi's been trying to use us as a scapegoat for whatever they can because of the domestic political pressure they're feeling from the agricultural crisis. The second they find out about this, I— I don't want to know what they'll do. It's going to get ugly, fast. They're not going to be shy about throwing their weight around."

"The minute they start to, Beijing will trip them up and then kick them once they're down," Li Jie grimaced. "You should see the kind of nasty stuff they pull to undermine us here in Taiwan. My parents would kill me if I mentioned specifics, but they stop at *nothing*. And all those infrastructure projects in Nepal, the direct investment into Pakistan, the bilateral trade deals with Sri Lanka—no offense, Vachan—"

"None taken," he waved him off.

"...it's all just maneuvering to contain and constrain India, give them no room to move, no room to grow. This will be a perfect opportunity to press the advantage, to paint Delhi a bad actor. If the prime minister blames the drought on this program and demands a ban, Beijing will play thoughtful and call for additional research while drumming up the risk of termination shock via their media apparatus. The farther Delhi goes, the harder Beijing will push, starting up their own program from scratch if necessary. And that's just the *public* stuff."

"There's no way the US sits back and watches this one pass without getting its hands dirty," said Daniela.

"Don't forget Moscow," said Aafreen. "This could turn into a Great Power bar fight in no time. Most of my job consists of not pissing off the wrong group of assholes, and let me tell you, it's harder than it sounds. This kind of thing... This kind of thing could really blow up."

Zia had to suppress a nostalgic smile. The conversation didn't just echo the arguments she'd made to Santiago, but also all the final exams she'd studied for with this tight-knit group, munching on potato chips as they spun out case studies late into the night in the chateau library. A bunch of kids playing at the intrigue their parents accomplished in earnest.

"I can't believe it's fucking *Tommy*," said Kodjo. "Having Zia kidnapped, calling a hit on Galang, framing Zia and Santiago, all to hijack this program and keep it under wraps."

"Oh, I can," said Aafreen, her expression calcifying. "You should have seen what SaudExxon got up to during the construction of New Malé. When Tommy got wind that Zia was meeting up with Galang, he must have assumed she might be about to leak Project Svalinn, which would have ruined his plan. So he attempted to kidnap Zia for leverage with Santiago, and when that failed, he had Galang assassinated, giving him the opportunity to frame them both. Then he could just move in and snatch Interstice without anybody finding out that he was really after the geoengineering program. The whole thing is only marginally more baroque than the visa scheme his colleagues were running with my second cousin."

"I knew that fucker was a snake," snarled Daniela. "Even back in high school."

Back on the beach, Tommy's blue eyes might have twinkled, but it had been the glitter of winter sun off polished chrome. His grin hadn't been easy. They weren't kids anymore. And this game had consequences.

"The program has to stop," said Vachan. "Ramp it down to zero as quickly and safely as possible. Otherwise people are going to start shooting sooner or later. You can't even prove attribution? This is way too much uncertainty for heads of state to handle. That's the thing about weather, it's always been an 'act of God,' even the insurance companies say so. The minute people start messing with it, other people have a target to pin all their problems on. It's pouring gasoline on the dumpster fire that is geopolitics."

"It's climate, not weather," said Kodjo. "And anyone who thinks climate change is an act of God is ignorant or kidding themselves."

"Yeah, but Zia's dad is doing it *intentionally*," said Daniela.

"At least if it's on purpose we can see what works and try to improve it," said Kodjo. "I'd rather have that than the status quo of pretending that something that threatens the biosphere is an externality. It's ludicrous."

"If Santiago hadn't been doing this, I wonder how many more centimeters sea levels would have risen," Selai murmured. "I wonder how many more Heat Waves we'd have had, how many other islands we'd have had to evacuate."

"Judging from our experience with storm surges in the Maldives, a lot," said Aafreen. "New Malé probably wouldn't even be viable anymore."

"So, what then?" asked Vachan, cheeks flushing. "The whole subcontinent goes hungry so that you can save some beaches? On a per capita basis, we've got a hell of a lot more people suffering because of this."

"So you think West Africa should take one for the team so you can have the monsoon back?" asked Kodjo.

"I'm just saying Delhi will shoot every drone out of the air before acquiescing."

"And I'm just saying that Accra will build its own drones and defend them if it means keeping farmers happy," said Kodjo. "The agricultural lobby will make sure of that."

"If Delhi shoots anything down outside its own airspace, Beijing will pounce," said Li Jie. "And there's no way they'll let Ghana do anything that might have regional impacts in East Asia."

"Ditto for Washington and the Americas," said Daniela.

"There's always the UN," said Selai with a shrug.

Aafreen snorted. "Take it from a minister of foreign affairs," she said. "Don't look for answers there. There have never been so many cooks in a single kitchen."

The debate was starting to pick up momentum, and Zia knew it wouldn't lead anywhere good. This was precisely the argument that would devolve into the kind of violence they were describing. Too much noise, too little signal. When tempers started to flare even among a tight knit group of friends, it didn't bode well for the public discussion to come. If this was the preview, Zia didn't want to see the movie.

It was time to make her play. Letting the snowball turn into an avalanche would do nothing but waste time they didn't have. Zia suddenly felt the stab of Galang's absence. His face belonged alongside the others. His snarky comments should be spicing up this conversation. If he were here, he'd know how to engineer a graceful transition. Without him, Zia just had to cut to the chase.

She unmuted herself—and wondered whether the real problem was that some part of her had been on mute ever since she lost her mom. When Zia was eleven, she wrote a book report on Ursula K. Le Guin's *The Wizard of Earthsea.* The teacher returned it covered in redline edits. Devastated, Zia showed the essay to Miranda, hoping for outraged sympathy at the teacher's mishandling of Zia's brilliant work. But instead of placating her daughter, Miranda had sat down with Zia and reviewed everything line by line, using each of the teacher's individual edits and comments to ask questions that challenged Zia to articulate her point of view with more precision, to hone thought's blade. *Clarity is not short sentences,* she'd said. *Or long sentences. Or sentences of any particular flavor. Clarity is forging your imagination into a pebble that, when tossed, will ripple through other minds.* Zia needed all Miranda's quiet strength now, all her poise, all her forceful eloquence.

"Look," said Zia. "You're all right, and you're all wrong. That's the problem. There's no elegant solution to this mess. But we don't need to find an answer right here, right now." They were all looking at her, even Santiago and Dembe. "The only way to sabotage Tommy is to make this public, and the sooner we do it, the sooner he'll stop hunting us—or at least the sooner he'll have bigger problems to deal with. We've got less than a day. That's not enough time to figure out what to do about Project Svalinn, what's fair, or even who should decide. But there's something we can do to avert the worst case scenario, that this sparks a—what did you call it, Aafreen?—a Great Power bar fight."

She took a breath and gathered her thoughts. This was it. If they agreed, the world might have half a chance, and if they didn't, they would have no choice but to roll the dice anyway. But the proposal was so patently ridiculous that they'd be right to just laugh in her face. "Selai," she said. "You understand the implications better than any of us and your uncles constitute a third of the Fijian cabinet. Li Jie, you grew up with President Wu's daughters. Kodjo, everyone and their mother in Accra owes you a favor. Vachan, your family exports more Ceylon tea than all the other estates put together. Daniela, you publish a pseudonymous singer songwriter who happens to be a justice on the Salvadoran supreme court. Aafreen, you've got the president on speed dial. I can call in a favor with President Kim and my dad knows the chief Indonesian economic minister because of all the approvals he needed for his island base. If we work hard and get lucky, we can get half a dozen heads of state on the line."

Vachan arched an eyebrow. "Uh huh, and what exactly are we supposed to tell them?"

Miranda had always said that the writer wasn't the author of an idea, but its vehicle—that her craft consisted of simply noticing things and cultivating them until they grew into book-shaped stories. Once an idea took root, it would spread like a weed through the garden of her mind, demanding to be shared with an overwhelming force that found release only through articulation. Just such a weed was germinating inside Zia, sending shoots in all directions, opening technicolor flowers, filling her head with drifting clouds of pollen, and releasing seeds to the wind. Only this idea demanded not articulation, but realization.

Zia shot a sidelong glance at Santiago, who nodded curtly. "My dad is prepared to immediately hand over the geoengineering program and the entire Interstice drone fleet to a coalition of countries who commit to creating a multilateral institution to manage it—and the climate. Imagine a new international organization along the lines of the Arctic Council or the International Atomic Energy Agency—coordinating with the UN but with few enough nations that things can actually get done. It'd be a sort of club, and we'd offer them the opportunity to become the founding members."

There was a moment of heady silence.

"I hate to be the one to say this," said Selai. "I mean, I'm a proud Fijian and all, but there's a reason we weren't the cool kids at boarding school. Let's get real. The powerbrokers we have ins with don't actually broke a whole lotta power. We're talking about Costa Rica, the Maldives, Fiji, Sri Lanka, Taiwan, Ghana, Indonesia, and El Salvador, right?" She counted them off on her fingers. "Your dad's company probably earns more every year than their combined GDPs, and the capitals that count treat them as an afterthought, at best. It's like if the Avengers all had superpowers like lightning-fast-bookkeeping or the-ability-to-suppress-yawns-even-when-everyone-around-you-is-yawning. I mean, that's cool and all, but it ain't gonna stop an alien invasion."

"Exactly," said Zia, gaining momentum. "What countries are powerful enough to take unilateral action? The big, rich, powerful ones. None of them would ever let any of the other major players control this kind of a program, and would wage war to prevent it. But if our group of poor, weak countries are in charge, Washington, Beijing, and the rest know they can comfortably sanction the coalition as long as the other big boys do too." She leaned closer to the camera. "If we go public by simply announcing what my dad's been up to, everyone will reach for their guns. But if we announce what my dad's been up to *and* that it's being handed over to a new international organization, everyone's going to have to at least take some time to consider the situation. By having a bunch of little guys assume ownership of the problem, we're giving the bullies an excuse *not* to take unilateral action. Our weakness is our greatest strength."

Kodjo narrowed his eyes. "Even if we're able to get to the people you want us to, announcing that they're taking over the program from a rogue billionaire who's going through a major scandal will put them in the middle of a media firestorm."

"It's a risk," acknowledged Zia. "But there's a substantial reward. They'll get to write the rules for engineering the climate. They'll get to define who else gets admitted to the club in charge of writing those rules moving forward. Our countries have done the least to contribute to emissions and suffer the most from the impacts of climate change. Now, we can finally do something about it, and we have more moral high ground from which to do so than anyone else. I'm asking you to be the messengers, to make offers they can't refuse."

"But you have to break the news *today*, or Tommy won't stop until he silences you," said Vachan. "How are they going to agree on any of these things over the course of a few hours? Treaties take *years*. I mean"—he exchanged a glance with Kodjo—"*we* can't even agree on what the right course would be."

Zia held up a finger. "We're only asking them to agree to one thing: to allow us to announce that they are part of the coalition that is taking over the program. That's it. We're handing them the reins. *They* get to decide how and where to ride. If my dad's the jockey on this racehorse when it hits the headlines, everyone will be as fucked as he is. If they take his place, we've got a fighting chance of turning an unmitigated disaster into a mechanism for unwinding environmental inequality."

"Your plan is insane," said Aafreen thoughtfully. "Totally, one hundred and ten percent, spectacularly insane. There are too many moving parts and there's too little time. It's historically unprecedented." She laughed a husky, faraway laugh. "Then again, the really interesting parts of history are always the unprecedented bits."

"So," said Zia, summoning every fleeting scrap of self-possession and letting the full force of her conviction blaze through her eyes. "Who's in?"

35

+

DEMBE RAPPED HER KNUCKLES AGAINST HER HELMET. "Remember your training and lead with your hips," she said. The visor magnified her amber eyes, revealing delicate green striations. Her stance was loose, relaxed. The more tenuous the situation, the more composed Dembe became.

Zia envied her equanimity. Her own heart was hammering like tropical rain on a tin roof. *Disembarking unconventionally*. It might be the best way to throw Tommy off their scent, but she was ready to call it off and take their chances. They could find some other way to cover their tracks. Her palms were damp inside the gloves. Acid burned the back of her throat and she couldn't stop clenching and unclenching her jaw. The best laid plans shattered on contact with reality. What had seemed clever now revealed itself to be suicidal.

As Zia opened her mouth to object, Dembe engaged the emergency release and the hatch exploded out of the hull. Frigid wind instantly filled the small cabin, tearing at their jumpsuits, sucking the breath from their lungs, and sawing away at any exposed patches of skin with a thousand tiny razors. Their ears popped as the pressure plunged and Zia almost lost her footing as a gust buffeted her.

Santiago's free hand found Zia's, and she squeezed—terror and determination leaping across the gap like electricity between two charged conductors. Then Dembe seized the front of Santiago's jumpsuit and yanked him toward the wound in the sleek skin of the aircraft that opened on the howling abyss. She helped him spread-eagle himself across the opening, gloved hands gripping either side.

A meter away, Zia's heart leapt into her throat.

Dembe tapped Santiago's shoulder once and he bobbed his head.

Was this the last time Zia would see her father alive? She had never shared how much the signed copy of *The Princess Bride* book meant to her or called him out for ditching her at the US Open. She had never admitted to him that her habit of challenging his every move was a serpentine homage to his single-mindedness. Despite years of hemming and hawing about it, they had never kayaked up the coast of British Columbia together. She had never told him how much it had hurt when they retreated from each other in the wake of Miranda's death.

Dembe tapped his shoulder twice and he bobbed his head again.

Zia could smell the faint scent of smoke, cinnamon, and sweat her father exuded, feel the muscles and tendons and bones through his skin, see his overlarge glasses fogging up one humid morning on a family backpacking trip through Costa Rica's cloud forests, her mother laughing and wiping them clean with the hem of a flannel shirt.

Dembe tapped his shoulder three times and Santiago disappeared.

One moment he was spread-eagled across the void and the next he was gone, and with him any hope Zia still harbored that they might make it out of this alive. You were supposed to have days of training and plenty of tandem skydives before taking your first solo jump. Dembe had done her best to run them through the basics, but this was utter madness.

Then Dembe gripped the front of Zia's jumpsuit and pulled her forward until their visors bumped against each other. Dembe caught and held her gaze for a moment.

"You got this, babe," she yelled, Zia could read on her lips the words the wind stole. Dembe bumped her visor against Zia's one more time and then shoved her around and helped position her over the aperture to infinite sky.

Zia gripped the edges of the opening with all her strength. Her muscles screamed. Her joints creaked. Her mind raged in denial.

Whatever you do, don't look down.

She felt a single tap on her shoulder and her eyes darted up, down, left, right. Nothing but nothing everywhere.

We'll never survive.

Zia nodded.

Double tap.

Nonsense. You're only saying that because no one ever has.

The wind was a solid thing. An avalanche. A demon.

Zia nodded.

She tensed her grip but the metal was beginning to slip away under her gloves. *Not too tight. Not too loose. Just right.*

Imagine you're holding a delicate little bird. This was her last vestige of control, her last thread of sanity.

Triple tap.

Miranda had tried to teach Zia to surf one summer when they were staying in Guanacaste. From shore, the waves looked like gentle, pastel, rolling hillocks. In the water, they were violent beasts rising from the depths. As Zia was paddling out, a blue-green monster reared up and flipped her over, tumbling her around underwater like a washing machine. Her lungs burned and she didn't know which way was up and she was spinning, spinning, spinning, and it was never going to end and then somehow her head popped up above the water and she gasped for breath and her mother was there beside her laughing her bright, kind laugh and saying, "*El océano es más poderoso de lo que podemos imaginar. No luches contra el. Sólo dejate ir.*" Zia could still taste the brine. *The ocean is more powerful than we can imagine. Don't fight it. Just let go.*

Just let go.

Against all instinct, Zia summoned a force of will she didn't know she had and released her grip.

Sky—the long-winged drone receding fast.

Sea—an endless dark expanse.

Sky.

Sea.

Sky.

Sea.

Sky.

Sea.

Zia was flipping, limbs flailing.

Sky.

Sea.

Sky.

Sea.

Sky.

She arched her body, brought her arms to her sides, bent her legs slightly, and thrust out her hips as far as they would go.

Sea.

Sea.

Sea...

She had leveled out, belly to earth.

Breathe. She had to remember to breathe.

Inhale. Exhale. Inhale. Exhale.

The Pacific Ocean spread out to the horizon in all directions. The last stars winked out overhead as pre-dawn charcoaled the sky in shades of gray. She was flying. She was falling. She was impossibly, heart-stoppingly free.

Zia brought her arms up from her sides, bent her elbows, and held out her palms on either side of her head. The air whisked away all delusion. All the heated arguments she'd ever made, all the fierce opinions she'd cultivated, all the false certainties she'd built up over a lifetime. What did it mean for a person to pass judgement on the world? In striving for rightness, for universal solutions, it was so easy to forget that reducing reality to a mental model meant *reducing* reality. Zia, and so many others, so often acted as if a single human brain could accommodate the universe—the fundamental fiction from which ideology sprang. Perspective could yield as much beauty as the grail of objectivity. Honoring limitations and uncertainty was a crucial aspect of truth. The fewer doubts a person harbored, the more you should doubt them.

Something grabbed her forearm and Zia nearly peed herself. She looked over to see Dembe falling beside her, grinning madly through the visor. Her expression was so genuine that Zia couldn't help but smile back. Dembe pointed with her free hand and Zia spotted Santiago a few dozen meters below. Navigating the air with the same grace as solid ground, Dembe adjusted her body and Zia mimicked her, both of them accelerating down, down, down until Dembe managed to reach out and seize Santiago's forearm.

He looked up in shock and then all three of them were beaming and shouting and laughing and crying—disbelief, relief, and the surreal joy of free fall fusing into pure overwhelm. They linked hands, each forming the point of a triangle. In the ethereal half-light, reality seemed to shift and surge around them, unable to contain itself.

Dembe let them go, checked their altitude, and tapped her wrist. Zia and Santiago released each other and all three of them separated from each other like dandelion seeds on the wind. Zia ran through her mental checklist over and over. Tilting her head, she found the ripcord. Then she arched her body and pulled.

The canopy filled with air. The harness yanked her up, slowing her fall to a gentle drift. Panic's emotional static faded. There was her dad and there was Dembe, both hanging from their respective canopies, testing their toggles by turning left and right in long arcs. The leading edge of the sun burst over the horizon, transforming the ocean from slate to deep blue and revealing the Fijian archipelago spread out below them, volcanoes jutting up through dense jungle and surf breaking against stranded atolls. And thousands of meters below, smaller than a child's toy bobbing in a bathtub, the fishing boat Selai had sent to collect them.

Costa Rica. Ghana. The Maldives. It was a start. Given the circumstances, it was the best that could be hoped for. El Salvador was on the fence and there was a chance Zia might be able to rope in Fiji if she was there in person. It might not be enough, but it was something, something she'd be able to use when she called Bonnie. With stories citing her friends' alibis undermining the original article, Zia was willing to bet that the veteran editor would welcome the chance to correct her mistake, issue a retraction, and break real news with the particular rigor of someone making good on a second chance, a sentiment Zia could understand all too well. And if Bonnie didn't want the scoop, they'd simply call a press conference.

Zia looked up past the edge of her canopy.

There, sunlight glinting off its fuselage as it ascended into harlequin clouds, was the drone. Dembe had instructed it to descend to an altitude where they could jump without oxygen. Now that it had offloaded its cargo, it would automatically return to its prescheduled route. Even if Tommy invaded Interstice's island base and noticed that one of the drones had returned without a hatch, its sanitized logs would reveal nothing. Nor would his analysts turn up any unusual activity at other international airports, exposure that would have been unavoidable if they'd landed the drone at any field with a long enough runway.

This crackpot stunt might have killed them, but it had bought them precious time—and if fate proved uncharacteristically kind, maybe future historians would look back on this whole geoengineering debacle and come to precisely the same conclusion.

The sea rose up to meet them, groundswell rolling through the glittering water. Zia inflated her life vest. The toy boat was larger now, and growing quickly. Selai was waggling shakas at her from the prow, shouting, "Yeeaaah, girl!"

Closer. Closer.

Peaks crested and crumbled into foam.

Zia flared the canopy.

Just let go.

Now.

She pulled the quick release right as her feet hit the water.

Salt had never tasted so sweet.

+36

IT WAS MIDMORNING, BUT BRANCHES FILTERED OUT so much light that the forest floor existed in a permanent state of dusk. Water dripped from rustling leaves and insects sang a deafening chorus. The air was so thick with smells that it was hard to distinguish them from each other, like myriad colors mixed to yield dull brown on a painter's palette. Mud squelched under Zia's boots, threatening to suck her down into the thick carpet of decomposing life into which rampant vegetation sank its roots.

Maybe it was Miranda's influence, but Zia had always found coffins to be strange and slightly disturbing. Life became new life. Every atom in every body had been a building block for countless previous lifeforms, and would contribute to countless subsequent incarnations. Why would you want to separate your corpse, however temporarily, from the never-ending cycle that was so very apparent in this jungle? Denying impermanence was like trying to light a match in a hurricane.

And yet, once a year or so, Zia woke up just before dawn convinced her mother had just been humming Celia Cruz's "Quimbara" from the other room. And yet, after her first official date with Dembe, Zia had automatically pulled out her phone to call Galang and tell him all about it before realizing they'd never be able to dish secrets again. And yet, Zia still couldn't believe Tommy had fallen victim to his own conspiracy.

SaudExxon didn't lose face lightly. Zia had called Bonnie immediately after Selai had offered them asylum in her house on the Yasawas. The story had broken the next morning, and with Bonnie's help, they'd made all the data and Santiago's explanation-cum-confession available to a team of investigative journalists from a cross section of leading publications. This new twist, combined with the alibis from Zia's friends, undermined Tommy's fabricated evidence, and Bonnie had been livid that she and her fact checkers had been duped. The implications had played out across the headlines for weeks, sparking vicious debate and condemnation of both Santiago and SaudExxon.

Riyadh wanted a scapegoat, and Tommy's cousins in the corporoyal family leapt at the chance to oust a competitor. He was denounced as a lone traitor acting on his own initiative and publicly beheaded—inviting even more of the same international recrimination the corpomonarchy had been hoping to sidestep by executing him. Fifteen countries had already retracted their concessions, and a few dozen more were under review. It was exactly the kind of irony that Tommy would have appreciated, and it had all happened so quickly, and in so brutal a fashion, that Zia didn't even know how to make sense of the fact that the shining, heartless boy she had fallen for all those years ago had bled out on a public square. Was his corpse in a coffin even now? What did SaudExxon do with the bodies of executed royals? Was he yet another death she was at least partly responsible for?

What is it like to kill someone? Dembe's eyes had been impossibly luminous when she had responded, *It's hard—until it's not. The better question is: what is it like to save someone?* If Zia had managed to save any lives by sabotaging Tommy's plan, they were the future millions who might have perished in a climate catastrophe had he been successful. But that was so abstract, so difficult to wrap her head around, let alone her heart. It wasn't the same as pushing someone out of the way of an incoming bus or taking a bullet for them. Then again, shouldn't diplomats be celebrated for averting wars that would have been? Hadn't they accomplished at scale what bodyguards did in person? Dancing with counterfactuals lacked drama, but was desperately needed in a world where technology had granted one man the power to change the climate.

Up ahead, Gilberto swore and hacked through a cluster of vines with a machete, derailing Zia's train of thought. The last decade had been hard on him too. He'd left guiding after Miranda's death and now spent three nights a week tending bar at a local dive, drinking more than he should. An anomalous beer belly jutted out from his otherwise skinny frame and, while he still wore his signature soccer jersey and flip flops, cigarettes had taken a toll on his lungs and he was clearly struggling with this climb as much as Zia was.

She slapped away a mosquito the size of a dragonfly and her hand came away bloody. Her calves burned and sticky strands of spider web clung to her face no matter how much she tried to get them off.

This expedition was her first break in what had turned into a six month odyssey of conference rooms whose polished glass, bad coffee, and besuited denizens had merged into a single, mind-numbing proto-conference room, a Valhalla for the hopelessly banal where the only food was stale sandwiches and you had to speak in acronyms—the most frequently mentioned, ESSA, she already half-regretted coining.

The Earth System Stewardship Agency now had eleven other members in addition to Costa Rica, Ghana, and the Maldives, bringing the total number of participating nations to fourteen. Himmat had formally taken over operations in Chhattisgarh, allowing Zia to help Aafreen draft the first official act establishing criteria for ESSA membership—pulling numerous all-nighters to get it done just like they had in high school. Any country could apply to join, but acceptance was based on low per capita emissions levels and binding mitigation commitments. That made China, the United States, the EU, Russia, SaudExxon, and most other rich, big emitter countries ineligible. To participate in making geoengineering policy and deciding what to do with Santiago's drone fleet, they would first have to make sweeping changes to their energy systems.

A number of those same heavy hitters had permanent seats on the UN Security Council, which had called an emergency session to evaluate ESSA's legitimacy. But by the time the session was convened, none could make a case for what should be done instead that wouldn't be automatically vetoed by their peers, and so, while they certainly hadn't approved of ESSA or its plans, they seemed content to let the question of legitimacy stagnate in bureaucratic purgatory, if only to have someone else to blame if things got nasty.

In the meantime, ESSA had officially taken over Project Svalinn, and Selai was working with leading researchers from around the world in a sprint to parse Santiago's secret database tracking the program's performance. Soon, they'd be able to map out what the best options would be going forward. The whole effort was funded by leasing back the drones' signal boosting capacity to Interstice, which was in the midst of a desperate search for new leadership.

Selai was also spearheading an educational campaign aimed at making ESSA comprehensible to the public. She had taken her gummy bears up in one of the geoengineering drones, and the images of them sitting in front of the windscreen looking down on Earth from the stratosphere had gone viral. Haribo hadn't known whether to be thrilled at the exposure or horrified at catching a political hot potato, but Zia had convinced the brand manager to double down and sponsor a contest for students in ESSA signatory nations to participate in a free climatology course culminating in a drone ride.

Zia glanced back to check on Santiago, remembering the terror of losing him in the woods en route to the island airfield. T-shirt soaked with sweat, he was stepping over stones and around puddles in the same steady, soldierly way that had always been his wont on their family backpacking trips. Even so, his progression from lean to frail was accelerating to match the velocity of his fall from grace.

In the wake of making his clandestine program public, he'd stepped down as Interstice's chief executive and pled guilty to unilateral geoengineering and data obfuscation in an ongoing proceeding at the International Criminal Court in the Hague. Zia was worried they'd come down hard on him, though at least the tribunal had promised to take the program's results, its transition to new management, and the extenuating circumstances surrounding its unveiling into account. Whatever the outcome, it would set the precedent for a whole new category of environmental crime. In the meantime, he was out on bail with a special dispensation to consult with ESSA on operations.

"*Aquí*," announced Gilberto, leaning on his walking stick and gasping for breath. "She wanted to come here. To visit the old trees. The big trees."

Zia and Santiago exchanged a glance neither could decipher, and then stepped through the overhanging fern fronds and into the grove.

Old growth rubber trees dominated this precious pocket of primary forest, Romanesque white columns stark against the shadowy green ferns of the understory. These silent sentinels exuded a palpable presence. Standing on the soft loam beneath them was to stand on a threshold between worlds. Passages from Miranda's books flared and faded in Zia's mind. Cause and effect fused. Time split and curled back like the petals of an opening blossom. Reality dilated—every color, texture, and smell becoming ever more itself.

"She would have been so proud of you." Santiago's voice was barely louder than a whisper. "And I am so proud of you. For doing what you do, for being who you are."

"She'd be *so* pissed at you," said Zia, swallowing hard. "Can you imagine what she'd have to say about the drones?"

Santiago managed a shaky chuckle.

"All too well," he said. "All too well."

"And she'd be pissed at *us*," said Zia. "For being such douchebags to each other for so long." Ten years. Ten years of unreturned calls and cancelled visits. Ten years spent fading from each other's lives. *The only important games are the ones we play against ourselves.* "And she'd be right."

Once shed, denial was as insubstantial as the raccoon's cotton candy.

Santiago's chuckle collapsed into a sob.

Zia wrapped an arm around his bony shoulders, reached out to graze her fingertips against smooth, creamy bark, and gazed up the towering trunk into the dense, shifting foliage of the rubber tree. Her mother had taught her that problems were inevitable—the universe was far too complex for humans to anticipate all the downstream impacts of their actions. Her father had taught her that problems were soluble—there was nothing physics allowed that human ingenuity could not accomplish. Problems were inevitable *and* soluble, yet all solutions were temporary and generated new problems to be solved. Zia was the daughter of a wizard and a prophet and maybe, just maybe, reconciling their respective legacies would be hers.

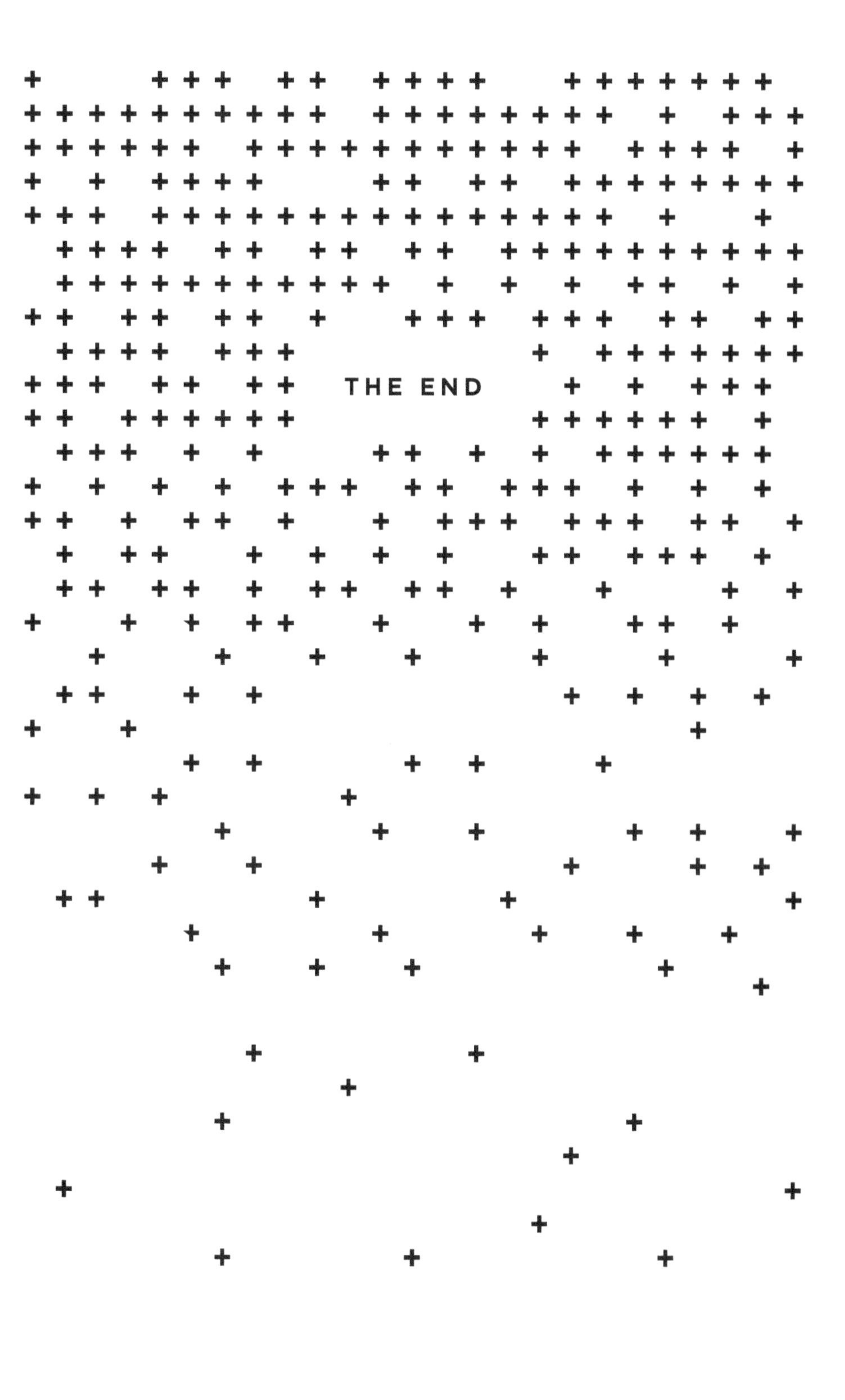
THE END

✚ Writing *Veil*

A few years ago I listened to a podcast interview with award-winning journalist Charles C. Mann in which he described scientists researching how to intentionally manipulate the global climate to offset the worst impacts of climate change.

While geoengineering proposals range from seeding the oceans with bacteria to sucking carbon dioxide directly from the air, only one approach is practical with today's technology. You fly planes into the stratosphere and spray inert dust that makes the Earth ever so slightly shinier, reflecting a tiny bit more incoming sunlight back into space, thus reducing the amount of energy entering the Earth system and cooling the planet. The kicker is that it would only cost two billion dollars a year to offset the current rate of global warming. That means that any country and even a few wealthy individuals could decide to create such a program all on their own.

Holy shit, I thought. *Someone needs to write a novel about this.* This scenario raises so many questions that will define the coming century: what does it mean to exist within an environment in which we ourselves are the primary agent of change? What will the future look like when technologies like nuclear weapons, CRISPR, the internet, and geoengineering can give a single human being the power to literally change the world? How can we harness our own natures in order to leverage such technologies to actually make the world better? I couldn't stop thinking about it. I read Mann's book, *The Wizard and the Prophet,* which had led to his podcast interview. It tells the incredible true stories of two little-known but highly influential scientists whose work and ideas shaped the 20th century. Norman Borlaug's high-yield crops saved millions (maybe billions) from starvation and William Vogt more or less founded the environmental movement. Their diametrically opposed views about humanity's relationship with nature and the kind of future we should strive to build have defined the debate over agriculture, water, energy, and climate change for generations. *The Wizard and the Prophet* embraces complexity in a way that illuminates deeper truths and challenges us to ask hard questions instead of settling for easy answers. As you may have guessed from *Veil*'s closing sentence, Mann's central metaphor stuck with me.

I like to think of literature as a single extended conversation, and *The Wizard and the Prophet* referenced Oliver Morton's masterpiece of scientific nonfiction, *The Planet Remade.* Rigorously researched, richly imagined, and compellingly told, it weaves the science, philosophy, and politics of geoengineering into a thought-provoking narrative that shows how this little-known field may take the world stage in the not-too-far future. I found it utterly fascinating and thought-provoking in the extreme. No matter what you think about geoengineering or climate change, this book will deepen and complicate your perspective.

In *The Planet Remade*, Morton quotes the leading political scientist interested in geoengineering: David Victor at the University of California, San Diego. As it happens I studied under Victor in grad school at UCSD and he was one of the best professors I've ever had—constantly challenging students to look at difficult problems from nuanced perspectives that reframed our understanding of the systems that shape our lives. I reached out to my old professor, and to Morton, and other researchers. I read more articles, books, and scientific papers. I watched as the topic emerged from academic obscurity into the pages of the *New York Times*, the *Economist*, and the *Atlantic*.

And *Veil* was born.

It would be convenient if the rest of the creative process could be aptly summarized by a 1980's film montage (Galang would approve!), but birth is never easy for anyone involved.

I had a great premise, but stories are about *people* and it took a while to find Zia and Santiago and Miranda and Dembe and Aafreen and Selai and the rest. It took even longer to figure out how their intersecting lives might reveal something interesting about the future in which the story is set, how their personal transformations might interact with the transformation their planet was undergoing.

I brainstormed. I outlined. I tested the patience of dear friends with extended bullshit sessions. Finally, I forced myself to sit down and start writing.

There's a funny thing about writing novels. I only ever figure out the heart of the story *as* I'm writing it. Rather than executing a clever plan, working through a manuscript sentence by sentence feels like hacking through dense undergrowth like Gilberto, following an overgrown path that might or might not lead out the other side.

As I explored this particular jungle, patterns began to emerge. Zia took on unexpected depth and started making decisions that surprised me. Her circle of friends came into focus. Santiago's scheme began to coalesce, as did Tommy's. Strange loops connected choices, objects, locations ever more tightly—opportunities to increase the story's density of meaning, a pocket universe reflecting itself not unlike the glimpse of infinite selves Zia gets while escaping in that mirrored elevator.

My wife and I were traveling. I wrote in Austin before sneaking off to explore the bustling music scene. I wrote in the farthest reaches of Patagonia. I wrote in cafés tucked along the wide streets of Buenos Aires. I wrote in an attic apartment in Bordeaux and in countless rural *albergues* as we spent five weeks walking the five hundred mile Camino de Santiago Norte. It was on that ancient pilgrimage route that I finished the rough draft.

But something was still missing.

Notes came back from my beta readers. Beloved sections they demanded remain untouched. Opportunities for improvement. I grappled with their feedback as we camped on the shores of the Arctic Ocean, swallowed raw herring in Amsterdam, wandered through ruined castles along the Rhine, and summited peaks in the Austrian Alps. Everywhere, we saw the impacts of climate change: receding glaciers, historic heat waves, flora, fauna, and humans struggling to adapt to a new equilibrium.

It wasn't until a long train ride through Italy—interrupted by a wildfire on the tracks during which conductors handed out plastic water bottles to sweating passengers—that my wife posed the ultimate question: *why* are you writing this story in the first place?

Only by answering did I realize the answer. I was writing this story to take readers on a journey that would challenge them to reflect on life in the Anthropocene. I was writing it because Zia and Santiago losing Miranda echoes how we have all lost capital-n-Nature—the ability to draw a clear line between humanity and our environment. By coming up with ever more ingenious tools that extend our reach from the subatomic to the cosmic, we have lost a neat metaphor for explaining the world to ourselves. Zia and Santiago had to find the courage to face their grief, to reconcile, to figure out a way forward. That is precisely the situation we find ourselves in with respect to the Earth system: we can no longer afford to pretend that our actions don't have consequences or that it's possible to turn back the clock. However difficult it may be, we must take responsibility for the extraordinary powers we've developed, and use them to build a better future together.

I had finally arrived at the heart of the story.

I needed that lodestone as I waded through numerous revisions. I needed that lodestone when my agent and I parted ways unexpectedly. I needed that lodestone when publishers passed on the manuscript. I needed that lodestone when I decided to publish it myself because this is the story I wanted to tell, a story I was happy to invest in.

If you've come this far with me, I hope you agree that the effort was worthwhile. Writing *Veil* changed my life, and my greatest aspiration is that reading it might enrich yours.

Just as Zia's success depended on her friends, *Veil*'s success depends on you. We all find our next favorite book through recommendations from people we trust. So if *Veil* means something to you, please leave an Amazon review and tell your friends about it. I know it might sound insignificant, but it makes all the difference in the world.

And if you'd like to get to know me better, I send a monthly newsletter recommending books I love that you might too and publish a blog where you can think alongside me.

You can subscribe to both here: *www.eliotpeper.com*

Whenever life threatens to overwhelm you, remember Zia. She'll be there for you. Always.

Cheers, Eliot

✚ Thanks

Josh Anon, Amy Batchelor, Brad Feld, DongWon Song, Lucas Carlson, Tim Erickson, and Craig Lauer read early drafts and gave invaluable notes.

Tegan Tigani and Amanda Rutter edited *Veil*—improving the story and sharpening my prose. Any remaining errors are mine alone.

Peter Nowell sketched an intriguing cover concept after a conversation about the themes the story wrestles with. Kevin Barrett Kane turned that rough concept into the beautiful cover you're holding in your hands right now, and designed the entire book, inside and out.

Tyler Cowen interviewed Charles C. Mann on the *Conversations with Tyler* podcast, planting the seed that grew into this book.

Oliver Morton's *The Planet Remade* was a constant point of reference as I worked through the rough draft.

Numerous scientists, journalists, analysts, and investors made time in their busy schedules to help a novelist better understand the implications of engineering the climate.

My brilliant wife, Andrea Castillo, was my creative partner every step of the way. Our dog, Claire, provided ample doses of much-needed distraction.

You read this book, bringing the story to life in the theater of your mind.

To all, a thousand thanks.

+ About the Author

Eliot Peper writes speculative thrillers that explore how technology shapes our lives. He is the author of *Breach, Borderless, Bandwidth, Cumulus, True Blue, Neon Fever Dream,* and the *Uncommon Series,* and his books have earned praise from the *New York Times Book Review, Popular Science, Businessweek, San Francisco Magazine, io9, Boing Boing,* and *Ars Technica.*

Eliot's writing has appeared in the *Verge, Tor.com, Harvard Business Review, VICE, OneZero, TechCrunch, GEN,* and the *Los Angeles Review of Books,* and he has given talks at Google, the Electronic Frontier Foundation, Comic Con, Niantic, Future in Review, Qualcomm, SXSW, and the Conference on World Affairs.

As an independent consultant, Eliot helps leaders think differently about the future and how to create change. Typical formats include talks, advisory engagements, and creative commissions, and his clients include founders, venture capital investors, award-winning designers, Fortune 100 companies, and government agencies.

Eliot pursued graduate studies in international affairs, survived dengue fever, translated Virgil's *Aeneid* from the original Latin, worked as an entrepreneur-in-residence at a venture capital firm, and explored the ancient Himalayan kingdom of Mustang.

Find out more at **WWW.ELIOTPEPER.COM**

CPSIA information can be obtained
at www.ICGtesting.com
Printed in the USA
LVHW051251230520
656337LV00011B/425/J